sweethearts

Novels

sweethearts

ELLE MITCHELL

SWEETHEARTS

Published in the United States by Little Key Press.

First Edition

Edited by Tessa Garrett
Cover by Elle Mitchell
Cover and heading font: Naomi's Hand by Naomi
Conversation hearts by MyCustomCandy

*For Mom and our many hours of road-tripping,
plotting and listening to Purple Rain.*

sweethearts

ELLE MITCHELL

November 17, 2017

Ada

FROM THE DAY I DISCOVERED Laura Hurst's body in Lynn Pond, I have been hiding. When my mother opened the door to her fifteen minutes of fame at the sake of my mental health, I hid my truths and regurgitated coached words. I told the rotund male 'journalists' I hadn't planned on being brave. They took notes and nodded, sinking into the flat cushions of our stained couch as if they were over for tea, not an interview. One woman, using me as her way into the industry, got tears of exhaustion along with my story. The stench of her sweat and desperation lingered long after she had gone.

I spent hours on the rose-patterned stool in front of my vanity staring into its mirror, practicing the perfect 'thank you for coming, but I'm sad you had to be here' mouth curvature. My older brother, Peter, would sneak in often to judge me. *You try to be perfect.* The memory of his frown still stings.

Now I'm caught between emotional and hollow. Part of me wants to blame it on Laura. Another part thinks it is the woman who left violet lipstick on Derek's pillowcase's fault. Most of me knows I would have ended up this way no matter what. But the result is the same: Peter rarely calls anymore, and Mom and I haven't spoken since my inevitable divorce four years ago. At least that may be for the best; nothing has been the same between us since the reporters and television stations stopped calling.

My left lash line throbs, as it does whenever cameras and lies come to mind. I grab the tweezers from my top drawer and turn towards the small oval mirror on my wall. I yank out the eyelash I'm sure is causing the most pain. Another swipe of eyeliner hides the sparse patch I've created because, of course, it's next to the two I pulled out this morning, and my naturally wide eyes make its absence more noticeable.

I straighten my dress and fluff my already frizzing iron-created curls then head into the café. Three eager women and two antsy men await me at the high-top tables. One woman, wearing a short skirt and a low-cut shirt, flirts with a man in a tailored suit. Given her interpretation of the typical interview business casual, she must have banked on me being male. The other hopefuls sit spread out, clutching purses, briefcases, and resumes. Only one person holds a coffee; steam fogs her glasses as she takes small, cautious sips. I imagine I'll pick her, as she has chosen to sample what we sell.

"Kelly Jellens?" I call after reading the cursive letters on her plain white cup and matching it to the interviewees.

I glance at my watch—the same watch I purchase time and time again after I wear it thin. The leather band is as simple as its light pink face; it tells me the time, which is currently 6:03 p.m., and nothing else. I'm exhausted, though I have only been at work for an hour. And I've spent most of that time pretending to be busy so no one will bother me.

Rachael, my therapist of seven years, has insisted that I revisit *the spot* on the anniversary of the day I started hiding. And after five years of comments, pokes, prods, and monologues about how

I will feel better afterwards, I admitted she was right. I have been listless with the weight of that knowledge for over a month. *I have to go back to Silynn.* Mental growth aside, I can't leave my business during a holiday week without a little extra help.

The scrape of chair legs brings my attention back to the short-ish brunette. She stands and half raises her arm. "That's me."

I take in her outfit: black and candy apple red striped dress, black flats with tights, and a long, thin gold necklace. Simple yet professional. I approve.

"Come on back," I say.

I open my office door wide to look inviting. I'd spent a whole fifteen minutes tidying up. Like me, it has secrets. Behind the photo of me and my best friend laughing is the deed to my ex-husband's new home. I stole it when I went to congratulate him on moving. I am not usually so petty, and I've only stolen three things in my life. But it wasn't my fault. He kept it where I had kept ours: inside the fourth hollow book on the third shelf from the bottom in the bookcase in the master bedroom. Rachael said it wasn't the healthiest thing I'd ever done.

Two joints and three hundred dollar bills are stashed inside the porcelain unicorn coin bank sitting on the edge of my desk. A longtime friend, Kirsten, bought it for me because of an inside joke I couldn't remember. When she gave it to me and started giggling, I mimicked her so she wouldn't know. That's the moment caught in my laughing picture—I am proud of how realistic my smile looks. If you shake the unicorn, you'll hear the *tink* of the money clip.

My desk hides darkness. I leave it unlocked as a sign of good faith to my employees; Larry seems to appreciate the ability to snag a new manila folder without having to ask. But taped underneath the bottom right drawer lives a single blade. I haven't needed it in almost two decades. Should that time ever come again, though, I would hate to resort to scissors; I'm not sure if my tetanus shot is up to date.

More secrets hide in and around my workspace: a small flask; newspaper clippings about the youngest versions of myself with scratched out eyes; my mother's favorite knickknack—she had blamed a neighbor boy for its disappearance; and a jelly bracelet that reminds me of simpler times.

Kelly's sensible shoes make little sound as she steps past me into my office. I appreciate the quiet nature of her entrance. Darling plastic, bright red glasses frame her round face and, being a shade off, clash with her dress. She smiles and waits for me to say something. As I'm about to introduce myself, a wave of memory slaps me. I am struck speechless. She smells like Lucky Charms. *Who smells like cereal?*

I want to tell her to sit or ask her to tell me about herself. I'm too caught up in the sickly sweet chalk my tongue is recalling.

After twenty-nine years, I still don't know why my curiosity took over that day. The shadow under the ice could have been anything—a rabbit, a tree branch—yet I couldn't run to it fast enough. I pull my sleeves over my scarred palms as I shiver.

"Ma'am? Are you alright?"

I can only imagine what I look like: frizzy hair, wrinkled dress, pale face haunted by a frozen dead girl. "So sorry! I'm not feeling too well. I'm probably just dehydrated; it's been a busy day," I lie.

Kelly holds a finger up and rushes out of the room. Before I can sit in my plush, ergonomic office chair, she is back with a cup of cool water. Her face reads, 'I hope you feel better,' and also, 'Give me a job, because I'm helpful.'

"Tell me about yourself," I say. *Can she hear my heartbeat?* My ribcage expands with each beat.

"Of course! I'm Kelly—of course." She chuckles awkwardly. *Nope, the loud thudding is contained.* "I'm a Junior at IU. I'm studying Business and Economics. I have very little work experience, if I'm being honest. I worked with my dad when I was a kid; he owns a hardware store in Little Rock. I like to call it a job, but really, I just rang things up here and there. In high school, I worked in a local ice cream parlor slinging cones and ice cream sodas. Since I moved here, I've just been in school. My goal was to power through Freshman and Sophomore year, which I did. Then I'd take more time with Junior and Senior year, which I'm doing. I guess you could say I'm driven," she says, getting more animated. "To be blunt, I was hoping this could turn into an internship. I'd love to follow you around when you got back. I'd do the grunt work too, of course. But it would be amazing to come out of college with a solid internship, a resume and—with any luck—a recommendation."

I nod, respecting a ramble that ends with an actual point. "Let's talk hours. I need someone from—" My eyes flick to my watch again. "5-10 p.m. this Tuesday through Saturday. If that works out, you can shadow me when I get back. I can even give you a fancy internship title. As for the recommendation, let's wait and see."

"That all sounds great to me—fits pretty perfectly with my schedule! I'll only have to leave a study group thirty minutes early. Would the hours be the same when you come back?" Her smile is infectious. I imagine she gets most of what she wants in life when she flashes it, despite two crooked lower teeth and an overbite.

"They would." She nods, and I say, "Kelly, you're hired. Welcome to the Cuppa family!" I pause for only a moment before I call Larry—a manager and close friend of five years.

White tufts of hair appear before he does. "What's up?"

The scent of roasted vanilla beans fills my office.

"This young woman will be your helper while I'm gone. Consider her your assistant. When I come back, she'll shadow us for an internship. Also, could you send the other applicants home? Be diplomatic about it, please."

He nods, but the twinkle in his eyes worries me. "Can you make espresso?" Larry asks Kelly as he leans against the doorframe.

"I had a French press a few years ago before my roommate used it while he was drunk." Her face scrunches. "So, no."

"I'll teach you. Learn quick." Ignoring her outfit, he asks, "Can you start now? I could use a hand closing up tonight." He walks out, apron strings trail behind him. He is wearing his favorite faded gray shirt. It has a hole by his belly button from an unfortunate lighter accident, which no one but Derek and I know about.

Kelly glances at Larry, then at me. Her voice is nervous and sweet when she asks, "Am I getting paid?"

As she is already standing, I make a snap decision my wallet may be displeased with later. "$12 an hour this week. $10 as an intern. And if you want to become a full employee after, and we have the hours, you'll go to $15."

"Amazing." *Damn.* She had not been expecting so much money for an internship, probably. Kelly gives me a quick hug and says, "I can start now." She leaves and jogs to the left, back towards the café.

Rachael will be so proud of me. I am all squared away to face my hometown, my demons, my mother, and Lynn Pond.

November 18, 2017

Ada

LANKY MONSTERS THREATEN ME. Their clawed branches reach from within the woods. Light splinters through the darkness they create.

It's as if only yesterday I was nine and my mother was driving me to the airport I just came from. I locked my eyes on a dark splotch on the famous green carpet—now an offensive blue that reminds me of multiplex theaters—as she told me how much I would love my uncle and aunt. Peter would join us in the summer, she assured me.

Flickering sun rays make my temples throb and tear away the thoughts of Peter's absence—my mother's absence—from my childhood. I still feel small, as if I never turned ten. Only now, I can drive and play at adulthood.

The winding road becomes a snake, and I ride its back up and around another chunk of mountain. When the rain comes, I'm in a jungle; I am a wild child at one with nature. Fried nerves smooth to a gentle buzz as the Hemlocks thin, and the sun streaks from the sky as if God herself is playing music just for me. Farmland stretches in front of me as far as my eye can see. The ground is dead.

In Silynn, winter begins no later than October 30th. If ice—but more likely snow—didn't crystallize on the dewy morning grass by November 5th, panic would abound. "The end of the world is nigh," the front page of *Silynn Times* would proclaim.

I will be in town this evening, so I'm likely to see snow. More importantly, I will be in town on November 25th, the anniversary of the day Laura Hurst became a part of me. Rachael swears being there on that day is an integral part of my healing.

I stare blankly at my ringless fingers. I will not focus on the lake—confusingly named Lynn Pond. It can be all-consuming. A raw, angry spot on my bikini line and the two gaping holes in my lash line flare hot. *Great.*

I unzip my jeans and reach for the second pair of tweezers I keep in my purse—one hair, maybe two.

As if a faerie waved her wand, the road, the trees, the sky itself is blanketed in white. I slow my speed to 25 mph to match the truck in front of me, and the hair follicle pain subsides. Yellow signs crop up all around, each cautioning me of another horror. I create a game to distract myself. With each new one, I create alternative meanings: "Indiana Jones Trap Ahead", "Slip 'N Slide Roads", "Suitable For Drifting", "Sneaky Deer". My younger self would be pleased—despite not knowing what drifting is.

The beat-up pickup's blinker turns on, and I imagine the loud ticking sound it makes. My uncle had one, and I loved to yank on the lever to hear its satisfying reply. Finally, the truck turns down an invisible path and leaves me alone an icy, open road.

There are tire tracks embedded in the ice; I try to stay in them. Every time I nudge the wheel too far, the rental hybrid swerves. As I rarely drive, taking advantage of car share services, taxis, and public transits, I don't have to deal with this often.

Uncle Carl has tried to buy me a truck more times than I can count. "Living in Bloomington means driving a truck. Too much rain and snow to drive anything else." I smile; he said that only last week when five inches coated the city.

A shoulder-less edge sneaks up on me, and I overcorrect. Swerving, balding tires miss the grooves many vehicles before me had created. The car spins, and my grip tightens. No one would find my body. I ease the car to a stop and headlights flash at me. Doing a three-point turn in such a small space makes me feel like I'm a dog chasing her tail. The lights flash again as the sound of skidding creeps in through closed windows.

As soon as I right the car, I drive away. I can't bear to wave or mime an apology to the stranger. I stay on edge.

Miles after the snow melted into another rainforest, my heart still clogs my throat. I wonder for a moment if I should stop to check the car as they do in movies, but I have no idea what I would be looking for. Rolling the window down, I take deep inhales of the earthy air. I wish I could close my eyes and dive into a daydream; I settle for calming my heartbeat. Once the jitters have faded away to the point of me nearly forgetting I almost died—*that old near-miss?*—the trip seems to take no time at all.

As I drive through another patch of snow, I play a game I used as a coping mechanism when the family drove to visit big news stations hours away. I created a new life for myself with each new landscape we went through.

When soft flakes wet the windshield, I am an Eskimo building an igloo. During a patch of flat land, I'm a farmer cracking into the frozen ground to retrieve a special kind of corn I name "Frorn". And when nothing but rock surrounds me, I become a rock climber prepping for a year-long hike up a mountain to meet ogres in the sky. Before I know it, I pass the exit for Lorla Falls. Lorla Falls is two hours away from Silynn. When I drive by the exit for the last cluster of fast food chains, which means I'm thirty minutes away, I zip my jeans, hairs still intact for the moment, and dread settles in my stomach, heavy and sour. My mother lives a mile and a half into town. My rental is two miles outside of it. I will call Rachael after I get situated in my room. *When will I call my mother?*

7:12 P.M.

THE CABIN I RENTED for nine days is simple. It sits in a small community of seven identical rentals. They are dark on the outside and—according to the static one-page website—light and cozy inside.

Musk with an overwhelming floral room spray pours out of the front door as I push in. I breathe through my mouth, ignoring the taste of poison, and head for the windows—cold be damned. The crocheted blanket on the back of the couch slides as I rush by it. I will be curled up with a book soon enough, so I leave it.

Once freezing fresh wind is sucking the manufactured flower scent from the air, I take my two suitcases into the bedroom. I have never been one to unpack in a hotel; it feels odd and too comfortable in a foreign place. Nothing changes despite my extended stay. Utilizing the dresser's top, I throw my smaller bag on the cheap, painted turquoise wood. One of the wheels clangs against the mirror, and I wince. I don't need any more bad luck or a hefty fee from someone my mother may know; I choose not to assess the damage. I carry my toiletry bag to the counter in the bathroom where pictures of coyotes howling at the moon and flowers on a mountainside litter the walls. I shift the leather band of my watch. It reads 7:21 p.m.

Okay, no more stalling. Before I find anything else I have to do, I pull out my phone and hit the icon of Rachael's face.

I frown as it tells me I have no service. I wander into the kitchen with my fingers crossed in hopes there is a landline. A piece of wrinkled, stained paper is taped to the refrigerator.

"THINGS TO NOTE:

— Some basic foods are in the freezer and cabinets if you need them.

— Toilets can't handle more than a small amount of toilet paper, so flush often. No feminine products, please!

— The thermostat is in the hallway.

— The wi-fi password is: LionHowlStorm23

— There is no cell service, so feel free to use the landline! It's by the kitchen sink. The cord stretches into the living room.

— We have a cleaning crew, but please put the dishes in the sink and the trash in the trash can.

— Please check and make sure you have what you came in with before you leave. We are not responsible for missing, lost, or stolen property."

I try not to overthink the last comment as I dial Rachael's number on the large chunk of plastic. It's like the 1990s in here. The first time the call goes through, a young male asks me if my China King order is for dine-in or take-out. The second time, I dial it correctly, and Rachael answers. "Rachael Young Therapy."

I inhale with the sound of her soft voice. It takes me a moment before I say, "Hi, Rachael. It's Ada Bailey."

"Hello, dear!" She sounds genuinely pleased to hear from me. *I bet she's like this with all of her patients.* "Have you arrived? How was the trip? Any trich troubles?" I await the rest of her unavoidable questions. "Did you think about the two things we talked about? How did you feel about them, if you did? And have you called your mother?" She huffs out a breath. "Okay. I think that's plenty out of me. Answer them in your own way, in your own time."

I picture Rachael twirling the one flat chunk of brown hair that frames her face. She does it every time she asks a question—out of compulsion or a hoping to make it match the other curls, I have still yet to figure out. The blue and gray striped armchair Rachael sits in while she shrinks me is almost as plush as the one I lay on, yet she never slouches. Perhaps it's how she stays so thin and fit. She is probably stiff-backed with tightened abs muscles as I formulate my words.

Why do I feel like I am about to disappoint her? I begin with a sigh. "Where to start… I arrived fifteen minutes ago, or so. I had one near-trich episode on the drive up here. I'm fine now, though." My hair follicles suddenly feel tight and itchy again. "Well, I was until I told you about it."

Rachael jots that down, I know. We have talked about my trichotillomania ad nauseam, *and* I have eyebrows again. Still, she wants more.

"The trip was a little longer than I remembered. Bits and pieces of memories came back during the flight. Nothing huge. I remembered my mother putting a cold cloth on my forehead when I was sick. I guess I'd forgotten she was capable of mothering. When I fell asleep, I had a dream about a weird abandoned swing set and angry boy eyes. And no, I'm not ready to address that yet. Oh, and dirt. I remember what dirt tastes like." I pause.

Rachael breathes out the question I knew she would. "Do you want to talk more about those moments of your mother's tenderness?

"Absolutely not, and sort of. Later," I decide. "When I get back. I haven't called her. *I know;* I've had weeks. But I have no idea what to say—still don't. 'Hey Mom, I'm in town. Are you ready to talk to me again, or do you still think I've ruined my life?' That will go over well."

Sam

LAURA SAW ME IN A WAY others never have. If she hadn't pulled her hand away, maybe I wouldn't be who I am today.

"Dinner's almost ready." *Already?*

The call interrupts what I'd hoped could have been my quiet time, time devoted to my sweethearts. Seems I'll go another night un-satiated. I leave the bedroom and head towards the scent of frying cow flesh and fermented beans.

Taylor is hunkered over our cheap wok, humming. Smoke fills the kitchen, and I worry about the fire alarm going off—and who would come if that happened. I have to think about these things.

"Smells good," I say.

"Should be ready any minute now. Take a seat." Taylor is short with me, but I never asked for a restaurant-quality meal; freezer meals taste just fine.

Steaming stir-fry is dumped onto my plate with the angst of a thousand teenagers, and a cold beer is set beside it. We chew in silence, because what is there to say?

"It's delicious."

"Thanks. It didn't take too long." *Sure.*

Our silverware bumping against the plates becomes the conversation we aren't having. Taylor scoops another helping of sticky rice onto our plates before either of us need it. We will be divorced soon; I can feel it.

I barely taste the last dribbles of food as I fork them into my mouth. "I'm grabbing another beer; want one?" I ask, to which I get a non-committal noise in response.

The floor creaks under my boots as I walk towards the refrigerator. I could go shoeless—this is my home—but there's something about being in boots that feels powerful. They remind me of younger days—when I told people I was a misunderstood misanthrope. I can't remember a time I've left the house in any shoes other than black boots—an angry statement refusing to die or utilitarian footwear choice, even I'm not sure. In high school, I hadn't been an outcast. But it wasn't as if football players and cheerleaders went out of their way to invite me to parties, either.

I'd gotten ahold of a flier once and showed up to a frat party. That had been a colossal mistake. Turns out a thirteen-year-old kid is only allowed into a college party after pounding five shots at the door. Despite the blurry night filled with inappropriate touching and forced dress-up, no one asked me to sit at the cool kid table at lunch. But I had friends. Some were even girls.

As I clear the dishes and scrape the uneaten burnt veggies into the garbage, I think about the people I cut ties with the moment I didn't have to see them daily: punks, soon-to-be womanizers, awkward nerds with halitosis, a set of twins who left Silynn the moment they could. I should've done that too.

I did everything one is supposed to do. I graduated from college and married Taylor—who cried when I said vows I copied from a book on weddings. We had a child who didn't start fires when she was small, as I had; she's off at college now.

"You want to watch some TV?"

I realize I'm still holding my plate, fork in mid-air over the trash can. *How long have I been standing here?* Not long, surely; I would've already heard nagging about my absence. "Sure. What did you have in mind?" I ask as I scrape at clean, already scratched porcelain. The sound grates my nerves.

"How about that 'your neighbor could be a killer' show you were watching the other day? That looked neat." Taylor's voice is light, but a seriousness lives behind it.

Things have changed for us lately.

"I'm tired of that show. Let's watch something less serious. I'm in the mood to laugh." I button the neck of my flannel shirt as if it will cover my lie.

The television is loud when it flickers to life and brings with it the memory of a scream my hand was barely quick enough to cut off. A commercial interrupted my thoughts—for the better.

"Come on down to Jake's Used Cars and More on 52nd Street and Tryon Drive! We'll fix you up a good helping of discounts!" If I were to look at the screen, he'd be wearing a turkey costume with the leg of his brethren in hand; I'd bet Taylor's life on it.

"Want a beer?" I try.

"I'm fine," Taylor says. *Of course you are.*

November 19, 2017

Sam

"YOU'VE REACHED TAYLOR. Leave a message at the beep."
Voicemail?

I'm not devastated—far from it. But when the beep comes, I don't even say that.

Instead, I say, "Hi, I understand. I'll wait for the papers. Jess comes home Wednesday night; text me if you're coming over for Thanksgiving."

We'd rolled away from each other to the edges of our mattress last night as if it were any other night. Usually, I'd wake up to the smell and sound of fat sizzling in my grandmother's cast iron skillet, which I'd never use if I were alone. Instead, I woke late to a note on Taylor's side of the bed: "*I want a divorce.*"

It's sooner than I'd expected. After the evening before, it seemed we would have another day of 'fine' ahead of us. It's a little sad; I looked forward to bacon and pancakes with over-easy eggs, all smothered in syrup with a side of freshly squeezed orange juice.

Without Taylor's breakfast, I pour instant oatmeal from a paper package into a mug and splash water in it. Two minutes seems long enough to cook dried grain and dehydrated cranberries, so I hit a button on the microwave and head back to the bedroom.

I've got to focus on the more important task of the day: I'm going hunting.

When I was nine, my father took me deep into the woods with a rifle, or shotgun, or some other long barreled gun, he described in detail when I was not paying attention. It was his attempt to bond after the matriarch of our house had been taken away two years earlier in handcuffs, spitting and spouting her usual lunacies. With my mother gone, I realized my father was a kind and decent man; he realized I had tendencies most children did not. Hunting was his way of trying to refocus my impulses.

While he cautioned me about gun safety and the importance of silence, I watched a small baby bird fall out of a tree and splatter onto a crooked root below. Its mother bird did not come to its rescue; the blue and black feathered female just continued to vomit in the surviving babies' mouths. As I mentally compared the bits of bloody brain matter to my existence, my father placed a gun in my hands.

The heft of it brought me back to the moment. We would watch for a deer, he said. We would hide and wait to murder a living thing. "If you kill it, you eat it."

A small doe with three tiny white spots on its forehead and another splash of light fur on its back wandered into view. My father shook his head, and I shifted the gun into a more comfortable position. A strong arm flew out in front of my chest, and his head shook with more vigor. I aimed.

My kind and decent father said, "No"; my tendencies pulled the trigger.

The bullet tore into the doe's hind leg. I barely heard the thud of its falling body for the violent ringing in my ears.

The gun weighed more as I handed it to my shaking father. Angry footsteps fell in step with the clanging in my head. He had to shoot the baby deer again. Its face both imploded and exploded into a gaping hole. I'd seen a photo like that once; the coroner's kid—eight when everyone else was seven—stole it from his father's office to scare everyone. A suicide victim who'd rigged some device up to kill himself with the tug of a string had been in full color; though the details of the person's death were fuzzy, the image hadn't been. Following the reactions around me, I'd recoiled. In reality, I'd wanted a closer look.

My father's disappointment was palpable, but it was his fear that suffocated me. He sidestepped me as he stomped to the car without the doe. I asked him why we weren't taking it home; he'd always said we had to eat what we kill.

And in one of my most vivid memories that doesn't involve my sweethearts, my father turned to me, and said, "It wasn't an honorable kill. We don't kill young things." My father had an odd way of talking. "So, we'll leave it for the animals. They can do what they will. You and I will go without meat for a while."

And we did. He didn't buy meat for months after. We also never hunted together again; I'm not sure if he ever went alone either.

I've hunted only once since; I was twenty-three, alone, and apprehensive. Tracey was nearly as messy as the doe. At least I was able to bring a piece of her home for my box; I wish I'd thought to do that with the doe—a chunk of the white fur patch on its back would look nice wrapped in Jessica's ribbon.

Last week, I began a new hunt. It's been nearly twenty-two years since I followed Tracey home from school. Collecting is usually enough; Silynn is close to so many rest-stops and gas stations, I haven't needed to try, to watch, to wait. But I need a break from the ease of opportunity. So, I'm taking extra care with my chosen sweetheart. My father isn't here to shake his head or put his arm out, and I don't want to miss or blow off a leg.

It's been three years since I've collected at all, and the need is growing.

A thrill runs up my spine as I picture red hair, green eyes, the way her older sister says her name, "Luh-orrrr-ee."

Ada

"HELLO?" Her voice is gravel under my feet. Pulling the phone back, I stare at the disembodied voice of my mother. *Speak.* "Hello?"

I revert to a younger self. "Mom?" The following pregnant pause makes my ears ring. I analyze an almost too perfect knot in the wood of the ceiling; there's a human-made quality to it. The swirls go both ways, from dark to light—the center is lighter than pine.

"Adelynn." I wince when she says my name. I cannot count the times I have asked her to call me Ada.

Clenching my fist, I respond with the opposite of how I feel. "It's good to hear your voice. How are you?"

A scrape in the background makes me think she's gone into the small dining room off of the kitchen. If the chairs are the same as they were a few years ago, they'll be wobbling as she pulls one out for herself.

"Is someone dead?"

Three eyelashes sear with pain. "No," I say quickly, so I won't lose my nerve and to give myself something to focus on; my fingers itch to yank at the burning cilia. "I am in town. I wanted to know if I could see you while I'm here."

"We haven't talked in a while." *Since the day after your fifty-fourth birthday, but who's keeping track?* "Why are you here?"

My body temperature flashes from hot to cold and back again, and I wonder why I expected anything but this. I have had a nicer conversation with a waitress at the end of her power shift on a Saturday at a job she hates.

"It's a long story." I reach for my water—ignoring its lack of clarity. A stress-induced dryness has filled my throat and made my tongue fat and sticky. I chug the whole glass before I continue. "I can tell you in person."

"Busy this week."

Neither of us has mentioned Thanksgiving or the day that follows it.

"I am only here for nine days, Mo—"

She sputters like a dying car. "Fine. How is Wednesday?"

My hands sweat; that's in two days. *Is my house ready? How's my hair?* I mentally pause. *Wait... what?* "Perfect," I say, as if I didn't just wonder if bangs would make me look younger. "Should I come over?"

"Okay. Around 2:30," my mother snaps.

Before I can respond, the phone goes quiet, and a dial tone follows. I tell the receiver I love it, pretending my mom didn't just hang up on me. Would she have said it back? *Probably not,* is what I come up with.

My energy is sapped. I should call Rachael; she would be proud. A loud yawn and grumble in my stomach demand my attention first. I will need a sandwich and an early nap—not in that order. The moment Mom called me Adelynn, I curled up in the nearest blanket. So I tilt against the couch cushions and let emotions and exhaustion take hold.

If only the sun could dim its rays, I would be asleep al—

1:30 P.M.

SILYNN IS A MOUNTAIN TOWN with a population of 1,512 and no hope of tourists—only truckers and adulterers looking for a cheap place to overnight. As I drive on the two-lane main street to a downtown smaller than my neighborhood, I pass only one unfamiliar sight—a new gas station, the opening of which must have been a red-letter day. The other shops are exactly as I remember, down to a tree stump near a 'major' intersection my mother called an eyesore. It is—and was—just a small broken sapling struck down by lightning before it had the chance to age.

Polly's Boutique sits at the corner of Trail and Steward Road. I shopped for an Easter dress there when I was five. We weren't religious, but a man who came around a lot—my mother's boyfriend, I assume—was. The yellow pastel dress made me look like cupcake frosting, only it crinkled. It was horrible, and I was promised I would never have to wear it again. Even as a child, I could tell she knew the man wouldn't last, but he was worth another few days.

The icing dress made one more appearance that year—to a cousin's shotgun wedding. That one was my choice. I still don't care for Diana or her taste in men. I believe she is on husband number six with nine children spread out between them. She's only twelve years older than me—now forty-seven. Like my mother, she has never left Silynn; it says a lot about her.

Polly's has a nearly identical icing dress in the window with pink piping around the ruffles on an adult mannequin—*horrifying*. Is this the local style? I wonder if my mother owns a dress like it now. If I have another wedding, will she show up in a cast-off gypsy wedding gown?

Few people wander the streets—it being just after church. The five rebel kids skipping lunch with the family or pot luck with the church walk in the same direction ten steps apart—not cool to be friends, I guess. A couple with a baby carriage looks downtrodden, or I could be seeing them through the Silynn-filter: young, already with a baby, and not at church. They seem to be headed the same way I am. Not much open on a Sunday.

I am in search of my favorite soda shop. As a kid, the sandwiches were the best around; as an adult, we'll see. I hope for better than lunch meat. I forget if I should turn right or left on Thompson; I choose right, because I always choose right first.

The gas station from when I was small is boarded-up—closed due to the new and shiny one, I suppose. Three teenagers with backpacks are smoking in the old parking lot to its left side. A floral shop I have never visited looks as new as it always did as if the owner never stopped painting.

I turn the wrong way. My U-turn is illegal, but no one is around. I see one or two small patches of ice left from what must have been a snowstorm, so I drive a few miles under the speed limit. *Good old Silynn.*

I pass the gas station again. The teens are gone. Up ahead, I see it: Sodas 'n More—otherwise known as the local soda shop.

It's busy and loud. There is no street parking for three blocks, and the wait is thirty minutes "or more." The hostess is a step away from filing her nails she's so bored with the current happenings. She stands behind her wooden podium in jeans and a hot pink sweatshirt; the black logo across her chest is a bottled soda with fizz bubbling into the first "o" of Sodas 'n More. Wooden pew benches in the cramped waiting area are stuffed with a goodly portion of Silynn's population, by the looks of it—church-goers and non.

A toddler shrieks, and I check my ears for blood. The mother sees me and glares; I know she thinks, *"City woman."* A man pats her hand, and she turns to him to resume their conversation. I can't help but want to laugh.

Another family, two girls and a mother—presumably—sit in silence squished between two couples. I appreciate how the eldest sister leans over to make the youngest laugh now and again. When the hostess calls for the Redfords, I nab a section of bench beside a canoodling couple and stare at my phone. It's useless for much other than calls in Silynn, despite being in the heart of the town, but I find comfort in the familiar motion. I check my watch; it has only been six minutes.

While I wait, I marvel at the decorations, the floor, the ceiling, the glass case with t-shirts and mugs in it. There does not appear to be a single new piece of art on the wall. The framed menus look as though they haven't been cleaned since I was last here. I remember focusing on them while my mother reprimanded Peter for his failing science grades. As a teacher, she had high expectations; as a mother, she had little time, little motivation, and even less maternal instinct to help us meet them. In some ways, I now believe that in her mind, she did her best. At the time, I tried to memorize the old prices of milkshakes instead of listening to her lectures.

I stare at the wall above the hostess's head and shiver. The photograph of three children with sacks over their faces is still upside down. I was always grateful for that—still am.

When I was thirteen and came back over winter break to visit Silynn, the owner of the joint, Fred, was having a problem with one of his syrup pumps. He decided to try and pour directly out of the twenty-gallon jug with the help of a young guy who had mole-like freckles and a lousy attitude. It went so well that the floor was coated in blueberry syrup. Somehow, the kid stayed clean. Artificial dye that no one wants to think about being in their food stained over a fourth of the cement dining room floor. I smile as I see it's still here—unabashedly uncovered.

"Ada."

My stomach growls. "That's me," I announce as if it is a different hostess.

Grabbing the plastic menu, she nods; her ridiculous dangling earrings smack the sides of her neck. She leads me to a plain wooden table with chairs to match backed with three unevenly spaced spindles. My back will hurt very soon.

"Your waitress will be with you in a second," she shouts over her shoulder.

I go to thank her, but she is back to leaning against her station.

"Hey there! I'm Hailey, and I'll be your waitress today," I hear from behind me.

Blood running cold, I do not turn.

Three thoughts race through my head. It could be anyone named Hailey. Maybe she won't be *my* waitress. She is too old to do this sort of thing; by now she would have a distinguished job. I am instantly ashamed of my third thought.

I am proved wrong on all accounts. Her ice blue eyes give her away. I look nothing like I used to, however.

"Adelynn! Is that you?" *Or maybe I do.*

I slide my hands under the table before I say, "It's Ada now. I haven't seen you in—"

"Around…" She counts on her fingers. "Jeez! Twenty-five years, or so? I heard you were in town. How are you doing? You look terrific. And oh, how you've grown!" Hailey laughs as she pulls up a chair; I clench my thighs.

I have managed to avoid her during every other visit thus far, yet this time I see her before I even see my mother. *Damn.*

Her hair is pulled into a tight bun, much like it often was when she was my babysitter *twenty-nine* years ago. She has thin, gray, square glasses that fit her face much better than the old plastic brown hand-me-downs she used to wear every once in a while.

I choose not to ask how she had heard of my being in Silynn

and answer her other questions in half-truths. "I am really good, thank you. I own a coffee shop in Indiana and am thinking of going back to school. You've grown too," I add. "Aging has done you a serious kindness."

Hailey blushes. "Thank you, Adely—Ada. A coffee shop, huh? Wouldn't have pictured that, but you were only in elementary school when you left. I'm glad you're doing well. What brings you back to small-town U.S.A?"

"Passing through. Thought I would stop to see Mom, check how everything has changed, that sort of thing."

"Where's your final destination?"

Now you're getting a bit nosey. "Haven't decided actually. Just wanted to drive on this coast for a bit. Enjoyed Portland, swooped by Tillamook, I think I may end up in San Francisco by the end of it," I lie.

Her eyebrows rise into sandy blunt bangs. "Must be nice. So, what can I getcha?"

With the shifted mood, I order my pimento cheese sandwich and Italian vanilla soda. I add a smile and quick thanks to break the tension.

"Of course, hon. Just happy to see you after all these years. Depending on how long you stay, maybe we could catch up? Been a while since I've seen a new face."

I am stunned by her suggestion. I nod nonetheless. *What else can I do?* I try not to seem like a liar or too eager when I tell her it's a great idea. I regret it as soon as I say it, but I tell her, "I am staying at the cabins. Cabin 4." There are only three places to stay in and around Silynn: the cabins, the hotel, and the motel. "Call me when you get off work tonight or tomorrow."

"Lovely! Your food will be out shortly."

It is so quick, I question if said food is pre-prepared. My pimento cheese sandwich is not as good as I remember, but the amount of cheese sticking to the roof of my mouth is the same. The Italian soda is better as if I can appreciate its flavor in a way I couldn't before. The syrup coats my taste buds and makes the last bites of my sandwich confusing and off-putting. I gulp them down quickly and go back to slurping the dredges of my soda.

"Hailey, can I get another vanilla soda?"

"At least some things haven't changed," she says. Her smile would be the same as it had been in 1988 if she still had multi-colored banded braces.

Back then, she snuck me sips of her soda while I had spoon-fuls of strawberry sorbet. My mother would not allow me to drink soda. "Rots your teeth," she'd say. But Hailey had let me do a lot of things I shouldn't have when I was six, including walk home alone so she that could spend time with her boyfriend, Billy. I believe she ended up grounded for going to Prelk Hill to neck instead of taking care of me, though; drinking soda didn't rate.

Seeing her, I know I still blame her a little for that day, even though I have long since forgiven her teen stupidity. If it hadn't been for Hailey, I would not have found Laura Hurst.

November 27, 1988

Hailey

IT'S NOT MY FAULT. I blame Billy. He told me it'd be alright, that Adelynn was old enough to walk home alone. "It's just *one* afternoon," he'd said.

The sun was still above the trees; it was cloudier than today. It feels like it was two years ago, not two days. Is that a sign of aging? Mom said time would seem different when I was older, and I should cherish my hours now. What if Laura's death made everyone lose emotional time—*was that a thing?*

The knock on my door is no surprise. Still, it jolts me. I've become jumpy. Suddenly, being thin is a curse; I'm no longer able to defend myself. With my litheness comes weakness. If I'd been with Adelynn, I probably couldn't have stopped her from running to the pond. And if I'd been with Laura, I wouldn't have been able to save her. Or so I told myself so I could sleep last night. I had nightmares of freezing next to them. I'll think different thoughts before bed tonight.

A second knock—more insistent.

I hesitate for a moment. Mom told me a cop wanted to talk to me, but it could be anyone. "Hello? Anyone home?"

I glance through the peephole. A badge is up against it, blurry and gold. Though the sign of authority releases hiked, tense shoulders, my hand vibrates as I turn the knob. I welcome the uniformed man in—wary in my fragility—and apologize for the mess we both know isn't there; Mom always did that, so it seemed like the right thing to do. He settles himself into my dad's chair and kicks his feet up, propping them on the just-polished cherry table.

When I offer him a drink, he jokes that he wants whiskey. He gets a soda in the can. Turning my back to him for even a moment frays my nerves again. So when I go back into the living room, I perch on the edge of our least comfortable chair. "Comfort makes you complacent," my workaholic dad says. He says it for a different reason, but it seems true.

I've done nothing wrong. Still, if 21 Jump Street has taught me anything, it's not to let my guard down. And if 21 Jump Street, Dad, and my instincts agree, I know better than to ignore them all.

Officer Barbour—according to his smudged nameplate— frowns at his soda can; he *actually* expected whiskey, it seems.

"What questions do you have for me, sir? It's not like I did anything wrong. I wasn't even there." That's the whole reason Adelynn found her, isn't it? My voice stutters a little as if I'm guilty of something, which I guess I am: *I'm a horrible babysitter.*

Officer Barbour stretches and yawns. With his orange hair and middle that's straining the buttons of his shirt, he reminds me of Tigress—Tiggy for short. My beautiful, tubby tabby was an indoor-outdoor cat. Three years, two months, and five days ago, she didn't come home for dinner. I still cry because I miss her. I swear I hear her collar jingle now and again.

"Where were you on the afternoon of November 25th?" he asks and coughs with the gulp of carbonation he just drank.

"I was at school until 3:15. I stayed a little late to chat with friends. Then, Billy took me to Preck Hill." I wince. Everyone knows what happens on Preck Hill. The cop's face screws up when I say it, and his eyes tilt downwards. *Ew.* Crossing my arms over my loose sweater, I continue. "I got home in time for dinner around 5:30. I know I was supposed to walk Adelynn home. She's only six. *I know.* But Billy said she could handle it. I agreed. I know how stupid it was now; I know how stupid *I* was." I almost say that Billy pressured me to have sex while we were at Preck Hill again, and I almost say that my mother should've noticed the hickies he was always giving me. If she had, I would be grounded and only allowed to take Adelynn home before coming straight home myself. Instead, I add, "We had pot roast and casserole a lot last week."

Officer Barbour is mentally taking notes of everything I say and do. I know because his face twitches the way Mom's does when she keeps track of my verbal slip-ups and mixed-up stories: a notepad with no pencils or paper.

"Hm, alright. That's what Billy said too. We just wanted to make sure everyone was on the same page. A few pieces aren't adding up, is all." Officer Barbour chugs his soda with a frown, and blood drains from my face. Why wou—*he knows what happened three years ago.* "Thanks so much for the hospitality. We may be in touch, just stay in town for the time being. Okay?" He chuckles at the idea of a teenager leaving town during school. "Thanks again." Standing, he strolls by me out of the house. The yellow lamp beside him seems to dim.

Struck still, I'm no longer afraid of him; I'm afraid of what conclusions he may be drawing.

November 20, 2017

Ada

"I'M SO GLAD YOU SUGGESTED THIS!" Hailey waves emphatically at the rows of liquor bottles behind her.

I did no such thing.

When I told Hailey to come over—after a short phone call filled with awkward silences—she brought a bottle of Jameson and a wicked smile. Somehow paper cups and warm whiskey turned into a car ride to a loud bar. On the drive over, she stuffed her ponytail holder in her back pocket and smudged on some makeup.

I had planned to be asleep by 11:00 p.m., needing my beauty sleep as I do. But my watch reads 12:03 a.m., and Hailey shows no signs of slowing. *Wow, this sloppy drunk used to take care of me.*

A guy at least fifteen years younger than me swims through the crowd as if he's a shark and I'm chum. His eyes unsettle me, but I don't blink away. I am no small fish easily devoured. "Well, hello there," he says when he is within speaking range. His voice plays at slick and polished.

Hailey swivels on the black pleather stool and nudges me. Smeared lipstick mouths, "He's cute!"

I shake my head; she can't be serious. He is a child predator—and not the kind that preys on children. Besides, his polo and two ounces of cologne would be a turn-off at any age. I begin with, "How old are you?"

Don't say—"Old enough."

I have met plenty of Old Enough's in my thirty-five years. At an Omega Theta party, I had at least five teen boys with bad fake IDs desperate to convince me they were old enough for a quick fuck. Follow-up: could they have my underwear afterwards? I'm sure it was for their thesis paper; if I didn't give up my panties, I would be depriving them of solid research material. They got neither.

Because I worried I might end up in bed with one of these Old Enough's whether I liked it or not, I avoided drinking at the few parties I attended. One of the worst parties I've ever been to during the end of my freshman year convinced me that one-night-stands should be with older guys in berets who smoke clove cigarettes that I meet at poetry slams, not drunkards who fall into me at frat parties. I enjoyed the phase that followed that realization.

My younger self had smarts but lacked the cynical irritability I carry with me now. I sigh and stare at the neon logo over the stunted brunette's head. As the sign becomes a pink blur, my eyes water. "I am not sure what you are 'old enough' for; I suppose drinking, which is good for you." I smirk, then turn to face the bartender and blink away the bokeh that's taken to blurring my vision like lubricating drops.

Hailey takes over the conversation with the young guy looking to bang a cougar. I hear the cushion squeak and assume she's shifted her tank top down a little. She has already done that twice in the last hour. Both times, she had gotten a booze-stained napkin with digits torn into it.

She giggles and flips blonde waves into my face. This isn't why I came to Silynn. *So why are you here, Ada?* I sigh at myself. Rachael would have words for me.

I stare at the bartender, as he is the best-looking thing in the bar-billiard room hybrid. He has five years on me, maybe ten. The lines creasing his eyes are from a life well-lived or from staying in a shitty town too long. Either way, they were sexy.

Broad shoulders scrub an invisible spot on the bar in front of me. His scruffy voice sends shivers down my spine. "I'm Luke."

"Ada." I lick my lips as I stare at his full ones.

He interrupts thoughts of those lips on my body with, "Would you like to get dinner tomorrow night?"

"Uh—um—" At first, I wait for the punchline. I'm in knobby-kneed jeans, an oversized hoodie that doesn't look fashionable and slouchy—it's just too big—and old boots. With my hair up in a messy bun, I look as if it's laundry day and I am on the way to a mat. But he's attractive, and my face heats up despite my confusion. "Sure. I'm only in town for a little over a week, though." *Who am I right now?*

"We'll see." *Wait, what?* He strides away to a man at the end of the bar who had been waving and calling him by name for a few minutes.

I watch him for a while. He slings beers and mixes drinks efficiently and doesn't glance towards the tip jar or at the receipts once. Back muscles ripple through his white tee, and his messy hair gets greasier as he runs his hand through it every five seconds. I picture fistfuls of it between my fingers as I scream his name.

Hailey smacks my hand. "Luke? Finally. He's why we came." She looks happy, jealous, even a smidgen angry. "He's a good guy, Adelynn."

Ignoring the barb of my real name, I say, "Wait, what?"

"He saw you at the restaurant and wanted to meet you. Anyhow, Luke's a catch."

A stranger saw me and wanted to talk to me? That's weird. But I guess I've done that; *haven't I?* I'm flattered, I decide before I roll down the rabbit trail of being creeped out.

"Okay." I take two amber shots and repeat myself, "Okay."

My mother, the English teacher, would be so proud of my extensive vocabulary.

11:45 A.M.

THE REST OF THE TIME WE WERE OUT, I was Hailey's wing-woman. I helped her get seven phone numbers of people she probably already knew; Silynn isn't that big. Drunk and under neon lights, neighbors and local farmers could pretend to be strangers. One person I am almost sure I had seen with his wife at the soda shop had less of a Southern accent and more of a blonde woman on his lap. What happens at Bar stays at Bar, I guess. Or they were all just terrible people.

Hailey and I never caught up, which had been the purpose of the invite to my rented cabin—a planned two-hour visit, at most. She never told me about the pale and wrinkled space where a wedding ring traditionally lives. I am very familiar with the months a thin tan-line screams to the world that you are newly alone. In defiance, I nearly replaced my wedding ring set with a colored band to hide the mark. I told myself, Derek didn't deserve to leave that visual ache. Instead, I put on a brave face and ate dinner, saw plays, and went to concerts by myself. Onlookers probably assumed I was on a rediscovery journey and may have felt sorry for me. I tried not to care.

I wonder if Hailey and I could have bonded over that reclaiming of ourselves. We are adults now. Maybe, if we had more than Silynn and our past in common, I could let my animosity go.

Hailey also never explained the off-handed comment she made seven drinks in about having a child once. To be fair, I never asked—even when I saw the dark stretch marks ripped across her belly as her shirt rode up and our eyes met. It seemed like she wanted me to, though.

After a slow drunken-drive home over two patches of black-ice, through five miles of lampless highway, I managed to get us to the cabin safely. Hailey crashed on the couch. I made a glass of cloudy sink water and wobbled to bed.

As my eyes fluttered to sleep, the bridge over the Lynn Pond came to mind. With that, I shot awake and wouldn't close my eyes again until my brick of a phone was in hand and the bedroom door was locked.

I woke early this morning, and Hailey was gone. She left no note, but the blanket I covered her with was folded and draped over the back of the couch. I made coffee and have been reading a cozy mystery until now. The heroine has stumbled over four bodies, kissed three men, bought a house, changed up her look, gone out to eat, and shared two cookie recipes thus far—and it's only noon. I have six hours to kill before dinner and only thirty pages left. She'll solve the crime in twenty, get flirty with the cop by twenty-five, and hopefully, it will end with her skirt on that cop's floor.

Should *I* wear a skirt? Did I bring a skirt? Am I really going on a date during *this* trip? My judgment of myself says something. I have yet to call Rachael to tell her about last night, and I have been awake for—I glance at my watch—five hours and twelve minutes. That says something else. I grab a left-behind generic root beer from the refrigerator and a sleeve of crackers from the counter and prepare myself.

After picking up the receiver at least ten times, I dial her number. She answers with her usual professional greeting.

"It's Ada," I speak softly in anticipation of the verbal whiplash I'm about to get.

"How's the trip? What have you been doing?"

I retreat to the couch; it seems like a good, safe place. At home in my loft, the window seat has served that purpose for four years. "I went out to eat at an old haunt where I saw my old babysitter."

She waits; I crunch.

As always, I cave first. My knees meet my chest, and I continue. "I invited her over to the cabin. It was supposed to be so we could catch up, but…"

Rachael disapproves of every moment of last night: the drunken babysitter, the bartender, allowing Hailey to crash on the couch. I know she is scribbling furiously because I can hear her pen as its sharp edge scratches through two sheets of paper. "Mmhmm." I would love to know what she writes on her legal pad and how many pages my story takes up. My guess is eight, four for what I tell her, four she'll throw away due to the imprinted words her heavy-handed writing leaves.

"I suggest you cancel your date," Rachael starts. "If you said that last night you'd had sex with a stranger, I would honestly not be concerned. You haven't slept with anyone since Derek, and it's okay to give in to urges now and again. That being said…" I hear rustling in the background and take the opportunity to shove a cracker into my mouth. I chug soda to wash it down; it bubbles on my tongue. She clears her throat and continues, "I don't think dating is something you should be considering here in Bloomington or anywhere else—especially in Silynn. I hate harping and telling you what to do. But Ada, you have to put yourself first."

"I thought that was what I was doing. He's cute." Even as I say it, I can tell it's an attempt to convince us both.

A stubble of a hair on my calf itches, and I clench my fist. My mouth goes dry. I take three small sips of the syrupy drink and find it unhelpful, at best.

"After what you said about Hailey's response, it may rock more than one boat there, anyhow. You aren't there for long, but you are there long enough that rocking boats can flip over. I hate to cut this short, but my next appointment is here."

I clinch the blanket I have covered myself with. I don't remember doing that. "Of course. Put this convo on my tab; I'll tally up when I get back." It's only sort of a joke.

"How about we cut the phone rate in thirds, and you don't worry about keeping track. That okay?"

It's incredible! Crumbs are still in my mouth, so I sound as if I am talking around cotton balls, as I say, "Totally fair, I appreciate you caring." I gulp down the last of my faux-sassafras soda. "Oh, before you go, I wanted to let you know I'm going to see to my mother tomorrow. I will wait to call you again until after that."

"Great, Ada. Talk to you then!" Rachael sounds chipper; she's already put on her new-client voice. I recognize it from the first few months of sessions. It wore away the deeper we got, and I liked that.

Okay, Ada. Are you going to listen to Rachael and cancel a *possibly* stupid date with a hot older man? Or are you going to go anyway?

Sam

HER GIGGLE IS INFECTIOUS. Tiny teeth show through soft lips. She can't see me smiling along, but I am. I imagine being beside her, hearing her tell stories. I would laugh, too, I bet.

A puffy jacket and green mittens hide her thin frame. She's shorter than the other girls in her grade. The ones destined to be basketball players or reach cups on high shelves are magnets to her natural shine.

Two cheerleaders in short skirts and leggings stand side by side. They hang off of each other's arm just as they do every word of Lori's story. I imagine them as the type of girls who steal lipstick and cigarettes from their mothers' purses so they can sneak a smoke in the bathroom. They enjoy the red smudges their stolen makeup leaves behind when their friend's lips curl around the filter. Imagining the smell of them—seedy bars and cheap whores—makes me gag. Lori needs no part in their delinquency.

Another follower has desperate eyes, as if she craves Lori. I could see her competing with me for a lock of Lori's hair—both of us having our reasons for collecting it. Shelly is her name, I think; she is lanky and plain with a greasy, stringy, brown mop on her head.

I remember that age, that grade, Georgia Keller. She was seven when I was ten. Soft, red curls framed round pale cheeks— so like my other redheads, Laura, Nancy, Tracey, and now, Lori. A recess in the spring, I'd chased Georgia down with scissors, tackled her to the ground, and snipped a piece of her hair. I still have it. It lost the smell of strawberry shampoo and fresh cut grass decades ago, but the memory clings. I wonder how Lori's hair will smell and how long it will take for her scent to fade.

The bell rings. Lori and her friends keep chatting as they run back towards the hallways of Silynn Middle School. Before the doors close behind them, she unzips her jacket. She is wearing a purple sweatshirt with rainbow hearts on it; it's the same sweat-shirt she wore last Tuesday and one of my favorites thus far.

The muscle inside my chest pounds. *"We don't kill young things."*

I drive around the block. From the corner of Salmon and Riverside, I can see inside Lori's classroom. She prefers the window seat towards the back; it's easier for her to pass notes without getting caught.

The music on the radio is new and popular; so, it's nails on a chalkboard to me. Preset number three is the oldies station. I turn it up as I wait for her class to start.

"This is KW95 in the afternoon. Thanks for listening in. If you are just now joining us, we're doing a Boston hour! We just played 'Hollyann', so you know we've been singing into our hair-brushes. Next up is another favorite: 'More Than a Feeling'. You all know this one. So turn it up, and jam with us! And don't even think about changing the channel after; we've still got another twenty minutes of Boston to go!"

My mother had the radio on often before she went nuts.

She'd dance around my room and sing. It was when the music stopped that my father and I were sure something was wrong.

The song starts up, and children funnel into the classroom. Lori takes her usual seat and sheds her backpack. When she takes her jacket off, shiny, ginger hair clings to it. I inhale the phantom scent of lip balm and pencil shavings I know surround her. Glitter on her sweatshirt sparkles almost as much as she does.

Lori grabs her book and tosses it on her desk. She opens it to somewhere in the halfway point, and I turn up "More Than a Feeling". Her mouth forms letters; I pretend she asked me to sing to her.

Changing thirty-year-old lyrics, I do. "And I begin dreaming / more than a feeling / 'Til I see Lori Michelle walk my way / I see my Lori walkin' my way." Stale licorice breath hits me.

I need a mint.

1:02 P.M.

WHEN I RETURN HOME, the answering machine blinks at me. The first message is a breath before a noisy click. Telemarketers. The second is from the pharmacy with a "final reminder"; I hit delete before they finish. Taylor doesn't want to take that medication anymore.

"Hey, Sam." I hear Taylor's voice over the line. "I don't know why I couldn't do this in person, but I couldn't. We'd been doing better, but I want more than better; we both should. We deserve happiness." The message stops abruptly, and I shrug.

Sounds about right; I figured it would end like this or in an addition to my collection. After all, I married for appearances more than love—normalcy is essential, I'd been told. My father made sure to add comments about that often. I think he knew one day I'd end up like I have. He wanted to make life easier on me, both in human interaction and interests.

I fix myself a sandwich and grab a beer without judgment. Plopping on the couch alone in the cabin Taylor and I built together, I get a sense of freedom rather than grief. I can leave my sweetheart's hair on the bedside table instead of in a box wrapped in a blanket in another box under the bed. I'll be able to spread Lori's photographs on the kitchen table to enjoy the hard work I've been putting into my hunting. I can pin the route to her house on the wall as I've always imagined doing. No longer will I have to pretend.

I'm getting a divorce; that's as normal as it gets. As for what comes after the divorce, well, I guess I'll see.

Jess's face pops into my mind. Should I warn her life will be different when she comes home? Mentally, I shake my head; I know that's unnecessary. She's an adult and can handle change. In that, she's like me more than Taylor.

I take a big swig of an afternoon beer and turn on a show about murderers in sheep's clothing.

Ada

I'M NOT DRESSED UP. I am in jeans without knobby-knees and a sweater that fits me; I only brought two of those. Snow is in the air, so I choose the crappy boots I brought just in case. I swiped on the lipgloss my friend's thirteen-year-old left in my purse. Now, I smell like teen spirit—all nerves and vanilla cake.

When Luke arrives at my door, I do not have to look at my watch. I know he's late by fourteen minutes, so I have written him off. If I'm honest with myself, I had been looking for a reason since Rachael judged me. I am pretty sure I wasn't *actually* going to leave the house with him in the first place. But his being late solidifies the worries I have worn into the blue-green ombre rug. Derek was late. Derek was having an affair.

"So sorry I'm late," Luke says the instant I crack the door open.

He's wearing a sharp sports coat over a thin sweater and slacks with shiny shoes. *Oh.* I can think of only one place in the Silynn I knew as a child where he wouldn't be considered so overdressed they may send him away. From casually asking me out at a bar, how could I have figured he had wanted to take me there? La Porot, they called it. I genuinely think they believed 'porot' was a word. It was an Americanized "French" restaurant with a name as ridiculous as the food.

As usual, I realize Rachael is right. I am foolish for treating this trip so cavalierly.

"It's fine," I hear myself say to Luke's insincere-sounding apology. "I can't go out anyway. I'm not feeling well."

He looks me up and down—dressed with my purse by the door. "Is this a new development? I can get you some soup, and we can stay in, watch a movie or something?"

I meet his eyes and wince. "Sorry. This was a bad idea."

"What?" Luke's face pales before splotching.

Embarrassed, I sputter, "S-sorry, I am only here for—"

He punches the door. "No! Not again!"

My eyes couldn't get any wider without pliers. Quickly, I catch the door and start to close it on his anger. I have done this bit already, too. Shutting the door on an angry man is not a new occurrence in my life. At least Derek had the decency to be drunk.

"You wouldn't be with me when you lived here before. Now, you're turning me down again?"

I blanch, his cologne and words make my head spin. "I have no idea what you're talking about. I left when I was nine; you would have been a teenager. I'm sure you have me confused. Either way, you need to leave." *Great.* My first date in god-who-knows-how-long, and I choose a crazy person.

Luke's face reddens, and he tries to push in the door I have nearly shut. He is stronger than I am, and my boots slip on the thin mat beneath me. I try to kick it back but fail. Luke snarls. The door flies open, and he charges—rabid with slobber dripping from his mouth. Anger and lust fill his eyes as he reaches for me.

I scream, "FIRE! FIRE! FIRE!" repeatedly. My throat shreds itself with exertion.

His hand reaches out, but he can't cover my mouth in time.

Noises from the other six cabins make their way in through the open door. As if he has been hit, he stumbles back. Luke's head swivels around the living room, searching. When someone calls out, their words are indistinct babel. Panic fills his eyes. Squeaky new shoes scuff the floor as he spins and runs out the door.

I need to close that behind him. I need my window seat. I need to call Rachael. *What do I need?* When my hand touches the doorknob, I fall over and begin to cry. I hear tires squeal in the not-far-enough distance.

Visitors and men who could afford to cheat on their wives in Silynn-style stood outside their cabins in various states of undress. I see them out of the corner of my blurred vision. Without a word, a fully made-up woman with wild curls brings me a blanket and glass of cheap, watered-down vodka.

I gush out what happened. She nods and coos through my story as if she has heard it a million times, and maybe she has. I shiver and tell her where I keep my pajama pants.

"Why would I need those?" She looks down at fishnet covered legs. Corset laces dangle from the back; the fabric gapes open in the front. I see enough of her smooth, tawny skin that I probably owe her money.

I gamble. "Because I don't want you getting arrested tonight?"

She hugs me as if we are friends and runs inside.

By the time the police show up, she sits beside me on the sidewalk in a cloud-covered two-piece flannel pajama set. She speaks for me until the questions come.

They jot down notes and nod with furrowed brows. I have to give them my real name, and they recognize it—recognize me. The tallest one has a mole by his left eye, and I would swear he pushed me off of a swing once. The other has such a forgettable face he could be anyone.

With every question they ask, my head spins more. Narrowing their eyes, they ask, "Did you know him?" at almost the same time.

I shake my head. "No, but he said he knew me from when I lived here before."

"Why did you agree to go on a date with someone you didn't know?"

What a dumb question. "Hailey knew him." Inwardly, I cringe. Namedropping is a nasty habit of a friend I see now and again in Bloomington. He talks of his adventures and the people he met there until he's blue in the face. More often than not, dinner will be over before he remembers to ask you how you have been. Often, I question spending time with him.

"What made him angry?" the dull-faced cop asks.

The nerve of these backwoods wannabes! "I told him to leave." I shiver with the thought of the look in his eyes. Derek had that look once; he charged right past me and slammed his fist straight into the wall. All the way to the hospital, he cried and apologized, begged for my forgiveness—which I have never given.

The cop towers over me. "And why did you do that?"

I want to tell them to go away. My left butt cheek is going numb from the cold. "Because I felt uncomfortable when he showed up."

"Why?" he asks, scribbling more than twice what I have said, and I wonder if he is writing a screenplay based on his sad life as a police officer in a small town. 'Adelynn Bailey gets attacked but not hurt' may be the biggest story he has ever encountered. Or he could be sketching me nude. He seems the type.

Before I can answer, the other cop asks, "And why would you scream, 'Fire'?"

My mind flashes back to my gym teacher, a pot-bellied man with one ever-stray eyebrow. He told us people are inherently selfish and horrible. Maybe he was just cynical, or perhaps he'd had a sad life. Either way, his sage advice has come in handy more than once. "You may think screaming, 'Rape,' 'He took my purse,' or 'Help me' will get you help. Nine times out of ten, it won't." I bet he'd had research to back that up. "No. You have to scream, 'Fire.' Self-preservation kicks in, and everyone runs. Even if they aren't running to help you, it may scare your attacker away. Besides that, sirens of some kind will show up pretty quickly."

As I am about to tell the cop about Mr. Poll and his rock-solid theory on humanity's suckage, Freesia—my new pajama-clad friend—pipes up. "It doesn't matter. He should have left without incident. And she had to scream something to make him leave, and it got our attention, didn't it? Why don't you leave Ada alone for now?"

They nod in unison.

I barely remember it, but it rings true that the cops were pretty stupid during the Laura Hurst investigation. Decades later, and Silynn still hasn't found decent police officers. One holds out a business card. "You're right, ma'am. Adelynn, call us if you think of anything else."

"It's Ada now. Just Ada." I stare at the misshapen mole on the officer's face as I accept the offered card. He should get that looked at by a dermatologist. I could recommend mine, but my doctor is in Bloomington. She's really good, though.

Short-cop nods. "Alright, Just-Ada. We'll be in touch. And please keep thinking about his comment. If he remembers you, there *must* be a reason."

"Sexist pigs," Freesia says, as they walk away. "Don't you worry about it, Ada. You didn't do anything. If he remembers you, if he's in love with you—" I check out. *In love with me?* I know she is still talking, but as I stare at her smeared, fuchsia pink lips, all I hear is, "Whah, whah whah whah. Whah whah."

I want to scream, *"I was nine when I left!"*

Three pubic hairs and one on my forearm scream for relief. I scratch at my arm with a vigor that makes me look rashy but can only wiggle for a minor relief under my panties.

"—lock the door. I can stay with you if you'd like," Freesia finishes.

Freesia's date—the grocery store owner, she told me—watches us; so do most of the guests of the rentals. The grocery store owner's short and thinning hair is tousled, shirt so hastily buttoned he had missed two. I know he is waiting for her none too patiently. I decide to give her the rest of the night off.

"Thanks, that would be great," I say with my eyes narrowed and locked on the grocer.

His huffs turn to stomps as he flounces back into the cabin alone.

I guess I won't spend too many nights by myself while I'm in Silynn. The wind picks up, and Freesia and I go back inside. Her arm around me is comforting, and I find myself drowsy. "Let's get you to bed," Freesia coos.

"Food and drink are in the fridge if you're hungry or thirsty." Distantly, I know giving free rein of someone else's possessions (and mine) while I am asleep may go horribly wrong. But as a fog of exhaustion rolls over me, I'm just grateful someone is there to tuck me in.

November 21, 2017

Ada

RACHAEL HAS STEPPED OUT of a session to take my call.

As I spill my irrational fears, they sound even crazier than they did in my head. "I can't help but imagine him lurking behind me in the woods that day. What if he did it?" I whisper into the phone.

Before my panic-call, I stomached overcooked eggs as I pictured a younger Luke watching me. I saw him drool as I tugged at my stockings. He touched himself when I bent over to adjust the buckle on my shoe. A rage made my hands shake, and I knew a therapy chat was in order. Now, as I talk with Rachael, I know I am being overdramatic. I have worked myself into a tizzy.

"Calm down now, that's a big leap. You don't remember him, right? You said that. No recollection of him at all?" she asks. *Click, click.* She plays with her pen when I'm nearly out of time.

"No…" I hedge. "But it still scares me. *He* still scares me. He said he knew me, Rachael." I talk in circles smaller than the phone cord wrapped around my reddening finger. "He said I wouldn't '*be with him.*' What the hell does that even mean?"

Rachael nods through the phone; I hear it despite not seeing it. "I understand, and you're right to want to stay away from him. Still, you shouldn't imagine him following you—or think about him at all. Just find a new place to stay, call me with the number —the police too—and work on the calming techniques we've talked about. You have no reason to believe he had anything to do with Laura. He said a creepy thing when he was pissed off, true, but that doesn't mean he murdered a little girl or stalked you when you were a child. He was being rejected. You, of all people, know men say crazy things when they're being rejected."

My ex-husband claimed he tampered with my birth control. He had said I could be pregnant, so we should stay together. When that hadn't worked, his excuses had become longer than the list of all the things I had to do to get a divorce—which had been substantial. The name change I was happy about, the apartment hunting was almost fun, but why did I have a lawyer to pay or a realtor to deal with? *Who cheated on who?*

I sigh, resigned. Rachael knows best. Honestly, what's new? If she wasn't on call, I have no idea what I would do. "You're right, of course. I will try and breathe." Floorboards creak behind me. I realize my voice has become a normal volume some time during my call. I wince and turn around to mouth, "I'm sorry!"

Freesia holds up the "it's okay" sign and opens the refrigerator. She takes out the half-empty jug of milk that came with the rental. I question its expiration date.

"I have homework for you," Rachael says. "I need you to start keeping a journal."

My face goes as sour as that milk probably tastes. "A journal?"

"Yes, Ada. I want you to write your thoughts and worries down. I'm here for you—always on call—just like we talked about. But sometimes you'll need an interim someone to talk to. Pretend the journal is that someone. Or me—it could be me. You can read it to me when we are on the phone or when you get back. I can read it too. Or, if you'd rather, it can stay private. What do you think?"

I hope my sigh is loud enough she can hear it. "I think you have been right about everything else thus far."

She is delighted and probably nodding as she says, "That's true."

"Thanks again for taking my call. I will find some paper and a pen. I can't say how well it will go, but I will try." Her patient must have more patience than I do. I would have peeked my head in by now and loudly asked if she was alright. It occurs to me that I may have rude tendencies. "Thank whoever is waiting, too, please!" I add.

"I will," she replies. She sounds happier than when she answered the phone. She must feel better about my mental health, or she's glad she'll finally be able to get back to her session.

I hang up first and turn to see Freesia on the couch. She's either staring off into space or trying to see what's going on in the neighboring cabins. I take the opportunity to wander to the bathroom and brush my teeth. The mint zings my gums, and I feel normal again.

Heading towards the living room, I see Freesia chugging the jug of milk. Her curls have created a static fuzz around them, and they transport me to the day a journalist from another state came to tell Laura's story through my eyes. My mother spent hours creating a shower cap of curls on my head so I would be camera-ready. I resembled a pageant child, and the newscaster ate it up. I refused to wash them out, opting to let my hair turn into a chia poof instead. Thanks to that nine minute and forty-six-second television interview, I became a hot commodity. My mother paid more attention to me for a while after that.

I clear my throat; either Freesia doesn't hear me or doesn't care, because she keeps drinking. Sinking into an armchair across from the couch, I smile. "Sleep okay?"

She puts down the milk and wipes her face with the back of her manicured hand. "Yeah, I slept great." Her cloud of curls moves in a mass as she nods. "Thank you. This couch is super comfy! Sorry I slept in."

I wish you had different hair. "No problem at all," I gush. I mean it, but it sounds like one of the forced, polite comments strangers said the few times my mother had taken Peter and me to church. I add, "Would you like to go to breakfast?" as if that will make me seem more sincere.

Smeared lipstick creases further with the broad smile she gives me. "I'd love to. Let me clean up first."

Well, crap. I didn't think she would actually take me up on it. I want to find a new place to stay, not sit down for food. That'll teach me to be insincere. "Of course. I better do the same. I'm still in my pajamas, and my breath is atrocious—don't get too close!" Cue canned laughter.

"You got a place in mind?" Freesia calls from the bathroom. The toilet flushes and garbles her next few words. "—place called the Silver Diner right outside of town that's got delicious pancakes and greasy bacon. Wait, you're from a big city, aren't you? Are you a vegetarian?"

My real laugh is quiet and stifled. Is that what people think of 'city folk' here? I suddenly feel disconnected from Silynn in a way I hadn't imagined. I am not displeased. "Nope, I eat meat. Rare meat, in fact." It seems I want to impress Freesia.

"Awesome." She turns the faucet. I hear two splashes and a long gargle before she says, "I'm almost ready."

I had freshened up before calling Rachael. It always felt wrong talking to her when I smelled bad or had unbrushed hair or teeth. Although this morning, I hadn't wanted to wake my houseguest, so I had skipped brushing at first; it has been the hardest part of the trip thus far. By the time Freesia is presentable

—save her outfit—I am by the door in a black, cable-knit sweater, jeans, green zip-up army-style boots, and a khaki scarf. When it comes to day-to-day clothing, I'm pretty one-note.

As she rounds the corner of the hallway, Freesia is fluffing her less-frizzed curls. "Whoa!" Her eyes widen, and I see more white than brown. "You get ready fast."

I tell two lies and a truth. "Learned habit. Besides, I'm hungry and excited to check this new place out."

In the short walk to the car, I learn that Silver Diner was built only two years ago, and since, Freesia's business has picked up substantially. She's unsure of the percentage, as she doesn't keep track. All she knows is that thanks in large part to the grocer, one of the gas station attendants, a math teacher, and the mayor's wife, she owns one of the largest houses in Silynn. I enjoy listening to her say the city's name as only a non-native would: "Sigh-lynn."

Freesia navigates, and I ignore the inclination to rub my finger along the thin, fishnet-created indentions on her thighs. They look so deep that I'm curious as to how long they will take to fade.

She tells me stories of her normal, suburban upbringing. Her "Roberts"—Freesia hates the name John—come with hilarious anecdotes, half of which I forget as quickly as she tells them to me. Though we drive for half an hour, and I learn a lot about her, she never tells me what led her to her lifestyle or how old she is. Both things are none of my business, but I can't say I'm not curious. Due to the two bathroom, three bedroom ranch-style house she owns, it could be strictly financial. If so, she had tapped into the right vein.

"That's it." Freesia points to the large sign off the two-lane highway that blinks in spite of the white sun.

It would have been impossible to miss.

I turn into the cramped parking lot and squeeze between a box truck and mini-van. Our doors barely open wide enough for us to slip out. I fully expect at least one side view mirror to be hanging by its wires when we leave. It wouldn't be the first time.

We traverse the frost-slick asphalt to an ordinary building. Despite its name, the Silver Diner is not silver; it doesn't even have a silver roof. It is a muddy brown stucco-like material with glass windows so wide they cover the majority of the front of the building. The interior is nothing special. If I was a betting woman, and I suppose I have been talked into it once or twice, I would bet this used to be a Waffle House.

"The wait is about fifteen minutes," a boy no older than sixteen calls from the center of the restaurant. He holds a black plastic tub filled with syrup-covered plates and half-eaten waffles sliding into leftover soda in scratched stackable cups.

Freesia leans into me, and whispers, "It never takes that long."

I nod. Pretending to adjust the leather band around my wrist, I take quick note of the time: 11:03 a.m. *We'll see.*

The elderly owners of the motor home parked partially in a ditch across the street canoodle as they try to unzip a fanny pack together. A group of five teens sit at a four-top and spit bits of napkin out of straws at each other; they are boisterous and happy. I assume they are townies taking a break from the prying eyes of neighbors and friends who report any activities back to their parents.

Before I get the chance to scrutinize the other customers, the teens pop up and throw a wad of cash on the table. "Thanks, Judy," they holler in a chorus of cracking voices and excitable laughs.

A woman in her fifties appears with a stained rag. Her breathing is labored. "Let me clean this off, and then we're ready for you!" After she stuffs the tip into her dirty apron, she wipes crumbs into her hand. The germ-soaked fabric leaves a damp smear on the table. "All yours! I'll grab you both some water."

My watch tells me our wait has been two minutes and forty-three seconds. *Not bad.*

·   ·   ·

12:49 P.M.

TIME HAS GOTTEN AWAY FROM ME. Freesia is an interesting human. With a single nosey, inappropriate question from me— "How did you choose your profession?"—she told me her life story and then some.

I still need a different place to stay. I have no idea how hard that is going to be to find, and it's ten minutes and fifteen seconds until one o'clock.

"Ready?" I ask after sneaking a glance my watch. We are nursing our fifth glass of water, and we have both had a full order of pancakes, that greasy bacon she mentioned, and eggs. If she isn't ready to go, I may leave her.

"Yep. This was fun. How long are you staying?" Freesia asks.

"Until the 27th."

"Well, winter is usually my dry season. People are always scared to stop around here; *I wonder why*." She laughs. "I mean, if they get snowed-in, how could they explain it to their significant other? So, if you have some free time…"

Another breakfast wouldn't hurt; I do have to eat. "Sure. I'll get your number," I say. "I need a new place to stay, obviously. Who knows where that will be."

Freesia buys breakfast. "Last night was rough on you," she says as she tosses out her plastic faster than I could unzip my bag. I had planned on getting it because she'd helped me with the police and stayed over. That being said, I have learned the hard way never to turn someone down if they want to help you.

"Where can I drop you off?" I ask as we step out into the bitter cold. I knew I should have taken a jacket with me. The restaurant was warm, and I had rolled up my sleeves. But the walk to the car has me clenching my fists and stuffing them into my small girl jean pockets.

"It's about thirty minutes from here—back through town. Sorry! I didn't think about that."

"It's fine," I say with only a hint of irritation. "Just lead the way."

I try not to stare at the clock as the afternoon ticks away. 12:54 p.m. 12:57. 12:58. 1:01. I play off the second time check by switching on the heat; it blows cold air on our faces. Not ready. With the fourth glance, I try the heat again and am rewarded with blissful warmth.

Freesia holds her hands up to the vent and sighs. "That feels nice."

We ride in pleasant silence for a while before I turn the radio on low—side speakers pipe in smooth jazz. I roll my sleeves up again and hum along, pretending I know the melody.

"Did you see that?" Freesia points to her right.

"No. What?"

She waves one hand emphatically; her other hand touches the glass. "I think it was a sign for a rental. Turn around!"

I hesitate for a moment. "Why not? Can't hurt to look," I say —to her or myself, I honestly have no clue.

Turning the car around is more of a seven-point turn than three.

Once I'm looking for it, it's easy to spot. Amongst the green and brown, the red and white "RENTAL" sign shouts at me.

I check behind me—no one is there. I slow to a stop, and Freesia jots the phone number and address down on the Silver Diner receipt with a cheapo hotel pen from the glovebox.

"Good find," I tell her, and her face lights up.

. . .

1:48 P.M.

As I slam the car door, I glance at the row of cabins.

Is he here? Is he watching? Is he inside? Why is my paranoia back? Should I leave my stuff and run away? Just call the rental and tell them I've checked out? Is he sneaking around my rental car right now?

I dart towards the cabin. The lock had been Ada-proofed in my absence. It takes four tries and five deep breaths to get inside. I rush to the corner and curl up on the floor the moment I lock the deadbolt.

Rachael's voice pops into my head. "You need to breathe during moments of rapid thoughts. We have to work on you gaining control of them. For you, I suggest you sit and let them come in all their chaos. It's okay to be overwhelmed for a while, to scream or cry. But once your thoughts start to go in circles, stand up—I mean it. Physically stand up and shake them off. Grab some water or tea, and do any activity that requires brain power: make a snack, get the mail, dust like you said you would for two weeks. If you can't, if that sounds like too much, then watch some TV or listen to music with lyrics. Cyclical thoughts will get you nowhere."

Taking six more deep breaths, I prepare to be overwhelmed.

Luke invades my mind. Dry, split knuckles swing at me as he shouts, *"You wouldn't be with me when you lived here before. Now, you're turning me down again?"* I shake my head as if I can free him from my swimming thoughts. Instead, I see myself at six with pigtails and wearing green overalls. A mouth-breathing teenage Luke hides in the bushes. I hear my mother's voice blame me for going the back way. She sounds pleased. For her, my finding Laura had been a mixed blessing; how much so, I have yet to figure out. Peter screams at me for ruining his school year; his round face resembles a tomato.

As if I'm in school and my thoughts are projector slides, the image clicks to Peter standing above me at my vanity. His voice plays at 'stern father' as he tells me my smile is too fake. He shouts, "Again!" I digress. I click to the next image. Luke's weathered, handsome face is young and smooth as he watches me, hidden. Rachael appears on my shoulder and taps her golden watch in my ear. *It's time, Ada; you've come full circle.* I glance at the pink face of mine. 2:23 p.m. Zooming worries have sapped an hour of my day.

I creak into a hunched stance and waddle my way to the phone, my knees ever-protesting. The paper with the rental number on it is hanging out of my back pocket, and my heart speeds up. *I could have lost it.* Before it disappears into the ether or joins the dust bunnies under the couch and is declared missing, I dial the number.

"Hello. I'm calling about the rental. Is it still available?"

"—ello? Y— it is. The key is insi— the —lbox." The man sounds far away.

"You're breaking up," I say. "How much is it per night?"

"—ty dollars," he replies.

"How much?" I ask in hopes it will break at dollars this time.

I know I should request a meeting or call back later, but I have the urgency to leave as strongly as I do to pee at the moment. If Rachael were on the other line, I would make her wait as I rushed to the bathroom.

He shouts, "—y dollars."

I mumble to myself, "What do I care?" Aloud, I say, "I'll take it. How should I get you the money?"

"Leave it —." It's as if the phone is testing me.

"Perfect! Thank you." I assume he will stop by for a check-in. We can figure things out then. Until, I'll assume $90 per night; the cabin costs $60, but it is not so tucked away.

. . .

I nearly missed my turn-off, as the sign is gone. The owner must have swung by already. I hope he is still here to give me more details; I don't bother holding my breath.

The long, long, *long* driveway is bumpy. By the time I pull to a stop at the end of it, my spine would swear I was just in a car accident.

A dented, metal mailbox is at the edge of the gravel. It's open, and white paper sticks out from inside of it. *Must be for me.* As I walk to it, I cross my fingers that there is a phone inside. I need to call Rachael and the local police to give them my new temporary address; some people may still need to find me. Inside a business envelope, I see a key and a note. "$60 a night. Call when you're ready to leave or if you have any problems."

Though I see the house, there is no paved way or even a stone pathway leading to it. My bags become the heaviest things I have ever had to carry by the end of the uneven five-minute trudge in the snow.

When I finally make it to the cabin, I discover it is more of a large boxy space. There are the usual suspects: living room space, bed in the corner, half-kitchen, small fireplace. The bathroom is unusual. The sink and toilet are in a small separate room, but the clawfoot tub is at the end of the bed. Every nook and cranny is lit up by sun and snow.

I drop my bags on the mattress; they bounce as it squeaks. That bodes well for my back.

After locating the phone against the wall in the kitchen—the place to keep it in Silynn, it seems—I call the police station. It takes a few minutes worth of repeating myself, but we are on the same page. They are surprised I would call about a change in location—despite their request. The law must be flexible here.

Rachael is the next order of business. When she doesn't pick up, I don't bother with a message; broken numbers and choppy letters won't help anyone. After I hang the heavy plastic up, I look outside. *Okay, now what?*

Resigned, I rifle through my bags and look for paper. I come up with another small pad from a hotel and a book. Ruthfred Suites notepad it is then. I have not journaled since I was a kid. When my mother found it and read it aloud to Peter, I decided yet another part of me was best hidden away.

Dear Rachael, I begin—feeling childish.

I feel safer here, I think. But is isolation the best way to handle problems? Oh, and I'll be having another breakfast with Freesia. Is this what I should be writing? I'm going to take a nap.

Bye?

I put down the crappy pen that missed inking a few letters and shuffle towards the bed. As I lay on it, I'm sure it has springs. Still, in the bright day, I sleep. I hope when I wake it will be dark.

Sam

A YOUNG MAN PASSING THROUGH Silynn is buying one of the ever-rotating hot dogs. The twenty-something covers it in bright yellow mustard and slimy relish from a jar with crusty bits around the lid. I bet those are the same chunks of shiny meat that spun under the heat lamp three days ago—the last time I came in to buy a six-pack of cheap beer and bag of black licorice. The relish is probably expired, but at least artificial mustard never dies.

Marly is behind the counter texting in between pushing buttons on the ancient cash register. She isn't apologetic. She's engrossed in the dirty messages she's receiving—if the rush of blood to her cheeks is any indication of the text's contents.

"Thanks, I guess," the guy mumbles.

He doesn't wait for Marly to bag his chips, soda, and rag mag. He snatches his purchases up and heads for the door. I push it open for him, if only to hurry him out; I have places to be. The stranger half nods at me but doesn't meet my eyes.

"Hey Sam," Marly puts her phone down to smile and starts in with her usual chattiness. "We haven't seen each other since my last shift… two weeks ago, was it? I haven't been able to work during my free period since, because our long-term sub was an ass. I'm so glad Mrs. Hope is back. Two weeks is *way* too long for maternity leave. How've you been?" I shove my licorice and cans towards her. *Hurry up.* "You must be so busy! What have you and Taylor been up to? Still remodeling the house?"

Taylor is much more polite than I am to clerks. Idle chit-chat is an art form I've never cared to learn; I've had to work on facial expressions as it was. "Something like that," I say. We've spent years "remodeling" things. That's what Taylor calls anything we do to improve the house; too many home improvement shows will do that to a person.

Because I don't give her much to go on, Marly begins telling me about her school year thus far. She's excited about her upcoming break. I nod occasionally. Maybe I even smile. Her new boyfriend, Chad—she broke up with Robby because he was a dick—is going to take her to the beach. Marly sees him as marriage material. "Even though we're only sixteen."

I'm not thinking about Chad; I've shifted to thoughts of my fingers squeezing her neck. I watch her eyes grow wide, the white snuffing out the blue. When she struggles, my fantasy shatters. She wouldn't be as satisfying as my sweethearts. Her fear would be different, angrier. The innocence Marly had once is gone. I see that in her tight, low-cut sweater and pushed-up breasts, in the texts that make her flush, in the way she talks about the hotel she and Chad may need to get if they got too tired to drive home. She has little innocence left.

"You hear me?" Her hands slip down to her hips, and she frowns.

"Sorry," I say. "Thinking about staining the deck. Have to do it before it snows again."

Her smile returns. "So you!" she says as if she knows me, as if

we're old friends. "Here's your stuff. I'll put it on Taylor's tab."
Marly winks; somehow, she knows I don't handle our money.

"No, it's fine." I didn't know even Taylor had a tab.

She coughs a little and nods. "Oh, alright. It'll be $9.98."

"Thanks." I hand her a ten and wait for what I've heard her
say numerous times.

"After all these years, I still love that we have no tax." And
there it is.

Maybe I could make an exception. An older girl wouldn't raise
suspicions. No one would think the Lake Killer is back. The
moment I think about the name thrust on me, I'm pissed. I
snatch the bag and stomp out; the rustle of the plastic reminds
me of kicking a kid in the face when I was eight.

I had a name all picked out for myself: The Sweetheart
Collector. The letter I'd planned to send after they found Laura's
body in the spring was going to include the one detail the paper's
had all left out: the pink conversation heart left by the edge of the
lake. It'd been a coincidence those were the candies I had in my
book bag that day in November—of all months—but it seemed
fitting.

My letter would have told Silynn that Laura was my sweetheart. There would've been no confusion over the candy then—or
any that followed.

3:13 P.M.

LORI SKIPS ACROSS THE WHITE DOTTED LINES, two streets
from her house. She hops over a patch of ice in a shady spot by
the corner. I have only moments. Once she turns left, neighbors
know her by name. I hedge almost too long.

When I slow my car close to her, she turns.

Perfect.

I expect the suspicion I've had time and time before, but Lori's unblemished face lights up. "Hello! Are you new to the neighborhood?" She's too trusting. Her family has done me a favor.

"No. I'm just passing through. I was hoping you could give me directions."

It's a valid reason to slow. The internet connection is spotty around town, at best. I made a big show of holding up my phone for anyone watching before I rolled my window down or talked to a young girl. *"We don't kill young—"*

Lori's voice interrupts my father's. "I can't help much with that. My parents should be able to, though. They know everything about everything, or at least they say they do." Lori laughs, and her chilled pink nose wrinkles. The wind has picked up enough to blow baby hairs around her head like a crown.

"I can drive you there." I try to appear casual as if her choice makes no difference.

She looks at me suspiciously for the first time. "No, thank you. I'm not supposed to ride with strangers."

I nod. Now is when I pretend to leave. "Sorry, I wasn't trying to be creepy! It's just really cold out there, and since we were going the same way... But I understand. Get home safe," I say and put my hand up to wave goodbye.

"It *is* very cold, and we *are* just two streets away." She shifts her pink backpack; it weighs heavily on her shoulders. I imagine the indentations the straps leave, the ones she usually hid from her parents. Because what good would their concern do for her? Lori's like that: sweet, considerate, and cares for those she loves. And she loves her family. I've seen that during giggles and glances at family dinners. "Okay," she decides.

"I promise I'll drive carefully." And that, I mean.

She stares at her hand on the door handle. I watch Lori's mind spin as she grapples. *Is she crazy or right to take this ride?* As the car door cracks open, my back starts to sweat, my pits stink.

"Thank you," she says and lets her book bag thud onto the floorboard. Now, she's just a girl in the seat of my car. Lori shivers and uses the vents to warm her hands. It's been three years since I collected Kendra, and suddenly, I'm shy and nervous.

"Of course." I forget to ask which way is her house, because I already know. But it wouldn't matter, we aren't going there.

Luke

"You able to come in today?" CK rarely waits for me to say anything when I answer his calls.

"You sure that's a good idea, boss?" I ask. "I wasn't planning on it because..." I leave the rest of the sentence for him to fill in and rub at the palms of my hands. They have deep half-moon slices in them, a sign of my annoyance and lack of nail clippings. Precious Adelynn should've felt these last night. I should be cutting them because she'd griped about scratches on her delicate skin, not because my hands are starting to bleed.

He pauses. *Maybe he hasn't heard.* "You mean 'causa that girl? Adelynn is just another hysterical woman. No one thinks you did anything wrong."

"You didn't even ask what happened." I don't know why I push the issue. No one's mentioned it, so he may be right.

Crinkles and crunches blast in my ear; CK loves his cheesy puffs. "Okay, Luke. What happened?"

"She invited me over for dinner at the cabin she's renting for the week. I show up, and she's already acting weird. When I start to come in, she starts screaming like a lunatic." I clench my fists again and wince.

"Mhmm. It's what they do." *Crunch.*

"—I hadn't even tried to hug her hello. Then, she starts darting around the room like I'm chasing her. I do for a second but only trying to calm her. CK, I wasn't going to hurt her."

Crunch. "Luke, yer a good man. Adelynn's got baggage."

Doesn't she ever. I nearly spit as I say, "She goes by Ada now." That's our problem, isn't it? Adelynn is the girl I fell in love with; Ada means nothing to me. I picture Adelynn blowing out eight candles as curls slip out of her hair. There was an innocence in her that I'd wanted to consume. Last night, that was all gone with her too-tight jeans and lips glossed up like a tween whore. Her usual scent of Dove soap and shampoo was lost to a fragrance reminiscent of Freesia after a visit to Mrs. Ore at the retirement home.

CK laughs. "Adelynn. Ada. What's the difference? You can put lipstick on a pig, Luke. In the end, it's still a fuckin' pig. I'll see you at six." The line goes quiet.

Clothes from yesterday are crumpled on the floor in the bathroom, so I'll wear those. It's dark enough in Bar no one will notice the wrinkles, or if they do, they'll blame it on their drunken eyesight.

11:06 P.M.

LIME STINGS MY HAND. The raw nail marks fade in the red neon bar signs. Gloves are in the supply closet, but I can't be bothered to get the key from CK.

"You okay, Luke?" a regular, Polly, asks. She often stinks of bourbon before she gets settled on the second bar stool from the right. "Your face is all screwy, and I'm sure that lime didn't do nothin' to you."

I look at the mangled fruit. Here I thought I was on my sixth or seventh lime; turns out, I hadn't grabbed but the one.

"This 'bout a girl?" Polly presses. *She doesn't know.*

"In a way." To get more tips and have women show up night after night, I say less, listen more, and aim for mysterious.

Having pounded five shots and two beers, Polly's finally slowed to nursing a whiskey sour; a water chaser sits untouched beside it. Her speech is surprisingly clear when she asks, "Wanna talk about it?"

Normally, I'd turn up the music, but it's the laid-back crowd tonight. "You know, Polly, I don't. How's your day been?"

"Weird, Luke, weird. I got a call from an old friend, is all. Said she'll be seein' her daughter for the first time in a while tomorrow." *Adelynn.*

"Huh," I try for supportive.

"That's what *I* said!" Polly slams the bar and winces, then rubs the outside of her hand. "Guess I'm stronger than I knew. Anyhow, so I ask her why she's tellin' me, and she doesn't have an answer. Says, 'Jus' in case she says somethin',' then hangs up. What the hell does that mean? So I take a quick sip, you know. It was like hearin' from a ghost, is all. Work was slow; only one girl came in browsin' for some dance in January. Don't remember dances in January. When I was in high school—" I check out. Polly does this from time to time, starts with a story someone may care about before rambling her way into the past. I can only watch someone disappear so many times.

A blast of cold air comes through the entrance door. It doesn't perturb Polly. I look up to wave, but when they see me, they shake their head and leave. It's the third shadowy figure to choose an evening of sobriety over being in my presence.

I begin to think people believe I accosted my Adelynn—no, the new, adult Ada.

I cue in to conversations around the sparsely occupied bar.

Kit—real name Joseph Kit—is carrying on about his wife being a nag to the five people who are still willing to listen. It's the same old, same old. If he'd take out the trash once and again, I bet we'd never see him. "She's always saying, 'Kit, if you just did your share.' I tell her not to start in again! I bring home the money, that should be enough. She mouths off after that. Always telling me she'll run away with my brother." Kit throws his head back at the thought, and his neck shows striations of tans and sunburns. He tosses an icy glare towards the back room's closed door. "But I ain't got a brother, though, *do I*?" he asks the same group of friends that have been having the same conversation for years on end. I tune out. Lacey—real name Chelsea—has pulled her shirt down more than it was the last time I scanned the room. The one out-of-towner has an expensive chain around his neck; that's enough to warrant her attention. His squeaky voice should've been a turn-off. But she's neck-deep in Red-Headed Sluts and already spent half her rent money on cigarettes and nail polish. The group in the back are old vets who come in from time to time. They talk about work, the good old days, and their nagging/wonderful/non-existent wives. For them, I leave my sanctuary every hour or so to bring three pitchers of whatever amber we've got on tap.

Someone comes in the front door again; I don't bother with the pretense of waving. If they stay, I'll say hello.

After I cut a whopping twelve limes up and tuck them in their plastic home beside the maraschino cherries, I look around to see if the patron stayed. She's in the back, getting settled by Joe and his posse.

"The nerve of some women." I turn and see CK grip the sides of the cash register. *Hadn't he left around nine?*

"What?"

"That bitch just strolled in my bar actin' like she didn't accuse my bartender of assault. A lotta nerve, she got—a lotta nerve."

The rasp of his voice matches dark circles under his eyes and a ten o'clock shadow.

Adelynn? "What are you talking about CK?"

He smacks the register, and it sounds like Vegas. "There. Adelynn, or whatever she's callin' herself now. She's back there with Kit and them."

"How can you be sure?" It couldn't be her, could it? *How had I not known?*

"Looks like her mama." CK doesn't slur, but he smells boozy and desperate, like Polly. "I've known Wendy for a long time now. We all have."

I hope he can't hear my heartbeat. It's so loud in my ears that everything he says sounds like lousy cell reception. "I'll keep an eye," I say.

CK nods. "Yeah, good. I'll be in the back. Got some work to do." He chose not to add, "*And I need to avoid the empty house waitin' for me.*" Few people know much about CK, like how lonely he is or that CK stands for Chuck Kit. He's also on a diet.

"Fill'er up," Polly slurs. Her cheek's on the sticky bar top.

"I think it's time we call you a ride home." Her husband, Stan, is her weekday DD; her boyfriend, Harvey, picks her up on the weekends. "I'll call Stan."

"Well, aren't you the sweetest thing."

"Sure am." I wipe down the spots around her head to see if she'd move.

Instead, she taps her empty glass. "Fill'er up."

"Nope, cutting you off. Sorry, Pol," I say, though I'm not. The quicker the bar clears out, the quicker I can see if that brunette is Adelynn. She sits differently; this woman leans a little to the right as if always contemplating what you're saying in a condescending way.

Polly catches me staring. "Who's that? Is it her? No! It couldn't be. Maybe so, though. Her mama *did* call. It's been a while since I've seen pictures, but she looks about—" She hiccups and holds her hand over her mouth. "I'll take that ride home now. Stan'll do."

Now two people think it's her.

Anytime now, she'll order a drink, and I'll know for sure. As if I'd said that out loud, Kit stumbles my way laughing. "Another round, and a dirty martini for our new lady friend."

Stay calm. "Who's that?"

"Pretty, right? She's visiting." I hear nothing else he says. Though it's Kit, so I'm sure he's still talking.

After I sling their drinks, I offer to take the tray to their table. I've never done it before.

"Ha." Kit winks at me. "Let me take a crack at her first, yeah?"

No one moves for hours. It's as if they're posed for a painting to be entitled, "Shitty Bar". Once, the woman stood. I held my breath, hoping that she needed the bathroom. Then she sat back down. A ponytail holder was in the back pocket of her tacky jean skirt. She offered it to one of the vets, her face ever out of view.

Around 2:30 a.m., the regulars start collecting their duds. It's been a while since I've had to tell this crowd it's last call.

CK appears from his office around 2:35. "She still here?"

I nod. *So are you.*

"I'll make it so she's the last to leave."

"Why?" My breathing shallows at the thought of being alone with her again. This time, no one would be near enough to hear her scream.

He chews on his tongue before saying, "Women shouldn't be spoutin' off at the mouth."

I get my closing list—the one I loathe checking off because I'm a goddamned adult who's worked here for years.

1. Check for people in the bathroom.
2. Check for toilet paper and see what needs cleaning while you're in there.
3. Take a shit now—it'll give it more time to air out.

My boss is nothing if not classy.

Re-rolling the toilet paper that's unwound to the floor, I hear a knock at the door.

"Didn't want to scare you," CK says. "She's headed towards the parkin' lot. I've got her keys, though."

I halt everything and wash my hands. *Breathe, Luke. This is what you wanted before. Maybe it won't get ugly.* How many martinis did she have? Four? Is that enough for my sweet little girl to forgive me for my outburst?

The music gets louder, and CK's behind the bar.

"Hello?" I hear a woman's voice shout in an attempt to rise above the beat. *She's here.* "I think my keys dropped out of my purse. Do you think you could turn some lights on so I could check?" As if I'm a teenager again, I watch Adelynn. Her head is ducked under the barstools, and her thighs are splayed a little with the bend.

Sandpaper calluses grasp my elbow. *CK.* Two fingers grip tighter into muscle and fat. "I'm glad we decided to go home without closin' up, Luke. It was a slow night, and we had no reason to stay after the customers left." He steps backwards and clicks off the surveillance cameras. Once the screens are black, he sets thin rubber gloves and the supply closet key on the bar. "Lock up on your way out."

Ada

TURNING THE LAMP OFF DIDN'T OCCUR TO ME until 10:34 p.m. The sudden blackness that filled the room was shocking even though I'd controlled it. A branch banging on the window set my teeth on edge, and I am still shaken.

Between a body stuck in fight-or-flight mode, an overeager owl, and the unavoidable worry over seeing my mother, I doubt I will sleep much tonight. After a certain point, I find it useless anyway. I get a lot done on nights I give in to insomnia.

I joke with Rachael that I have too many diagnoses to be logically functional. I try not to think about them all. Most of them are occasional and only mildly irritating. As if I said "Trich" three times, one of my pubic hairs begins to burn. *Fuck.* I tug at the culprit; it doesn't rip out easily, but they rarely do. If it had been near the smooth, bare patch I had created in the past few years, I wouldn't feel it. Instead, the momentary eye-watering pain and frustration have me screaming at the owl and my cyclical brain to shut up.

My eyes flick towards the pad of paper on the floor beside my bed as I wonder if there are things I should tell it, tell Rachael. It would all come out whiney, so I don't bother. Hopefully, exhaustion will claim me soon. Another sound echoes in from the outside as if to say, "No, Ada, it won't."

April 3, 1988

Luke

WHY MY FATHER INSISTS ON MAKING US go to church on Easter is beyond me. We don't go any other day of the year. Then again, when I look around, I see other heathens like us. Fellow eighth graders wave with the same dead-eyed stare through the cloud of borrowed cologne. I was told I had to wait until I was fifteen to wear it. Fine. Doesn't bother me any. The scent makes me sad; my father smells desperate when he uses it, even though he and my mother have been married since the beginning of time.

Our meet-and-greet session takes entirely too long, as we see most of these people as often as we want to. If we wanted to see them more, we would. And now the pastor or preacher or minister or guy who thinks he's closer to God than everyone else is asking us to stand and pray with him. I know this is the routine, but I'd rather be outside on this miraculously sunny day in April.

I stand but do not pray. What is there to pray for? I know my mother prays for me to get better grades in school. My father prays to get a better paycheck or for me to get a girlfriend—he's been on me about that for ages now. The day I turned thirteen, he sat me down and told me about his days as a ladies' man. It was gross and uninteresting. I'd been warned about that long talk a few years ago, though. I was at a friend's house, and his older brother gave us the what's what on life. Dads always want their sons to be like them, he said. He also told us it was okay to take sex when you wanted it; he said his dad taught him that. It didn't sound right, so I left before the pizza showed up. My friend chased me down me with an apology, but in the same breath rationalized why his brother hadn't been wrong. Seems certain things run in families.

"And bless us—"

Under more words I don't care about, I hear quiet clicks and a woman's voice say, "Hush." I turn and see the most beautiful girl I've ever seen. She's in a hideous dress, no doubt her mother's doing. She doesn't look happy to be here, neither does the older boy who looks like her; her parents don't look happy to be late. They are all rushed and frantic to find a place to sit down.

Don't ruin this. I wave them over.

"Thank you," her mother mouths. When they get close enough, she leans in and touches my shoulder. "You're a lifesaver. Always awkward to come in late on Easter."

I nod. "Glad I could help," I say, hoping I sound adult enough for *her*. She hasn't looked my way yet. Her fluffy, yellow dress has snagged on a splinter in the pew. Once she's torn herself free, she grabs a bible and sits before the longest prayer in history is over. I like her style.

"Amen," the congregation says together.

The holy-man tells us to, "Be seated."

Now she looks like part of the flock. But I know she isn't. I see her for who she really is—someone special.

The pastor tells us of the importance of Easter, blood and

sacrifice, love and friendship. When he asks us to worship with him and a solo guitar starts up, I'm relieved. It won't be strange for me to look her way now.

Singing, singing, singing. Who cares. Her face goes red. That, I care about.

"Adelynn, stop it," her mother says. "I won't tolerate this behavior today." *Adelynn.*

"It's so loud, Momma." I want to cover her ears for her.

Voices crescendo around me, "...I am happy all the day!"

Church may not be so bad after all.

They don't stay for the potluck after, not that I blame them. All I know is, now that I've seen her, I'll never be the same.

"Son, you're smiling. Did you find God or something?" My father chuckles.

"Or something."

November 22, 2017

Sam

LORI IS IN LYNN POND NEAR THE BRIDGE, which should ice over anytime now. Was I too nostalgic? *Too late now, Sam.* My other sweethearts are all over Silynn. There are still a few areas of town that have yet to be used; the ditch by the pharmacy will be great once the ground is softer.

Yellow light streaks in and blinds me. This early in the morning in November, it should still be dark outside. The sun is cruel, though. We should've moved to a valley. As I blink spots away, Lori's wide eyes come into focus.

Yesterday, as I drove out to my favorite side street off the smaller highway ten miles from my cabin, Lori was silent. Her shallow breathing heated the car. With each passing minute, I tried but couldn't choose which lock of hair I wanted. None were right, and all were perfect.

Her stare was blank—until she saw the scissors. The sound of metal slicing thin fiery strands made her blue-veined eyelids crinkle. Her panic was so beautiful, my heart slowed. Lori never saw the ribbon I chose to match her emerald eyes. It looked perfect around her neck; I wish she could have seen it. When those green eyes popped open for the last time, they stared at me, then at the sky. I shifted my gaze to the fraying fabric in the snow. Slivers of the silk darkened as we melted winter.

I wrapped the lock of her ginger hair in the wet ribbon and put it in an antique tobacco tin. I don't know how long I'll keep it there before Lori will join my others.

"Thank you for letting me take care of you," I told her as I put her in her final resting place. I have done that with all of the sweethearts that came before her.

I drove home filled with nervous energy and a high I've only experienced nine times before. My ability to come home, dirty and shivering, with no questions asked, was a cherry on top. As soon as I showered and washed away the frigid mud that had soaked through my jeans, the craving hit again; she wasn't enough.

My tenth wasn't enough.

I've waited too long, and now I have years to catch up on. I only hope the scent of Lori's lavender mint shampoo will linger until I'm sated.

I dreamt about yesterday all night—something I rarely do. Each time it ended differently. Sometimes my terror of her being found leaked in. Once, Lori stabbed at me violently. As she ran away, her screams of fear and fury woke me. When I fell back to sleep, I relived the moment again. Then, jagged, unclean finger-nails clawed at my face as Lori fought back. Shocked, I fell back-wards. Instead of running, Lori grabbed her ribbon and wrapped it around my throat. After the fourth time, she pulled the green satin tight. I jumped away with my hands on my neck. I knew it was a dream. Though I'm far from the spry young kid I once was, no sweetheart should be able to take me down. Still, when I shook myself awake at 6:00 a.m., I gave up any more attempts to sleep.

Now, I dress for the cold. The temperature is going to drop down to 28°. My long-johns have grown scratchy from too many washes and running out of fabric softener.

I try to ignore the itch as I throw jeans and a green flannel button-up over them. I have a bit of a drive ahead of me with two objectives: keep an eye out for news of Lori's disappearance and find a sweetheart worth following her. I plan on watching this one, enjoying her from afar much longer than I had Lori. I'll need to draw it out, as I can't keep up this momentum

The wind has kicked up, and it bites more than I'd antici-pated. It's as if I'm wearing nothing rather than two layers of shirts, a sweatshirt, and a thick coat. Escaping into the car is no *real* escape. Inside is a still-cold; it's better, but I can't shake the chill in my bones.

If I want to beat traffic, I have to start driving before the car can provide warmth. I shift a little and put the car in reverse. As I clench the wheel, my palms throb. I don't have to look to see faint remnants of the deep impressions made by Lori's ribbon yesterday. When I turn left, the muscles in my usually under-used, now tired and burning, hands stretch.

Ada

IN MERE HOURS, my mother and I will be in the same room for the first time in over four years. Tomorrow is Thanksgiving. This weekend, I'm going to visit Lynn Pond. *I'm not panicking.*

In honor of not having any food, I make a small grocery list for my solitary turkey day. I do not expect to spend it with my mother. Even if she asked, I'm not sure I would accept.

I contemplate just munching on the one sleeve of rosemary crackers I found in the fridge for breakfast. Ultimately, I decide against it. I have always hated shopping in the mornings, but it must be done.

The parking lot is almost empty. One car is near the front, and a station wagon is in the other row, facing outward. I turn off the engine and fidget with the seat buckle as if it's a foreign object. Nerves have my fingers vibrating. If this were a life and death situation, I wouldn't make it out.

Freezing air sneaks in through vents that never warmed and seeps into my bones. I breathe through frozen lungs. This must be what asthma feels like. Every thought I've ever had about my mother's love rushes at me. I assumed she hated me when she sent me away. Once that pain ebbed, I ran through the stages of grief backwards and forwards during the growing pains of being a know-it-all tween and teen. Spots fill my vision as my fat tongue sticks to the roof of my mouth. *Ding, dong, Avon calling: I'm having a panic attack.* With no cell service, a quick call to Rachael for a guided meditation or a reminder that what I need is within is out of the question. Shaky hands assure I can't reach for a pen or paper to write my feelings down either—not like that would help. Pills forgotten on the new rental's kitchen counter ensure I can't rely on pharmaceuticals. Hell, with the steering wheel in my way, I can't even put my head between my knees without opening the door to more cold.

I crank the seat back as far as it will go and picture the night sky. I count stars in a constellation shaped like a watermelon; there are twelve. A cow-shaped cluster is made of twenty-six. It's a game I played when I was nine and suddenly dropped in a new place with an uncle I didn't know. I found it so helpful, it stuck. Another thirty-one stars create a dream catcher resembling the one I stole from a gas station on the way to said uncle's house. I still have one of its turquoise beads in my jewelry box next to my scuffed wedding ring and a tooth I found near railroad tracks when I was nineteen.

The muscles around my ribs unclench, and the blood pounding in my ears dwindles to a dull thud. I click the driver's seat to an upright position slowly—cracking my eyes a little as I do. Finally fully vertical, I stare straight ahead at the cement wall. Clear vision signals the end of the episode, and I attempt to change my focus. The grocery list is in my lap, so I stare at the word "eggs". The here and now. The here and now. *I am in the here and now.*

Shakily, I open the car door to get out of the space I feel trapped in and am surprised to find I have already begun to adjust to the weather; I hadn't turned the heat back on during my moment of fear. On quasi-steady legs, I meander towards the tiny grocery store. I am in no hurry—rushing myself can lead to old patterns of more panic attacks, lying in bed for hours, panic attacks as I attempt to leave the hole I've created, descending into darkness until it's time for bed, then more panic attacks. After a week or so of that cycle, I would emerge a few pounds thinner with no eyelashes, sparse eyebrows, and raw, bald spots everywhere else hair exists. *Not great.*

Frosty double doors are ajar when I reach the entrance. The grocer is by himself, standing off to the left by a modestly sized checkout counter and meat scale. He is bundled in two coats and a fuzzy hat; still, he shivers.

You could just close the door.

He glances my way, and I picture Freesia's near-nakedness jogging from his rented cabin room. As if he knows the inner workings of my mind, he turns to his newspaper and flicks a page loudly to flatten it open.

My watch becomes interesting: 9:41 a.m. I choose not to address the amount of time I spent in the car and turn my attention to the list:

- Eggs
- Wine
- More cheese
- Gummy candy
- Chocolate
- Frozen chicken
- A frozen dinner meal or two
- Salad stuff?
- Root beer

It is not quite twice the size of a convenience store, and the aisles are narrow, so I carry a plastic hand basket to collect my food items. I should add milk and bread. *Isn't that what adults do?* I start in dry goods and work my way to the lackluster frozen section. By the end, I have added carrots and a large jug of water, because Silynn is getting really cold. All through my shopping trip, I struggle to remember this place from my childhood. It looks like it's always been here, though—maybe longer than the town.

Rachael's voice pops into my head like an alarm. "Don't push things when you go back. You may have repressed some memories. Let them come if they will, but it's okay if they don't," she said, as I handed her my card to pay for our last session.

"Hey," I say, as I drop my overflowing basket onto the linoleum countertop.

The grocer starts scanning. *Beep.* Off-brand root beer. *Beep.* Eggs. *Beep.* Blue cheese salad dressing—sadly, the only kind they had. *Beep.* Bread.

The eggs will break, and the bread will get squished if he doesn't separate them. He doesn't. He tosses them in the same bag; it rips at the corner, and I'm unsurprised. How can he be bad at bagging? He's the only one who does it.

I shift uncomfortably. "Looks like snow." Weather is how everyone communicates, right?

Beep. Merlot. *Beep.* Merlot. The second bottle earns me a judgmental eyebrow raise. *Beep.* A half gallon of 2%. *Grunt.* He nods.

Why won't he talk to me? Because he is a sad, lonely man with no social skills to speak of, probably. Thanks to Freesia, I know at least one thing about him to be true: he likes to be hog-tied and called "Piggy." I have tried to shake the image, but his round middle and flushed pink skin make that impossible.

He smells like pumpkin guts; it's festive, if not a little off-putting. "Happy early Thanksgiving." *Piggy.* It's my last ditch effort.

Holding my chocolate bar, he stops scanning. His unremarkable muddy eyes meet mine as he asks, "Are you Adelynn Bailey?"

A new kind of panic sets in. "Wha—"

"I heard you were seeing Wendy today." He sniffs in and wipes a glob of snot onto his sleeve. "What brings you back home?" As he fondles the rest of my groceries, I notice a wedding ring—*so much for being lonely.*

I try to keep track of which of my groceries he's touched so I can sanitize them before I put them away. "Where did you hear a thing like that?"

"Around town. You're the talk, you know. There's even an article about you in the paper." He flips a few pages in, smacks it, and folds it in half before pointing to a three paragraph blurb about me. "See?"

My cheeks burn, yet I try to stay calm when I say, "Oh."

"You can keep that." Something about the way he says it makes me not want to.

"Thanks," I say anyway. I fear if I'm rude, I will get *four* paragraphs on tomorrow's *front* page.

"I'm Dave, by the way." He drops the *Silynn Times* in one of my thin plastic bags, then holds out his hand.

Awkwardly, I shake it. I'm desperate to clean it immediately. "Well, you already know my name." I hand him my credit card, which thank goodness he accepts without any more conversation or a quip about how he only takes cash—a thought that had not occurred to me until now. Without any more conversation, I grab my things and head towards the exit.

As I kick open the front doors with five bags juggled on and in my arms, Dave calls out, "Adelynn?"

I sigh. "It's Ada. What's up?"

"Alright. Ada, why *did* you come back?" Nosey man—Silynn is filled with nosey people.

The bags cut into my arms. "Not to talk to your wife, if that's what you're asking." I know I have just added myself to a list I'm sure he has.

His eyes cut. "Have a nice visit with Wendy."

I am numb as I walk to the car. I practically throw the groceries into the passenger seat so I can scrub my hands with globs of quick-drying sanitizer before heading to my home away from home. During the drive back to my new rental, I realize I forgot to get lettuce to go with the salad dressing I don't like, and I didn't look at the expiration date for anything. Somehow, that feels important when shopping at a place like Dave's.

When I arrive at the cabin, it's isolated and scarily removed from the town rather than safe and out of sight as it was yesterday. It's a good thing I'm leaving again today. I think I need a break from my head, even though I've not been alone for more than five minutes since arriving in Silynn.

1:54 P.M.

FROM THE STREET, my childhood home is the same as it was. The memory of losing my family still lives trapped in a time capsule on 4512 Filsen Drive. *This is a mistake.*

I see a figure as I park in the driveway. My mother is waiting on the stoop, so I can't back out now. She doesn't wave. Instead, she puts a loose fist on her hip before skulking in, leaving the screen door hinged open. I can hear her now, *"You can let yourself in. I can't have the cold seeping in because you're taking your sweet time."*

I don't take my time, though, because I cannot get warm. I have a feeling there will be plenty of stifling heat in the Bailey residence. When this was my home, I thought the fireplace was magic. I never chopped wood, Peter never chopped wood, my mother never chopped wood; hell, to my knowledge, we did not even own an axe. But the fire ever-roared and the house always verged on too stuffy.

A picture of me rushing out the front door without a coat flashes in my mind. I try not to think of frozen skin, bitterly freezing water, Luke watching from the bushes. Grabbing the edge of my sleeves, I revert to hiding and try to focus on my impending doom, not the past. When I reach the door, the familiar warmth emanates through the beat-up wood and grounds me in the present—for good or bad, we'll see. I touch the metal knob, expecting it to burn me; it doesn't.

"Mom?" I call, as I push in the door. A slam of crooked cabinet doors answers me. Clicking the lock behind me feels like a sentencing of some kind. "Mom? I'm coming in now. You in the kitchen?"

I step over the two pairs of shoes in the foyer and veer right. The stairs to my left demand my attention. *Do not run up them.* I tamp down my racing thoughts.

She meets me at the kitchen entryway. "You look good. Tea?"

We are playing pretend, it seems. Things are fine between us in this game. "That would be lovely, thanks." Briefly, I wonder if my voice is as shaky as my legs.

"Head into the living room." With pride, my mother adds, "I got a new couch." Nothing but said couch has changed—even its location hasn't. It's a fine couch, but I don't say as much. Mom looks good too—healthier than the last time we saw each other; I do not say that either. I deserve an apology. Without one, I will never compliment her again. Venom sits on the tip of my tongue.

A second later, my mother appears holding Nana's metal tray. I have laid claim to it; once my mother dies, I will be able to display it on my steel and glass tea cart. Nana loved bees and honeycomb-patterned anything. Two cups of steeping tea, a bowl of sugar cubes, and a couple of spoons sit on the rectangular tray. Once, it was a bright and sunny yellow. Now, it has dulled with chipped enamel, but the decoration remains. "Bee Mine" is written in honeycomb-lettering, bubbling from a trio of smiling bees with black hearts on their tummies.

"Sugar?" my mother asks, breaking me away from the image of Nana's sweet age-spotted cheeks.

I nod. "That would be great, thanks."

My first-grade class photo is still on a side table, I notice. She clears her throat when she catches me looking at it. "So. What brings you here?"

"As in Silynn or to your house?" My middle finger digs into the crevice between the nail and the flesh of my thumb.

"Both. I thought we were done, you and me?" She squeezes exposed skin below her rolled-up sweater sleeves; purple and blue veins darken with the pressure. *Like mother, like daughter.*

Rachael would be proud of me; I resist the urge to scream, cry, break the framed forced smiles and unfilled vases around me, or quietly tweeze out leg hair and rip at bits of skin. "That was your choice. I have done nothing wrong here. I came to Silynn because I can't sleep, I can't eat, I can't exist more than a week without thinking of Laura Hurst. It has been twenty-nine years, and she won't leave me. Her screaming mouth, her fingers tangled in my—" I break off. "I have not been ready to deal with it, until now. And I guess I stopped by here to see if we couldn't work something out too."

"So, what? I'm on a checklist?"

I begin to think all of this is a mistake. "Sure, Mom. You put yourself there, though," I say with such defiance I almost clap for myself.

She twists bits of her dyed chestnut hair but stays silent.

I had my first gray hair at twenty-two. The underneath part is salted now. I have decided not to dye it. Unlike my mother, I enjoy aging—except the aches and pains. I want to ask her why that's happening early—another thing I won't do.

Standing, Mom adjusts jeans which probably have long-

johns under them, as they usually did in the winter months—
even if it wasn't cold, and even though the house is hotter than
Silynn in summer. She takes the tea bags from our cups, drops
them on the largest bee's face, and stomps into the kitchen with
the tray cutting into her soft side. I have seen her do that so
many times, I could be any age. I imagine Peter rounding the
corner in a baseball cap carrying a bat, in a bright orange jacket
with the duffle bag our mother never looked in, in the tux I
never saw him wear to prom, in the blue suit he wore to my
wedding. My heart seizes. Everything would be easier if he were
here. *No, Ada, it would be harder.* He'd just be another person
with baggage and issues with me. If only he were still a kid—if
only I were.

"Okay. You wanna talk? Let's talk," she says, as she comes
back into the living room.

Wrinkled jowls set as her eyes settle on her new couch—gray
and fluffy, while the old was khaki and deflated. I am expected to
remark on her fucking piece of furniture; that's how she wants
this conversation to start.

Never blinking, I release a held breath. "Why did you stop
talking to me after Derek?" Her face pales. I have verbally slapped
my mother. I am not sure whether she would have looked more
shocked if my hand had actually made contact with her face.

She stutters out, "I thought we were going to talk about
Laura."

"We will get to why you kicked me out of the house the
moment reporters stopped caring about me in a minute. I want
to know why we haven't talked in years. What made you think—
of all times—cutting me off after a divorce was the right thing to
do?" I shake off the coat I wasn't sure I should earlier. *Settle
in, Mom.*

"Because you couldn't do better. He's a great man, Adelynn."
I shudder at the sound of my name. By the flicker of hurt in her
green eyes, she notices. "So he made a mistake. We all do that

sometimes. Not forgiving him is the stupidest thing you've ever done. And you've done a lot of dumb things."

"How would you know?" I snapped. Rachael's many mantras beg me to calm myself. "You haven't been around much. Derek was never the best to me or for me. His cheating worked out just fine in the end. It was the final straw I needed to do what I hadn't had the strength to do before."

My mother's thin hand flew up. "But did it work out? You're still alone."

"I'm not with an abusive alcoholic who doesn't love me enough to be faithful anymore. That should matter to you; it matters to me. My happiness is more important than having a husband."

"Your happiness is important to me, of course." Her voice is curt. "Happiness isn't all it's cracked up to be." She casts her eyes down.

The story of my mother's life is tragic. Her parents were monsters; she has demonized them in every story she has ever told me. I don't know where their acts end and her flourishes begin. After leaving her house, she fell into my father's arms. When I was young, he ran out on us. I like to think I'm compassionate, but her lack of happiness shouldn't affect how she treats me.

"Is this about my father?" I accept the can of worms I may have opened by mentioning him.

Mom chuckles sadly, still not looking up. "No, Adelynn. His leaving was my fault. I kept you and Peter out of selfishness." Her right foot taps the wood flooring—*tap, tap tap, tap, tap tap tap, tap.*

"Wait." This goes against everything she has ever told me. Her tapping makes my eye twitch. "Are you saying he didn't leave us? He left *you?* What did you do?"

"Have I not told you? I slept with someone else. I could have sworn I tol— Oh well." Mom shakes her head. "So, is that all?"

"What!" My mind explodes. Her obsession with my forgiving Derek bursts into clarity. For months, she called to see if I had taken him back. When I signed the papers, the calls stopped.

"Is that all you needed? Do you feel better now? You can blame me for the lost years between us, and you can blame me for the loss of your father. Go ahead and blame me for finding Laura too; I'm sure you can make a connection there if you try hard enough."

I blanch. Unable to address my mother's infidelity, I say, "I did not come here to blame you for anything. I came to… I don't know, make things right. We don't have a lot of family; it's just you, me, Peter, Uncle Carl, and Aunt Susan." Now I wonder why one less person would bother me so much.

"I haven't talked to Carl or Susan in years, either." *So no Christmas party or family reunion.*

"You want to blame me for that? It sounds like you want blame to be thrown around," I snark.

She takes a deep breath. "I'm not blaming you. I know why I haven't talked to them, but that's between us." I know too.

Uncle Carl told me he couldn't stand even the most surface of conversations with her while she and I weren't on speaking terms. He had raised me through my formative years. In some ways, I am his daughter as much as I am my mother's. I know he and Aunt Susan are disappointed in her as a mother.

"So, can we quit the blame-game and talk for a few minutes?" I ask over a held breath. It is *a lot* to ask.

"About what? Laura? Your father? The weather?"

"We'll unpack Dad later. I need more than two minutes to take this all in."

"So, Laura?" I nod. She is all I can take now. "What is there to say, Adelynn? I didn't know what to do with a maudlin kid when there weren't tons of people around. I was falling apart, and—"

"Why?"

My mother rolls her eyes and blots at them, and I watch a television contestant hopeful create tears. "A lot happened after you found her. It wasn't as simple as you finding a dead girl."

"Simple?" *I will not laugh.* I'm sure she has more to add, Lucy will 'splain herself.

Clouds must have heard my confusion because the room falls a shade darker. A memory comes back to me: my mother whispering through a mostly closed door to a disembodied man's voice. She slid to the floor and cried in her hands the moment he was gone. I'm almost positive that was the day after I found Laura.

"Do you remember your grandmother's pie? I made some of it a few days ago. Want a piece?"

"What?"

"I froze some berries in June and was craving her strawberry pie. Making it always reminds me of—" I picture narcissists as vending machines. Their stories are queued and waiting to be chosen before you engage them. F1 and F5 are particular favorites of my mother; they have to do with cooking. She rarely cooks, which is why the moment she has any reason to bring it up, she drops the F's—whether they matter or are relevant or not. I am flabbergasted. She gave me F1 when G3 and A2 are more sensical. But F1 had been primed long before I walked through the front door; by the time she brought tea, it was dangling out of its coil. G3 is the story she uses to shut everyone up; it's an uncomfortable and sad memory from her teen years. A2 is reserved to guilt Peter and me into doing everything her way; she tells us of childhood woes and harrowing events—real or fabricated. Why then would she not use her traumas to explain away bad behavior? "—and I had three slices before dinner!"

I stare at her. Maybe the next story the machine known as my mother drops will be relevant.

"Oh! I was cleaning up the attic last year and found some of your old stuff. There are three boxes stacked up in your old room." She stands up, and it's like a balloon popping—jarring and loud—though she has made no noise. "Do you want to see?"

What's happening? "I would rather know why you were falling apart. But sure—why not?"

She is blowing me off with nostalgia, *great*. I leave our now useless conversation and head up the stairs. I turn left towards the first door on the right; the second is the only full bathroom in the house. My old room is empty save a coffee table, three boxes and the vanity my mother swore she would take apart and mail me (I even sent her a blank check she never cashed for the shipping costs). The last time I was in this house, I was twenty-eight. I didn't go upstairs then, like I hadn't gone upstairs any other time I had visited as an adult. So I am surprised to see the light pink paint and ballerina border still present and hanging on—slightly worse for the wear. I wonder if Peter's room looks different. *Has it become the home gym all parents are supposed to get when their children leave the nest?*

"It's not changed much, huh?"

I jump; I hadn't heard her footsteps. "Thought you'd stay downstairs to putz or avoid me."

She shakes her head. "These are the boxes," my mother gestures towards a stack of partially crushed cardboard. "ADE-LYNN'S OLD STUFF BOX 1-3" is sloppily written in fat black marker on the top and one side.

"Thanks. I'll pack them up..." I trail off to see what she suggests. I'm still unsure why I am in my childhood bedroom staring at packed-up memories rather than having an adult conversation.

"You could look at them here?"

I shake my head. "No—better not. That's a memory lane I don't want to walk down right now."

Her shape in the doorway brings me back to arguments with Peter and her rushing to his aid. She would block the door so I had to listen to her berate me until she got bored or tired.

"I understand," she says. Her eyes look past me and through the only window in the 10x10 room. "It was hard, you know—to feel the way I did and deal with two kids. I know that's no excuse, but it's the truth. I couldn't handle it. That's why I sent you away."

"It was hard." Nope. Not good enough. "What was hard?"

She shuffles her feet like a teen waiting for an answer to a prom proposal. "Being a mother." We both know she's copping out and not saying all that needs to be said.

The urge to peel at the wallpaper becomes so strong I have to make my hands into fists. My curled-in pinky finger brushes the thick skin of my palm scars; I swallow the flash of rage that follows. Mom wobbles a little as if my anger rippled the air.

"Will I see you again before you leave?" *I guess we're done for the day.*

My watch pronounces our visit has been forty-two minutes—more awkward silence than I had expected.

"Do you want to?"

She shrugs. "I think so."

"What an answer."

"I mean—"

"I get it." I sigh into a hunch. "We have always been complicated. And now, I don't know what to think. You're clearly hiding something about why you sent me away, and you have spent thirty years lying to me about why my dad left. Why fill me in on it now, right?"

My mother's gaze shifts down, and she blinks rapidly. *Here we go with fabricated tears again.* "We have been, haven't we? As for hiding something, I'm not. I couldn't handle being a woman and a mother at the same time. Peter was old enough to be more self-sufficient, which is why I didn't send him with you. And I should have told you about your father a long time ago. The other man was nothing but trouble. After everything, I still lost both men I lo—"

"Wait. You loved him? So it was a full-blown affair? Is that who came to the house the day after I found Laura? Who was he?"

Her face goes hard, and I know my mother has shut down. She turns and grabs the top two boxes of my past life and shifts them onto the bare coffee table. "I can carry the biggest one. These two are mostly stuffed animals, blankets, stickers, and pictures."

Our talk is over. We pack the trunk in silence—quickly and efficiently.

Before I know it, I am standing by the car with the door open. My bones ache from the cold; my heart aches from the rejection I swore I wouldn't let her cause me again. It all happened so fast. And now the car's electronic beeping makes the moment feel urgent as if we have mere seconds to decide what to do. But neither of us knows what should come next. Expectations are ugly. So I do what I've always done: I go first.

"So, I—um, let's—" I stammer. "Why don't we have breakfast before I leave? Sunday?"

Her poker face is solid. "Sounds good for now, but let's play it by ear." That is my mother's code for, *"I'm going to blow you off."* I asked a few too many questions, it seems.

I squeeze her. "Bye, Mom. I love you."

She mutters, "I love you," into my shoulder and jogs inside without looking back.

As I drive away, the end of our conversation seems more like a shrug than a goodbye. Maybe we *will* see each other again. It won't be for a while, though. When we do, it will probably be on my mother's terms. I hate that after everything, I'm alright with that.

Sam

I WISH I'D SPENT MORE TIME WITH MY FATHER. Somehow, he understood things I still don't. It could be that my mother taught him something useful before she tried to axe his face in half —*could be.*

As I muse on the highlights of the mothering I received, I see her. A woman drags her out of the rest stop's restroom by her small, plushy arm. When she releases her in front of their car, pink fingerprints remain. The small child cries out, "Momma, that hurts!"

Bad mothers disgust me. More than once, I've considered collecting them instead of my sweethearts. Then I look at their unwashed hair and gray skin and the way they walk—downtrodden and irritated. For the same reason I couldn't squeeze the neck of the busybody checkout girl, Marly, I'll never be able to collect one of them. Their innocence is gone.

Shoved into the backseat, the girl is left to strap herself into her car seat, and my opportunity is lost. Their license plate is from Wyoming; she would've been perfect. I sigh as I look at the clock on my dashboard. Tomorrow is another day. That one may have been too young anyway. I would've had to ask; that's hard when you've only got moments, and children are told not to talk to strangers.

Mary had talked to me. I'd been twenty at the time, and she said I seemed nice and "okay because of my clothes." Her daddy had to poop, she told me as she kicked her still pudgy legs back and forth. Soft flesh bent against the wooden bench with every swing.

"I'm six and three quarters," she said without me asking. *Young.*

But no one was around. Mary's father was taking his sweet time as if encouraging someone to collect her, and I was on a high from Jessica. A town-wide hunt had begun the day before— only 24 hours after her disappearance, not the usual 48—and no one suspected me. I was just another college student, a face in a sea of faces. Why would they? It made me feel untouchable.

I took the auburn-haired sweetheart-to-be to my car to give her one of the toys I was taking to donate. Mary assumed I worked at a nearby hospital. Her plastic jelly shoes clicked as she skipped towards the backseat. Later, when water splashed around us, the right one flew into a briar patch.

I still don't know when her father came out.

I had to take a break after Mary, thanks to one nosey reporter. Gracie Pearce wore a severe bob, too much makeup, and spoke loud enough that she never needed a microphone. "I believe Laura Hurst, Jessica Thompson, and Mary Louise Keller are related. I think they were all killed by the same monster: the Lake Killer," she'd told local and national news cameras, creating a serial killer and naming me in two short sentences. For the time, it was still progressive for a woman to not only make connections but share them. With no proof, though, the theory died down. Soon the murder of Laura became another mystery that *somehow* made it to the show Unsolved Crimes. Jessica and Mary became rest stop warning tales. And I took a year hiatus.

My knuckles begin to ache as my grip on the wheel tightens just thinking about the stolen time. I blame Mary and the irresistible situation she put me in.

I turn up the heat to its maximum. I've wasted my afternoon, and now, I'm in a bad mood. The drive back to my home is twice as long as the drive there due to unnecessary traffic. One thought bounces back and forth in my head like Pong as I stop and inch forward with the rows of irritated skeletons covered in skin: *did I hide Lori's body well enough?*

6:02 P.M.

OUR DAUGHTER Jess took after me with almost white blonde hair. The last time I saw her in person, it was down her back. A week ago, she posted a picture of it dyed dark and cut to her chin. It doesn't suit her. I hit the heart below the image obligatorily all the same, just as I told her she looked beautiful in the comments section under seventy other people. Only I used fewer adverbs and emojis than they did. We haven't spoken since, but she's shared photos of her lips on her boyfriend's, staged studiousness at her college's library, legs and high-heeled boots on top of a bar at a neon club, and her new manicure holding a cocktail at a moody bar.

I've tried to adjust to her new hair ever since by staring at the blunt edges, by imagining my scissors slicing through new chestnut locks. It hasn't worked. Her haircut has accentuated her smallish black speckled blue eyes and made her sweet, round face look soft and pliable.

And now the last visual connection to Jessica has been severed. At age eight, when Jessica became my sweetheart, her ponytail was so blonde, the sun made it almost as white as Jess's virgin hair. It was always tied in a simple ponytail and pink ribbon at the crown of her skull. One of those ribbons holds a chunk of her hair now. In honor of my Jessica and Laura, I never let Jess wear pink or peach hair accessories.

Before our daughter left for college, I cut a piece of her hair and wrapped it in one of the ratty white bows from her single-digit years, as she called them. It's underneath my sweetheart's locks, safe and sound.

That reminds me of the work I haven't done to prepare. The counters, my bedside table, even the walls hold my truth. Jess can't know. I park, glad to be out of hours worth of traffic, and rush in. Each piece of my sweetheart collection has had a place for so long, it's muscle memory putting them back. Freedom has been so natural; it feels dirty to hide again. But it has to be done.

Taylor knows about one of my sweethearts and suspects there's another. It's the darkness alluded to when we fight, the thing I'm prodded about in joking ways—probably as a way to get a confession. After our divorce, I may have to leave Silynn or go into hiding. Taylor will have no reason to keep my secret. I don't have time to dwell. I glance at the clock. How is it 6:35 already?

I take the town map off the wall and curse; in my rush, I tear a corner. It's the same map I've had since my high school class on local government. All of my sweethearts are marked in two places. Where I found them is a dot, and where they are now is a heart. Rolling it up, I try and look on the bright side. It's lasted nearly thirty years without more than a crease in the center. The week I bought it, I folded it the wrong way all because I was up late studying and wanted to move it off my bed. I should have been more patient.

I slide the cigar box under the bed and roll the map up in a leather tube that's tucked behind the toolbox in the garage. Lori's lock of hair stays put in the tin, and I breathe a little easier.

I'm sweating, but Jess could arrive at any moment. A new coat of deodorant is all I have time for.

I fill up the water filter with tap water and chuck it back in the fridge, then check to make sure we have ice. Taylor put new sheets on the guest bed last week and cleaned the floor a few days ago. *Good enough.* Everything will look normal.

Okay, Jess. I'm ready for you to visit.

7:04 P.M.

I HAVE WILLINGLY BECOME the couch's hostage by the time the doorbell rings. Standing to answer it is trudging through the mud and snow to hide Lori's body. I shiver; my house is too cold. I tick the thermostat up to 69° on my way to the door. The doorbell chimes again three times in a row.

"Hello? Anyone home?" Jess's voice is muffled by the thick wood and double insulation Taylor and I installed.

I realize I still have on my dried, crusty boots. Taylor's mopping was in vain. I shuck the evidence of my crime off. I don't want to be asked any questions about where I've been.

With enthusiasm I don't feel, I swing the door open. Jess grins. A fluffy hat covers her too-short hair. She's wearing the sweater we bought her for Christmas and balancing three bags in her arms; another suitcase sits beside her. Jess drops it all the moment she sees it's me and not Taylor. Without a doubt, I'm her favorite parent.

She throws her arms out and rushes forward. "Mom! I've missed you!"

Ada

I AM STILL HOLDING MY BREATH when the sandwich I forgot I ordered arrives.

Hailey touches my shoulder, and I jerk. "Oh, sorry!" she says. "I didn't mean to scare you."

Shaking my head, I attempt a laugh; it comes out as a sad choke. "No, it's not you. I'm still processing something my mother said five hours ago. I haven't been able to talk to my therapist about it."

"Wanna talk to someone else about it?"

"Unless you want to dig into who my mother was sleeping with when I was a child, I doubt we should." *Damnit, Ada. Shut your mouth.* I'm far too candid.

She winces. "I'll be right back."

"Sure," I say, nodding. I understand; I wouldn't want to talk to Hailey about her parent's infidelity.

I pick up the… ham and cheese, apparently, and bite into it. Processed cheese that still tastes like its plastic film wrapper fills my mouth. Yum. I am pretty sure even the meat came from the sandwich section of the grocery store. The french fries are delicious, at least. Fresh frozen, perhaps. They are likely 50% potato, 50% words I can't pronounce, which is why they're so tasty. I shove three fries drenched in ketchup in my mouth just as Hailey sidles up across from me at the square four-top table.

"I'm taking my break," she announces to no one in particular and pulls her apron over her head; her bangs muss. "Now, spill." It's as if we are best friends, or at least old friends. Rather, I have been wondering if she is to blame for my trauma. Before I say as such, I remember that she is older than me. Maybe she heard gossip back then; maybe she knows about my mother.

Guarded, I say, "My mother told me my father left, because she cheated. Then, I think—*I think*—"

Hailey doesn't try to hide her shock. "So it's true? She slept with him?"

Goosebumps erupt on my arms, and my heart speeds up. "You know who it was?" I almost scream at her and demand answers. But I'm an adult, and adults do not throw tantrums in public.

"Well, I heard rumors. I was just a teenager then, remember. I heard rumors all the time. Dina was sleeping with our English teacher; my boyfriend had herpes. The mailman dealt coke to the football players, and our neighbor had a secret family in another town. I heard all sorts of things, Adel—Ada. Most of them weren't true."

"But this one was," I say in one breath.

"But maybe not with who I thought." She gathers her apron. "I don't know what I saw—I mean heard. On second thought, it can't be true. I've got to get back to work."

With semi-checked emotions, I whisper, "You saw something? What did you see, Hailey?"

"Nothing, really. I was a kid too, remember? I'm so sorry you got sent away, 'cause she did the wrong thing. It's not fair that adult's decisions affect children as much as they do." I never told her that's why my mother sent me away. I revisit the tantrum idea. "But since they do," she continues, "and since you still want answers, maybe ask Polly. She and your mother seemed to be good friends back in the day. I have a feeling she wouldn't have just rumors. I'll be back with some more water and an ice cream sundae on me."

"Hailey, what did you see?" I ask again.

She's gone back to scooping up dirty plates from the table beside me. She knows; but yet again, I am a child in the dark. Anger bubbles in my gut and curse words threaten to spill out of my mouth. I came to Silynn to face demons, to sleep better at night, and focus on rebuilding myself without a shadowy past. *What do I get?*

Before I can answer myself, the two unremarkable police officers burst in the door. "Adelynn Bailey! We need to talk to you."

Hailey disappears into the back room, and I cannot help but hate her for a moment.

I should be worried or scared as the two cops storm my way, their eyes hard and lips pursed. Indignation hits me first. *Well, this is unprofessional.* I stay seated and wait for them to come to my table. The packed soda shop buzzes; this is the equivalent to the stars of a box office movie waltzing in for dinner where I live.

"Adelynn Bailey, where were you last night?" the cop with the mole asks.

His raised voice solidifies my curiosity. He definitely shoved me off of the swing once. I had a scab for a week. I couldn't stop picking at it to watch the unreal red ooze down my pale skin. His name was Logan in my mind. I would have to look at his card to see if that was right, but all bullies have been named Logan at some point. He could have been the one who triggered that.

"Well?" his partner prompted.

"At the rental I told you about. Why?"

"And all by yourself, I assume? That's nice and tidy."

I pick up my drying bread and slimier ham sandwich and take a bite. "Yeah. I came alone; you know that," I mumble over the gummy globs of food. "Why do you ask?"

"Ada! Is that you?" I hear over the silence of the cops' lack of response. *Am I in a dream?*

Freesia clomps over in six-inch lucite heels. Wild curls bounce almost as much as her barely covered breasts. The thong and thigh-high socks left 2% to the imagination.

"On your way home?" I ask, ignoring the police who have been nothing but a disruption.

"Work, actually. I came to get a slice of cake." She leans in and whispers, "She likes to watch me sit on it."

"To each their own," I chuckle and pick up my soda, which leaves a ring of condensation on the table. With my chewed straw, I stir melting ice cubes; they rattle against the glass.

"What's going on here?" Freesia asks the mute officers who should be scolding us for telling secrets like children in school. Instead, they are drinking her in. When polished nails drum curvy hips, their eyes move with them. *If I walked out the front door right now, would they notice?*

My voice is loud and clear. "I have no idea. They charge in here and start questioning me like I've done something wrong. You walked in at just the point where they were *definitely* going to tell me what this is all about." They had only asked me one question, sure, but it was clearly accusatory.

"If you have any more questions for Ada, you can ask them with her lawyer present." I snort as Freesia says, "Did I forget to mention my husband is a lawyer?" *What?* "Well, we aren't that close yet, so that makes sense."

She can tell me about the Robert who wanted to fuck her feet but not that she's married to a lawyer? Silynn is an alternate universe, and Freesia is my guardian angel—both statements I would not have believed five minutes ago.

The boring cop's voice wavers a little. "Miss Miller, we were just asking Ada about her whereabouts last night. There was a Jane Doe found by Lynn Pond. As Ada has a history with the area, we just wanted to cover our bases."

A Jane Doe found by Lynn Pond. There must be details he is leaving out—like that she's a child with red hair. How else would finding a body in the same place where I found Laura nearly thirty years ago mean anything now? Questions swirl in my head: who is she; how was she found; what happened to her; when did she die? I assume they thought *I* did it.

The mole above Logan's mouth wiggles as he speaks. "Maybe we should take this to the station. You go ahead and call your husband." He turns back to me as if only just remembering that I'm here. "We have a few more questions for you."

And I have some—no, *a lot*—for them. "Am I a suspect?" I ask before Freesia can say anything else.

They both clear their throat.

"Well, am I? I don't see why I need to go to the station if I'm not. And shouldn't you be arresting me if—"

Freesia shoots me a look, and I go silent. "Let her pay the check, then we'll follow you. I've got two calls to make while she does that."

Logan nods and mumbles an irritated, "Fine."

I finally take a second to look at the boring cop's name tag: "Officer Frueller". He crouches a little; it's his first attempt at privacy. "You come back to town and—" He hesitates. "It's her location, Adelynn. It's not too far from where you found Laura Hurst. Just doesn't look good. We can't not question you, understand?"

"Sure, yeah." *No.* Substandard food curdles in my stomach. "Feel free to have a seat while I pay. No need to stand."

"We'll be by the door," Logan murmurs.

With each step the cops take towards the exit, the chatter around us swells. Snippets of conversations rise clear above the buzz. Those are the women and men horrified that I am not in cuffs. I've killed another girl, and the police haven't taken me straight to jail. "Everything is wrong with this picture," they're saying. Already low spirits sink to the core of the earth. The townsfolk think I killed Laura? *I was a child.*

Freesia spins towards me, frowning, and sits. "Okay, what's going on?"

"No clue. Apparently, I'm a murderer. I came here to have a sandwich and clear my head. A few hours ago, I found out that my dad left because my mother was a cheater. And it seems my old babysitter knew about it. Now, this! You know, I'm so normal in Bloomington. No messy family, no cops, no stalker, no Jane Doe, just a successful coffee shop, a nice apartment, friends that like me, and a bunch of issues I can keep mostly in check because of Rachael." *I'm cracking.*

"Breathe." When Freesia leans towards me, her nipples show a little. I pantomime breasts spilling out, but she's already reaching for the phone in her purse. "I've got this." Does she? *Can she?*

7:48 P.M.

INSTEAD OF DRIVING TO POLLY'S BOUTIQUE, practicing what I would say and how I would politely demand answers as to who my mother was having an affair with, I'm headed to the police station and picturing Jane Does. They are all dead Laura Hursts, screaming and frozen in fear. Some of the Janes are hidden beneath the lake, shadows just as I remember. Others I can make out eyes, lips, hair; they are clawing their way out of the water. Women lie limp, half-nude, littering the snowy banks of Lynn Pond.

I rip at my eyelashes when a girl who looks like me when I

was a child screams that I shouldn't have come home. *Some daydream*—more like an eveningmare.

When Freesia pulls into the parking lot, I slide up beside her. She hops out before I turn the car off. Somehow, during our short drive, Freesia managed to change clothes. Her sleek jeans and sweater make her look more put-together than me; I fluff my flat hair out of insecurity. As I scooch my sleeves down my arm, I curse the thick scar tissue that reminds me of the moment I found Laura. The police don't need any more physical connections; it's the reason I'm here, as it is.

A man in a suit is waiting by the steps of the unassuming gray building I must have blocked from my childhood. He looks tired, yet alert as he waves.

"Honey!" Freesia shouts.

He rushes over to her. "Everything okay? Is this Ada?"

"Hi." The car door slams, and I jump. "Nice to meet you..."

"Timothy. But you should call me Tim. Nice to meet you too. Sorry it's under these circumstances. It sounds like you two have a habit of this." *He knows about Luke?* I wonder what else he knows. "Speaking of, Freesia, were you able to visit Mrs. Ore?"

"Nope." She looks disappointed. Pointing in her car, she says, "But I've got the cake already."

Question mentally asked, and verbally answered. Wind bites through the sweatshirt that I feel frumpy in now. I have a lot of things I want to ask Tim, but I would rather be inside with the cops. It can't be as cold—even being questioned about a murder —as it is out here.

Tim turns back to me. "I believe there are people inside who want to talk to you?"

"So I hear."

"Well, let's face the music. Maybe we can get a late night breakfast after all this is done. Freesia can join us after she visits Mrs. Ore. I think we'll have plenty to talk about." He is so casual about it all that I bet he's not from here either.

I'm curious to know how he pronounces Silynn. I'm afraid to say it first in case he parrots me.

Our footsteps are loud on the cracked cement parking lot. The officers are waiting inside the double doors.

"Wondering if you weren't gonna show up. We had plans for a manhunt, in case." *I'm a woman, though.* Curiosity finally gets the best of me, and I read my bully's brass tag: "Officer Curt". Curt seems fitting. Logan Curt. That sounds about right. If it isn't his given name, I have given it to him all the same.

Freesia's hand flies to her hip before I can formulate a response. "You saw us follow you." Her voice is indignant and annoyed enough for both us of, so I say nothing.

Tim turns to her. "You know. It might be better for Ada if you head out now."

For a moment, she looks hurt. "If it's better for her, then okay." Glancing around at the dirty walls and scuffed linoleum, she sighs. "It's sad here, anyhow."

We both get a quick hug before she leaves.

"Hello, Mr. Miller. You and Ada come on back to my office," Officer Frueller says.

The building is shared. Other businesses reside in this space, though I cannot tell what kind. I assume that's on purpose. We stroll past empty cubicles devoid of personalization save a vacation photo here or inspirational calendar there. It reeks of toner and lost dreams.

"Here we are." Body odor wafts with his overextended wave towards his office. His pride stinks of days without a shower. "Have a seat. We have a few questions."

"Alright," I say. "Shoot." *Poor choice of words, Ada.* Did you forget you were in a police station about to discuss a dead person? *And when did I start using phrases like that again, anyhow?*

Frueller's frown reads his displeasure with my word choice too. "Okay. So we established you were at the rental off of—" He grabs a notepad and flips a few pages back. "—Highway 43.

Address: 3258 Hwy 43. Correct? About what time did you get there?"

"What's this about?" Tim interrupts my prepared response.

"Last night, a woman was murdered out at Bar," Logan Curt snaps.

Tim puts his hands out—quick and tense—like he's telling the officers to "stop" with both hands. "Why are you questioning Ada about a woman at Bar? You said this was about Lynn Pond. Did you check the security footage at Bar? We agreed last time there was an incident there that they would have to get four security cameras. Was she on the tapes?" *Last time?*

Both cops shrink at his scolding.

"It appears as though she was moved. As for the cameras, they were out. CK is looking into it. Until then, we've interviewed everyone already, and we only have the words of folks we know."

"And a bunch of drunks' words are enough?" Tim challenges. Though his posture is rigid, his face stays impassive, smooth—calm, even.

Frueller shakes his head. "He wasn't drunk. He said she must have come back for revenge." Blood running cold, I wait for his name. "Luke's been trustworthy up until a few nights ago."

Without missing a beat, Tim counters. "When he attacked my client." My fancy-pants lawyer knew a lot about me. I'm glad Freesia's a talker. "She comes to town and decides to go on a harmless date. Then, she nearly gets assaulted by a man shouting about how he's known her since she was little—which, if you consider their age difference is mighty disturbing. Does that sound like a man we should call *trustworthy?*"

Officer Curt throws a slew of images on the desk in front of us. One of them slides off and lands by Tim's polished shoes. It's the yet-to-be-named woman. The top image is of dark walnut hair matted with strawberry jam-like gore. Her head has been bashed in and is covered with a dusting of snow. A zoomed-in shot of her feet shows a low black heel on her left foot and a bare right one. Seven deep stab wounds shred the sheer shirt she wore over her tank top; bits of fabric are stuck into her back like a jammed slot machine, yet there is little blood under her. Her skirt's ripped a little at the right seam but is otherwise intact. Several images underneath are from Bar. One is the handle of a bloodied beer tap. Another is the wooden leg of a chair, the bottom of which is now burgundy.

I blanch. "You think *I* did that? You think *a woman* did? How the hell could I have moved her?"

They both mutter over each other for a moment. Frueller comes out ahead. "We see a possibility. You show up, and this happens."

Anger at what Silynn has represented for me leaks out. "A plus B equals C, is that it? Really? What possible reason would I have to do this?"

"Ada," Tim's voice warns.

To calm myself, I focus on the three silver-framed photos on Frueller's desk; the glass on each of them is smudged. None of them have him in them, and everyone is smiling *just* right. I'm familiar with that trick; they are the stock photos that came with the frames—nothing like an imaginary happy family to brighten an otherwise shitty life.

"We're just looking into all possibilities." Frueller sounds less cocksure now.

Tim grabs the photos and flips through them. When he gets to a close-up of her face, he stops. We both gasp at her round eyes and pouty lips, soft chin and sharp cheekbones, fivehead instead of a forehead.

"What?" Worthless-Curt asks.

"Does this woman resemble anyone?" Tim sounds astonished that he has to ask.

"A pretty brunette?"

"And if it was dark?" Tim leads the horses to water as he picks up the photograph on the floor. It's a full shot of her under the

Lynn Pond bridge at an angle at which you can see up her skirt. Her underwear is on and un-torn. *Thank god.*

Their eyes get big; they see it.

Curt speaks first, "Um, it could be a lot of women."

"Sure," Tim says, as he collects all of the crime scene photos and taps them together on the desk. Once in a neat pile, he places them face down in front of Frueller.

Frueller gets back to business. "So, when did you get to the rental and how long were you there?"

This is all for pretenses now. No one in this room thinks I killed her anymore. Still, I answer like it is a serious question. "I had a late breakfast with Freesia, dropped her off around 1:30, stopped by the old rental to get my things. After that, I went to the new rental. I called you as soon as my bags hit the floor. Got settled and read for the rest of the evening. I didn't leave until almost ten this morning when I got groceries." I assume from the television I've watched, that's what they care about. "Feel free to check in with Dave—I think he said his name was. He and Freesia know each other," I couldn't help but add.

Both cops shift uncomfortably.

Officer Curt moves the conversation along. "Have you been to Bar?"

"I have. That's where I met Luke. But you already knew that. How did you figure out that's where she was murdered?" I counter.

"Okay, then. I think we're done for tonight; we got what we need. Thanks for coming in, Ada. Don't you leave town, now. We'll be in contact," Officer Frueller says.

"Sure." I wonder if their contact will be to arrest me. "I haven't done what I need to here anyhow." Still, going home is a better idea than staying for mental health reasons. With my safety at risk, Rachael would understand. But then I'd look guilty.

As Tim and I leave, I am a droopy wet paper bag.

Tim strides tall and proud. His client isn't guilty! Well, she's at least walking free for the night.

I forgot my jacket in the car, so I'm back to the bitter cold. It matches my mood, so *sure, why not?*

"You ready to get something to eat? We'll get coffee and warm up."

When will Freesia meet us at the diner smelling of vanilla cake and strawberry icing? Though breakfast with a progressive husband and wife sounds exhausting, Tim and I do need to have a chat.

What I want to say is, *"I'll come by your office tomorrow morning. We can talk more; you know, just in case the police somehow connect me to a murder I didn't commit. We'll work out the billing then too. Night."* What I do say is, "Sure, I'll follow you there."

His smile must be one of the reasons he's married. It was one of the reasons I married Derek. He had pearly whites—like Tim —which he flashed at everyone—like Tim. In moments like this, I actually miss him. Derek and I started like most couples: sweet dates, sexy nights, wild adventures, talks about our future until three in the morning. The lustful teenage version of us was perfect. He is still the only person I allowed to really see me. When we had to grow up together, I found I should have stayed in hiding. To date, it is my only real regret. I wish I could say I regret chasing after a shadow under ice twenty-nine years ago, but I was a child. I cannot blame myself for curiosity any more than I can blame a wasp for stinging a person who smashes its nest.

"Good." Tim interrupts my rabbit trail. He runs the back of his hand across a fake sweaty forehead. "That was a close one. Figured you'd want to go home after that. Heidi always says food's good for the soul."

"Heidi?"

"Oh! Freesia. She changes her name with every move. But she'll always be Heidi to me. Five names ago, I met her in high sch—you're shivering. Let's get to the restaurant before I start reminiscing."

My teeth chatter as I decide to go with my first instinct. "Wait, you know what? Could we meet tomorrow for breakfast at the diner? I really need to go home, take a long hot bath, and get some sleep."

Tim puts on a smile. "Of course. That does mean you'll have to listen to more stories. You won't be able to claim sleep as a reason to bail." He hugs me and opens my rental car door. "I'll tell Freesia what happened. We'll see you tomorrow. 9:00 a.m. too early?"

"9:30?" I counter.

"Perfect. Night, Ada."

It isn't until I am near the cabin that I remember tomorrow is Thanksgiving. I wonder if Tim forgot about that or if he and Freesia are like some of my friends who choose not to recognize the blood-soaked holiday. Either way, I'll show up. I've got nothing else going on.

10:58 P.M.

SLINKING INTO THE CLAWFOOT TUB that takes up as much space as the kitchen is a sigh escaping tight lungs. I have bird-bathed for two days, and it's catching up to me. There is something about a tub that makes me want to cry, call someone important, or have an orgasm. I choose cry today, because I can't call Rachael, and I need a release. "*An orgasm would be unhealthy and avoidant,*" Rachael would say.

I take a sip of the full coffee mug of red wine before sobs wrack my body. My spine hits porcelain, and it's sobering—in that, I don't want to be sober. Chugging cheap, dry Merlot should make me gag, but I haven't stopped crying. Salt drips into my glass; I barely notice the taste. After my third cup—which is the whole bottle—I pull the plug to empty the water that's run cold and turn on the hot water nozzle again.

Another bout of crying threatens me as my skin tingles with warmth. Lamplight breaks through the bubble of tears hovering on the few lashes I have left. The moment I blink the watery blur away, I see myself with a clarity I hadn't before. *I'm crying for me.* Knowing that, a relief rushes through my veins, followed by a heavy dose of guilt and fear that have me feeling dizzier than the wine. I should cry for the woman who probably lost her life because I rebuffed a crazy man. But that's not what I am focused on. Laura deserves my tears too. *Oh god.* What if they were murdered by the same man? *Luke.*

When the same eerie branch hits the window and scares me out of my pity party and spiral, I check the watch next to the empty bottle and mug. 11:47 p.m. *Holy hell.* Without drying off, I wobble out of the tub and slip my way to my wrinkled sheets. They smell of slobber and sadness.

Body odor resembling Officer Frueller's hits me when I cover my shivering nakedness. I forgot to wash. In the end, my soak left me more depressed and aware of my stink. I grab the pen and paper by the bed and jot down feelings. I wish I could call Rachael instead.

My handwriting is wonky, and the drunken sentences aren't as coherent as I'd like. It also turns out that my spelling is atrocious, but it's something.

Dear Diary/Rachael,

It's 11:46 pm and I smell bad. I tried to cry my damages away. Didn't work. the dead woman that looked just like me, didn't she? My mother's faults. I didn't want to think about them. But I'm am.

That catostrophic thinking that makes me feel like I've experienced it all over again. I'm doing it. I'm reliving being kicked me out. I'm experscing a trauma I can't explain, too. Luke's fault! He murderered my lookalike. Whered she come from? Silly to write in a journal. I should be running, calling the cops At home, they'd care.. But here, they don't. Maybe Logan wants me dead. Should learn his name for real. Lukes gunna kill me. Just like he did Laura. I think he did at least. Pretty sure he did. And my mother will never love me the right way even after i'm dead. Where's Pete? I'm tired. Okay, that's it for today. Fear and exhastion are the words of the day if I had a calender for that sorta things. I think I'm bad at spelling.

Night.
Me, Ada.

November 26, 1988

Wendy

MY BACK ACHES. It isn't until the staircase creaks and Adelynn asks me for dinner that I realize why. I've been on this damned floor against this damned door for hours. *What a mess I've become.*

"Momma, did you hear me?" she asks again. Her voice is smaller than her body.

I'm an automated mom. "Yes, honey. We're having leftover pot roast."

Nodding, she turns and jogs back up the stairs. She clutches the stuffed bear, Beary, her father had bought for her at the hospital the day she was born. After a few steps, she lets her arm dangle. It looks as broken as I think her insides are.

I could comfort her. I *should.* Instead, I stretch into a hunch and amble to the kitchen. If Polly were here, she'd tell me to pick myself up and brush it off. She'd say he'd ruined enough, and he shouldn't take any more of my time. Polly would be right. That's why I'm not talking to Polly right now.

The refrigerator blasts me with the cold air I've been combatting with the fireplace in our living room. I stare into the bare-shelved void. The dish with a three-day-old roast is coated in shiny fat and nearly empty. *Right, I sent a portion with the kids for lunch today.*

After yesterday's ordeal, Adelynn should have something better than leftovers, but I'm so tired. I fix Lucky Charms for the kids, hoping they'll be happy to have sweets. There isn't enough milk for both bowls, so I splash in a little water in each. That's all 1% milk is, isn't it? Watered down 2%. That's why I refuse to buy it; it's a rip-off.

We have a few potatoes left; looks like I'll have a baked potato with the last of our sour cream and a sprinkle of cheese. The grocery store calls my name. Maybe I should go now. Having to decide between twelve different kinds of canned tomatoes sounds like a manageable problem compared to Adelynn, Laura, and *him.*

"Peter! Adelynn!" I shout, sounding angrier than I mean to. I soften my tone before calling, "Dinner!"

In reply, the steps moan. Peter isn't wearing his boots. Though I'm relieved, it's concerning. He put them on after the man (who the police claimed must have been a drifter) broke into our home earlier this year. The moment I heard about Laura, I thought of his face—Justice, my daughter said he told her. My stomach cramps when I think about his walk through Adelynn's room to me. She still doesn't understand what happened.

"What's for dinner?" Peter asks. He swivels his head around the kitchen, and I'm reminded that he needs a haircut. "Not *just* soggy cereal, right Mom?" He's right. The thin milk's gone pink; even the marshmallows are nearly dissolved. *That was quick.*

"No, baked potatoes too. They're going to need a bit longer, so I thought this might help."

Adelynn nods in silence, that bear still in her grasp like a lifeline. "Thanks, Momma," she says.

"Suck-up!" Peter raises his hand.

"Don't you touch her, young man. We do not do things like that in this household. What have I told you?" My voice spits the venom seething in my heart.

"I know. 'Don't hit women. Don't hit anyone. It makes you pathetic and weak-willed. Only small people resort to violence.' *I know.*" He says it mockingly, but his remembering it gives me hope he won't turn out like some of his friends, or their fathers, or mine.

"Well, there you go. Now eat your food before it becomes a glop of sugar." I ignore his response—it may have even been polite.

The four shriveled potatoes will do just fine; they can each have two. I'll eat the last of the Lucky Charms. Dry Lucky Charms for dinner. *Oh, joy.* As I carve out the eyes and dark spots from the potatoes, I can't stop thinking about him, about us, about that goddamned conversation.

Four years ago, he approached me at a barbecue. It started innocently, with a graze of the hand here, a compliment there. Eventually, he grew bolder. First, it was a kiss on the cheek as Gary, Adelynn, Peter, and I left block parties. Then, it moved to a brush of my breast as he reached for another roll during dinner when our spouses sat mere feet away. Almost a year later, he had me pinned against the hospital bathroom sink.

We were tacky. I should've known that any man who'd start an affair on *that* day—with my daughter in the hospital and his devastated—wasn't worth my time, wasn't worth shredding a family for. I was stupid.

We almost announced our relationship after Gary left, but he said it would be "too much" for the kids.

The day after Justice, he said the same. "I want to, I really do. I haven't had sex with Carla in ages, and I don't want to." It was a weird thing to add after I shot the man who tried to sexually assault me—hindsight is everything.

Now, he's broken it off like we're teenagers, jumping from one boyfriend/girlfriend to another. I understand his reasons. The unthinkable happened: his daughter was just murdered. It's as if the cosmos have cursed us for our infidelity—first Justice, then Laura. Still, I assumed he'd want support from the woman he loves at a time like this.

"Mom?" Peter says in a way that makes me think it isn't the first time.

"Yes, honey?"

"Can I go back to my room while we wait?" His voice is weary, a traveler after a long journey. His cereal bowl is empty, milk and all. "Please?"

I nod. Adelynn is gone before he stands.

"Hey, Peter?"

He blows a raspberry of frustration. "Yes?"

"Why aren't you wearing your boots anymore?" I almost add, *"You know, your security blanket since Justice."*

Peter stiffens. "After yesterday, it's clear to me that preparedness doesn't matter." He pauses. "Can I go now? I have homework."

"Sure, okay honey. I'm here if you—"

As he leaves, I'm left feeling that he'd rehearsed those words all day. *Why?* Because he sounded mechanical and hollow. *Well, that could be your fault, Wendy. You're a shitty mother.*

I pop the overly stabbed potatoes in the warming oven and head into the living room. Lying down seems like a good idea. When I close my eyes, I see Mike's face. It's tear-stained and desperate. I smile a little; maybe he will come to his senses once the initial shock of grief wears off. A lot can happen in a day, in a week, in a month, in—I shudder—a year. Yes, we'll be together again. Carla can lean on him until then.

November 23, 2017

Ada

I JERK AWAKE, FREEZING; the warmth of splashing blood left with my consciousness. I run my hands along my body to check for the dress made of Laura I know isn't there. In a way, I miss it. There is nothing but naked, sticky skin. I resist the urge to sit up to look for the woman with a thin wrist who tossed the bucket on me. Hidden in shadows, her face was obscured by darkness.

Sleep tries to claim me again, and I picture the wintery woods I had been in before I woke. Bits of the nightmare stay with me: a low-hanging moon, hot breath on my shoulder, eyes peeking out from tree roots—*his eyes*. I shudder before I forget everything.

9:01 A.M.

I WAS RAISED TO BELIEVE in platitudes and obligations.

Though I have tried to carve away that part over the years I've been away from my mother, I still feel compelled to call the few friends I have.

None of them will judge me if I don't call on a bullshit holiday people use as one of two excuses to spend time with extended family to stave off guilt trips throughout the year, which is good because I can't. Unlike most people, the ones I surround myself with allow themselves to devour four slices of pie without counting calories any day they want. My mother, and most of the people I grew up around, pretended we could only do that two days—*ahem,* two months—a year.

My boxed-up childhood laughs from its home by the door. I know what my day holds: breakfast with a couple that will make me feel lonelier, wine, unpacking memories, and a hodgepodge of food from Dave's.

Happy Thanksgiving, *Adelynn.* I grimace.

Now, which sweater that I've already worn doesn't smell?

9:28 A.M.

I AM TWO MINUTES EARLY, and drinks are already on the table. They ordered me water, coffee, and a tea of some kind.

"Hey!" Freesia says. She shrugs out from under Tim's draped arm and rushes to me. Her elbows dig into my shoulders with the neck hug. "Happy Thanksgiving! How are you? I heard about last night— what a load of shit! You should have protective custody or some-thing, not be questioned about a dead girl. And those pictures—you shouldn't have had to see them! I wish Tim hadn't either. He had nightmares all night—damn near punched me, thrashing so much."

"Me too," I get in edgewise.

"See?" she says to Tim. "I knew it would be okay to tell her."

I squeeze her to signal the end of our embrace.

"Nightmares, huh?" I slide into the booth and hope I didn't just invite him to tell me about all about them.

He sighs. "Yeah. It was you beating me with that beer handle thing. Only, you had fangs and—"

The menu gets my full attention. Wow, they have steak AND eggs. I bet they have waffles AND pancakes. *Oh, look*, there they are. I picture the different Adas I could be throughout the day depending on which food I choose.

Steak-Ada does not exist. Egg-Ada would probably have more energy. She would go for a brisk walk before addressing the hateful boxes. Pancake-Ada or Waffle-Ada may be a little more lethargic, stuffed with carbs. Maybe she would go for a drive to clear her head before diving into her childhood.

"Ada?"

"Yeah? Sorry." *How long has it been since Tim finished recounting me murdering him?* Somewhere between Egg-Ada and Pancake-Ada, I suspect. "Got lost in food."

Freesia chuckles. "Happens all the time. We were just asking what you were getting, anyhow."

I think about the Adas. "Waffles with two scrambled eggs."

The hovering waitress says, "Did I hear waffles and two scrambled?"

Creepy, but, "Yep. And a little milk, please." I am not sure I have ever had creamer from a plastic container on a table, and I do not intend to start.

As I hand her my menu, Tim sees my *usually*, artfully hidden palm. He doesn't shy away; he doesn't ask questions either. If we weren't in Silynn right now, if they lived in Bloomington and we had a chance to get to know each other past one or two exchanges, I may tell him about it.

"And for you two?"

Tim orders for them both. "She'll have a short stack, an order of bacon, and two orders of sausage. I'll have a waffle, an order of sausage, and two over-medium eggs. And hot sauce, please; it was missing from our table."

"No problem, Tim. Coming right up."

When we came in before, the waitress didn't address Freesia by name. As if I'm a detective, I file that away in case I need it. Maybe in Silynn, I *am* a detective: Detective Ada of the SPD. I'm better than the police. Already, I had figured out the killer and the motive. *Right?*

"So," Freesia says. "Let's talk about this dead Jane Doe who looks like you. I hear she was visiting family too. What a time to have a doppelgänger! Is it horrible that I'm happy you weren't there?"

I hedge, "No, I'm happy too. Maybe relieved is a better word. Then I think, *Could I have fought him off?* Knowing what I know, maybe I could have been prepared. But could I?" I sigh. "She was blindsided."

Tim shakes his head. "None of this. We aren't going down this road, ladies. No good can come of complex emotions before breakfast." He laughs. We don't.

"So, if we aren't going to talk about that, then why am I here instead of wrapped up in a blanket with a morning wine?"

That Freesia laughs at. "Unlike Tim here, I still want to talk about it. Do you think it was him?"

Skip the bullshit. I knew I wouldn't mind seeing her again. "I do."

Another round of coffee for Tim arrives. Our waitress seems sweet on him. I want to ask about that and about how two seem-ingly-educated forward-thinking adults ended up in Silynn. Instead, Tim breaks our conversation about Luke short.

"I don't think I can talk about death on an empty stomach." *But dreams of me murdering you were on the table?*

"Let's talk money then. How much do I owe you for yester-day? And how much is your fee, should I need you again? I'd like to think they've figured it all out by now, but who knows. They may keep me as a suspect for a while out of stubbornness. The one with the mole was a monster of a kid."

"A monster of a man, too," Freesia adds quickly. "I heard he's punched cars to intimidate people. He's not right."

"I wish I was surprised."

"Ada." Tim reaches across the table with his left arm—the free one—and grabs my hand. "Freesia hasn't liked anyone like you in a while." Cheeks flushing, I'm shocked she didn't smack him. "Because of that, whatever you need is on us."

"Is this because I wear crappy sweaters? I have money. I own a coffee shop." *What am I doing?* Rachael's voice pops into my head; she tells me to stop talking, and be grateful. "I mean, thank you. I'm not used to this type of thing."

"I can tell." Tim's wry smile turns wide as our food arrives.

"Sorry to interrupt, but I thought you might want it fresh." The waitress says this with a twinkle in her eye. I believe she wants admiration for doing the minimum job requirements.

I throw her a bone. "Thank you."

We're of the same mindset; we eat in silence. Tim moans a few times and insists I try a bite of the sausage. Freesia offers me a pancake. I take nibbles of both and find myself having fun. I didn't think I could enjoy any part of today.

I eat the last bite of my waffle with intense satisfaction; it was probably cooked in a seasoned waffle iron—which I find both gross and delicious. Since I moved in with my uncle, I eat slowly. He always cautioned me of getting fat if I ate too quickly. When I look back on my childhood, it was the only detrimental thing he ever did to my mental health. I watched what I ate a little too closely, ate a little too slowly, and ran a few extra times if I saw skin that looked like it *could* be flab.

Tim and Freesia take turns interrupting each other to fill in the blanks of their love story. I laugh and smile at the appropriate times, just as I had for the picture on my desk in my office at

Cuppa. Soon, the fun is gone, and I am back to dreading the boxes at the cabin.

They finish telling me how Freesia happened into being a prostitute during a road trip, and I know it's time for me to leave. I can't keep the facade up any longer. If we aren't going to discuss the dead woman—and what is there to say, *really?*—then I should be alone.

"I need to journal," I blurt in the first moment of quiet.

"Oh..." Tim's voice trails off with confusion.

Freesia, however, nods. "I totally understand. A lot's going on in that head of yours. Maybe we can get together—just you and me—to talk about the rest of your trip." I know she means seeing my mom and going to Lynn Pond.

"That sounds great," I lie. "For now, though, I think I need to process. This has been great, but some stuff is settling in." That's what people say, right? It seems so because Tim waves the waitress down.

"Grab two slices of—" He turns to me and asks what kind of pie I like. "Blackberry pie and another waffle to-go. On my tab."

"Can you wait that long, Ada?" the waitress asks me but stares at Tim.

I slurp the dredges of my over-steeped tea. "Sure."

Sam

"Did you see this?" Jess shouts to me from the open front door.

I shiver as I yell, "Close the door! I don't pay to heat the outdoors." My father used to shout that, and I regret saying it the moment I do.

"You sound like Grandpa." A nearly audible eye roll follows.

Jess remembers little of my father; his name coming from her mouth throws me off guard—a seldom occurrence. When Jess sees this, she rushes to hug me. Her body is bigger than I recall—even from last night. Every second she isn't in my arms, she reverts to a slight twelve-year-old, so it's always a momentary shock when her adult figure is almost my size.

"Sorry, Mom. I know hearing his name still hurts," she almost whispers.

It doesn't. I nod anyway. Inwardly, I cringe at "*Mom,*" though. The word still holds memories of a woman gouging lines and drawing tear-shaped red droplets along my crayon-drawn fairy's neck. Whenever Jess is around, I feel more. I think it's why I agreed to have a child; I heard about the connection women have to things that come from inside of them. I hoped it would work like that for me. I think I even hoped I wouldn't need any more sweethearts. Then I collected another. No child could bring me what that does.

"It smells like cookies! Did you bake while I slept?" she asks.

"No," I say. "I wear vanilla behind my ears sometimes." *To make me more approachable.*

She takes a big whiff. "Maybe I should do that too! But then I'd always crave sweets and get super fat." A pregnant pause. "So, I've slept, I've gotten the paper, I assume you're going to let *me* make some breakfast soon-ish, *now* can we talk about Dad?"

I cast my eyes down and nod again—my go-to for emotions I don't understand. "Yes."

"So you guys split up. At some point, I figured you two were a stay-together-for-the-kid couple." She goes into the kitchen and grabs a mug from the cabinet by the stove. "Want one?"

"Sure, thanks." I wait a moment. "So, do you have questions?" She's an adult, so I hope she doesn't.

The gas burner *click, click, clicks.* "Will I get two Thanksgivings and Christmases?" Her eyebrow sounds raised, even though it isn't.

"Do you want two?"

I watch Jess's lip twitch as she considers it. "No." She pours milk into a saucepan. "You guys should put up with each other for me, if possible."

"You got it. Your dad will be here around noon."

"Perfect. Now, did you know about *that*?" She pokes her elbow towards the two newspapers she brought in from the stoop.

I shake my head. "Probably not. Before we switch gears, you don't have anything else to ask?"

"What is there to ask? You two weren't happy. Last night, you seemed happier than you have in a while. But you were a bit blurry, so you could have been frowning." She shrugs. "That about right?"

"Yeah."

"Well, there you go."

"Okay then," I say. "I'm glad you're okay."

"Thanks for waiting until I moved out, though." She pulls out a pan and takes eggs out of the refrigerator. "Now, what's going on with that headline?"

"Ice Storm On the Way," I read aloud.

Jess grabs a bowl and fork-scrambles eggs with a splash of milk. It's so advanced, I stop paying attention. "Not that one." Jess sounds exacerbated. "The other one. It says a Jane Doe was found."

My face goes cold, and I assume I look as if a vampire had its way with me. "Oh?" I gulp, then turn and head towards the bathroom.

"I haven't read it yet, just saw it, and thought you might have heard. Not a lot of crime that I can remember," Jess continues.

"No, there isn't."

Papers rustle, and Jess clears her throat. "Early this morning, a Jane Doe was found under the bridge at Lynn Pond. How sad!" Everything goes white. She stops reading, and I hold my breath. "Looks like the police aren't sharing much, just that she wasn't murdered there, and they have persons of interest. That's about as helpful as anything. The article is only two paragraphs long—a bunch of buzz words and hype. Whenever I see all that, I figure they don't have much, and they're banking on someone calling in with information. You alright in there?"

Who me? "Yeah. Yesterday's frozen lunch is catching up to me." I steer the conversation elsewhere. "How's breakfast coming?"

"Don't rush perfection. I'll flip through and see if anything else is worth reading about. Our papers are so huge, filled with violence, corrupt politician scandals, government policy changes. Silynn has twelve pages. Twelve pages! And one of them is an ad for a new dentist in Lorla Falls. I forget how different the world is here."

They found Lori. They found Lori. Nostalgia is going to ruin everything. Should I get rid of my sweetheart memorabilia?

"Wow."

My heart skips a beat. "What?" *No more bad news.*

"Silynn was hurting for news before the Jane Doe. Some woman named Adelynn Bailey coming back to town made it to page four on the day before's paper. Apparently, she found a dead girl from Lynn Pond a long time ago. That place sounds like it has bad juju. Those poor families!"

"I wonder why she's back."

"Who?"

"Adelynn Bailey," I say. Sometimes I worry medicating Jess as a child was to her detriment. If she hadn't taken pills when she was thirteen, Jess might be a bit smarter.

"Wait. Why? Do you know her?"

Clearing my throat, I say, "No, but everyone knows her name." *At least, those of us who have a stake in her memory—or lack thereof.* "It's just curiosity, really."

"See? The papers did their job: made news from nothing. Hopefully, my visit will make the front page of the *Silynn Times* tomorrow! Samantha and Taylor Pruette's daughter returns for the holiday!"

I sound as dismissive as I am, as I say, "Maybe so."

Hiding in the bathroom can only be a solution for so long, I know. I flush and wash my clean hands before heading back out to keep up the facade.

"Perfect timing," Jess says, as I walk into the kitchen. She wipes a little chocolate splatter up with a white and red polka-dotted towel and grabs a ladle. "Hot cocoa and cheesy scrambled eggs are ready."

"Great, thanks. Looks delicious."

My face must show my worry over Lori being found. *I didn't leave any trace of me.* Adelynn Bailey's presence in town adds another layer of stress. She doesn't come home often—*why now?* And why is this happening when I need to sneak away to find another sweetheart?

"Mom," Jess says and puts her soft hand over my white-knuckled fist. "Everything will be okay." *Will it?*

12:11 P.M.

"I CAN'T BELIEVE HE'S STANDING US UP." She's clutching her third cup of cocoa, but her hand may as well be on her hip. "And on Thanksgiving!"

"I'm sure your dad is only running late." We both know Taylor never runs late.

Jess slurps down the last sip of chocolate. "I'm grabbing another. Want one?"

"Might want to slow down there."

"I can have as many as I want." I see a five-year-old version of Jess stomping around in her favorite mermaid jellies.

"Yeah, you're right." I'm in no mood to pick an argument. All I want to do is move this day along so I can find out what the police know about Lori.

The front door shakes with a knock.

"I guess you'll get your wish; I won't have another cup of cocoa now." She throws a smirk my way before racing to throw the door open. "Dad!" she squeals. "Where were you? It's fifteen minutes past when you were supposed to be here. What was I supposed to think? You and Mom split up, and what? I'm chopped liver? Not cool, Dad. Not cool."

. . .

I imagine my daughter as chopped liver; then make Taylor into ribbons of onions. It suddenly becomes necessary to consume my family. I salivate and reach for my mug—empty. Looks like I'll drink Jess's fourth cup of cocoa for her.

Taylor is speechless.

"Enough of that," Jess says, shaking invisible dirt off her. "I've missed you!"

Taylor's deep-set features soften. "Me too, Rugrat! It's been too long." I turn away from their hug; it's intrusive to see affection.

Jess waves towards our—*my*—living room. "Come in, Dad. I've been waiting to tell Mom something until you got here."

Taylor sits in the recliner. Its old hinges squeak. "Okay. Shoot." *I can't; my father's gun is locked and under the bed.*

"Cole and I are getting married!" I can see Jess spinning around with a bouquet in her hand. Her hair is as blunt as it is now, so she's an ugly bride. Jess pauses only a moment before adding, "And I'm leaving to meet his family in Prague tomorrow night. My flight is early the next morning. I'm sorry I'm leaving earlier than planned. And he's so sorry he couldn't make it. It added $400 to the ticket price to come here for a few days, and he didn't have it. This has all been so crazy."

Taylor chooses platitudes to buy time to process. "Wow, honey! That's big news."

I'm not nodding. "You're getting married?" I ask for double-clarification.

"Isn't it wonderful?" She sighs. "I've never been this happy!" My daughter is a frog with an open chest. I envision a heart beating from within the y-shaped incision. Our beats are out of sync. It turns out she is nothing like me.

I remember March 10th, 1993 like it was yesterday. The flowers reminded me of a funeral home. *Fitting.* In some ways, my wedding was a celebration of my independence dying. Formaldehyde filled my nostrils instead of the dabs of vanilla extract on my neck and behind my ears. I stared in the mirror and touched my face. I was warm and soft, not like my grandmother; she had been cold and waxy. Her skin had slid a little as if it were a mask lying on her skull.

Taylor was supposed to be the love of my life. My face had been frozen in a grimace I'd forced into a smile before I trudged down the aisle.

My father held my arm loosely. We'd grown apart over the years, but he'd insisted on being involved. As I strode past my grandfather, his cologne overwhelmed the imagined scents of death. Taylor's best friend, Maggie, cried—not for us, but for herself and the loss of what she never had. She'd loved Taylor long before I came into the picture. I felt calm, bored despite the mourners around me.

A smiling Taylor waited for me under a small arch suffocated by twinkle lights. I think the ill-fitting suit was the one worn to a co-worker's wake the year before. Knowing I wouldn't care showed that Taylor understood me as much as anyone could and accepted that I could never be more than I was—than I am.

That was until a few days ago. Will the same thing happen to Jess? She hasn't dated much, so she's never experienced heartbreak like most people I've watched. If someone breaks her heart, I won't be able to do anything. I can't put a broken thing back together.

Ada

NEARLY FOUR HOURS, and the soft snowfall shows no sign of slowing. It appeared like a plague. I made it home without incident and have no more plans for the day. Even so, I worry about my last few days here.

I have found out my mother had an affair that tore my family apart. For no rational reason, I spent time with—and ended up a wing-woman for—the woman who was partially responsible for the most significant trauma of my life. I befriended a prostitute and have been questioned about my doppelgänger's murder, not to mention pissed off that woman's probable murderer who may have loved me since I was a child.

But have I talked to my mother about Laura like I had planned? *No.* Gone to Lynn Pond? *Not yet.* Driven around to trigger memories despite Rachael's advice? I glance at the fluffy white flakes pounding on the window. *May not be able to do that at all now.* Called Laura's parents and asked to talk to them? *Nope.* I also haven't called Rachael lately. I *have* journaled as requested.

It will be an interesting read for her when I get back—nonsense and words that shake out to a fear of the dark and anger revolving around that. It's just not enough.

I use the cordless phone and dial through each number for Rachael I have. Being Thanksgiving, it's no surprise she doesn't answer. Her work number and professional cell have sweet messages about calling a hospital or suicide hotline if it's an emergency. The personal number she gave me for this trip as a "just in case" goes straight to voicemail.

"You've reached Rachael Weski. I'm probably eating pie and enjoying my family's company right now. If you leave a message, I'll get back to you when the laughter dies down." Kids squeal in the background for emphasis.

Wow, she changes her message for different holidays? Mine has been the same for six years now, passed down through three phones.

"Hey, it's Ada. Leave a message at the annoying beep if you'd like." That was the married, happier version of me. I should rerecord it. "Hey, it's Ada. I'm in Silynn trying to get over my demons right now. Leave a message if you absolutely have to, but know it's doubtful I will call you back." That sounds more honest.

I decide to leave a message—despite the moroseness of it all —and hope it won't ruin her Black Friday shopping plans after she listens to it. "Hey Rachael, it's Ada. I'm sorry to leave a message here—or at all really. I know if I don't, though, I may go insane. My mother sent me away because of an affair. That's the reason my dad left too. Also, the police found a dead girl who looks a lot like me. Luke tried to point the finger at me, and the cops questioned me—like that made any sense. I think he did it. What if he finds me? I just keep feeling like someone's watching me. Rachael, what if he's the Lake Killer? What if he has been killing all this time." I sigh into the receiver. "I know it's all so far-fetched, but that's Silynn for you."

The lady on the other line interrupts my next sentence as she asks if I want to hang up or rerecord—what a short attention span her answering machine has. I suppose my long pause could have triggered the woman. Either way, I press to rerecord.

"Hey Rachael, it's Ada. Sorry to bother you on Thanksgiving. I'm just having a hard time. I should have called yesterday; you would already know about the dead girl that looks like me—the one I can't stop thinking about. There's a hair on my right nipple that's stuck under the skin. I have to get it out. I'm staring at three boxes of my stuff from before my mother sent me away. I'm not sure if I should open them. Anyhow, I'll try again tomorrow." I stop talking and wait. When the automated woman prompts me again, I push one once more and hang up, crossing my fingers that it won't even register as a message.

I shove myself away from the counter I have been relying on to keep me upright. Before I get drunk, I should make my dinner. Despite my grocery trip, I'm unhappy with my options. With no frozen meals worth eating, I bought little *real* food: a pack of frozen chicken, eggs, dressing I don't want, bread spotted with mold I missed during my two-second scan, a block of cheese, and carrots. Setting the old oven to low broil, I toss an unseasoned chicken breast and half of the bag of carrots onto a warped tray I found in a cabinet by the sink and into its cool belly. Its cook will be uneven, and its taste will be bland, if not a little sweet thanks to the carrots. It should keep me from having a hangover in the morning, though. Hopefully.

I grab my faux-journal and jot down a list of worries.

1. Being murdered.
2. Being arrested.
3. Going to Lynn Pond.
4. Not going to Lynn Pond.
5. Being alone forever.
6. Never seeing my father again.

7. Getting stuck in Silynn during a snowstorm.

8. Dying alone.

Okay, now that I have been excruciatingly honest with myself, opening boxes will be a piece of cake. Torture on a holiday, what's more festive than that?

Once I fill my coffee mug to the brim with wine again, I drag a box to the edge of the bed where I curl up in defense. No. *For warmth.* The first box has two layers of un-sticky tape dangling from the top. Not only had my mother packed my childhood up and not sent it to me, but she had revisited it later and *still* hadn't sent it to me. I wish I were shocked.

The first thing I see peeking out from beneath the cardboard flaps is matted fur. I recognize the color and am horrified. She had sworn she didn't have Beary—whose name I jokingly changed to Bearable when I told semi-filtered stories of my childhood to acquaintances at parties. I tug him out and clutch him to my chest. I had begged her to find him. After she sent me away, I cried every night for months. I missed her, Pete, Silynn, but I also mourned the loss of Beary. If I weren't already buzzed, I'd call her right now.

Underneath Beary, I see green pilling fabric. My mother kept the jacket I should have been wearing that day. *Why?* A visceral memory accosts me: sticky sweet dehydrated marshmallows clinging to my teeth and wedging into the small grooves, the taste persisted through two brushings.

I feel the wine before I see it. Lukewarm liquid runs over my hand onto the blanket around me. *Shit.* I can't move. Merlot blossoms into a purple ink blot resembling the stamp apples and acrylic paint make. I know I have forever changed the patchwork quilt, yet I remain seated. Still shaky, I wipe my hand off on my pink and white striped pajama bottoms, ignoring the stain I am creating. It'll wash, or it won't.

Cooked chicken smell fills the room. I don't think I've been sitting here long enough, but my nose is usually right about food; it's time to flip it. I toss the quilt over my shoulder before I go to prove an ability that has never done anything but make me a nag to my ex-husband.

As usual, I'm right. After flipping the breast, I run cold water over the wine spill. I manage to lighten the inky splotches to a palm-size patch of mauve tie-dye.

Knowing I have ruined someone's handmade quilt—probably some sweet great-grandmother who is long gone from this world —reminds me where I am and what day it is. Thanksgivings in Silynn brought on a feeling of unworthiness. My mother always attempted to cook a traditional meal using canned and frozen foods—no spices in sight. Peter and I would try to smile through it. But when one of us couldn't control our faces at the tinny taste of the wobbly cranberry sauce or chewed too long on the over-cooked turkey, my mother would cry. She had "slaved over" the meal, and we were "ungrateful." Her food "wasn't good enough" for us.

After I was sent away, my uncle and his wife went out of their way to make the holiday homey by requiring family time. At first glance, it was lovely. But it became exhausting, and I craved alone time. The food was better, though. Turkey *and* chicken with stuffing made from real bread, not a box. And pie—the pie was hard to pass on.

I remember the slice of blackberry pie and waffle I have in the fridge, and my stomach growls. I eat a lot of desserts now, to make up for the days I passed on it.

The moment the chicken's done, I wipe down the pan and toss Tim and Freesia's generosity on the tray and into the oven. Until the better food is ready, I stab at bits of bland chicken and softened carrots with disappointment. I should have looked for salt, at the very least.

After four bites, I remind myself I have eaten cold food before, I can do it again. I pull the pie and waffle out of the oven.

Somehow, the pie is a little warm, just not enough to make the sauce oozy. Without whipped cream, that bit doesn't matter. My waffle is a bit chewy, almost as if I'm eating less squeaky styrofoam. They are both tastier than the unseasoned chicken.

Licking the plate of purple goo, I sigh as if I had eaten a real Thanksgiving meal. Reaching for another glass of wine and Beary, I become a fetus. For the moment, I feel safer.

Pretending that tryptophan is lulling me to sleep and not wine, I try not to stare at the green fabric peeking from within the open box in the corner. I do not succeed.

Sam

JESS IS CONVINCING US that we should go into town after our early dinner. She seems unperturbed when I tell her little will be open.

"It's fine. I just want to revisit some old haunts."

"Do you have places in mind?" Taylor asks.

She nods. "I thought we could drive past the school, maybe go through downtown; it's been ages since I've seen it. After that, we could see about getting a milkshake. You know, if Sodas 'n More is open." I doubt they will be, but we toss on our coats.

Taylor shouts from the kitchen. "Hold your horses, ladies. I've still got to put the turkey and stuffing away. Your mom only helped a little."

"Then why doesn't Mom take me? We'll be back in a bit—hopefully with milkshakes." Jess smiles and shakes stray short hairs from her high jacket collar.

Taylor's face crumples. I've never dealt with disappointment well, so I avoid a look that means to ask if we'll wait a few minutes.

I turn away and say to Jess, "I can do that." I grab my wallet and keys and open the front door. "Thanks for cleaning up," I call over my shoulder.

"Yeah, thanks, Dad!" Jess bounds to the kitchen in three long gazelle strides to give Taylor a quick kiss on the cheek. "We'll be home soon."

"I can't believe nothing's changed," Jess says, as I pull over in front of her old high school. "I bet the paint on the sidewalk has at least worn away." She's thinking about the time she and her friends volunteered to paint backdrops for the school play. They got into a paint fight, and it splattered everywhere. Some nazi-kid who claimed he was in charge went nuts. Jess hasn't been able to let it go. "I'm still floored he wasn't expelled. I mean, what if he'd had a disease? I may have had a cut or something!"

"We should go." I hate when she gets overly emotional.

"No, I'm fine. It's just still so shocking. If I were his mother—"

"You'd have grounded him then taken him to a shrink." I know this because she's said it numerous times.

Jess nods. "You're right. He needed help." She kicks a pebble, and it flies into the trashcan nearby. The unexpected *tink* makes her jump and shakes her from wherever her thoughts were headed. "So many memories," she whispers, more to herself than me.

Jess had enjoyed high school. She'd been a cheerleader since age seven; Taylor had been the cheer-parent. I couldn't be for lack of enthusiasm and the similarities Jess had to Jessica when her hair was in a high ponytail and she held pom poms. She, too, had been a cheerleader. I often wish I'd named Jess anything but. Nostalgia had gotten me then as well. Popularity had come with

Jess's cheerleading. The only two boys she's dated besides her fiancé were another perk. They bought her jewelry and a slew of other Valentine's Day-like crap weekly. And her social life earned her the nickname Jessibuzz. She's never stopped being the busiest person I know. *How did I help raise this?*

It was a horror beyond horrors when some mentally unstable teen tried to rub blood on her because she got paint on a sidewalk behind the school. Why blood? Who knows. He just sliced his hand open and shouted, "If you want to share things, you can share some of this!" It was one of the first big bad moments in her life. She was devastated and confused, but I didn't comfort her much. As with many of her memories, though, she's blurred and shaped it to fit her purposes. That moment became her clay seconds after it happened. And the way she tells, I was a stellar mom who'd demanded an expulsion. I didn't, and he wasn't, but her version of the story is better than the truth: I did nothing but take her home. We went to the Perrin Mall for a new pair of jeans that weekend, though—Taylor's idea.

"You ready?" I open the car door. There is a scuff by the handle. I don't remember it being there before. I checked my car inside and out for mud, hair, fingernails, small rocks, scratches, even bugs, two days ago.

Jess's ugly bob bounces as she skips back towards the car. "Yes! Thank you."

"Where to?"

Her eyes glisten in the amber lights that surround the school. "How about downtown? We can drive for a bit, then head over to Sodas?"

I wait for the click of her seatbelt—because that's what parents do—before I drive. "Downtown it is."

The drive is short—fifteen minutes or less. I listen to Jess tell me all about her soon-to-be husband and the lead up to the proposal. It isn't a great story. "Wait!" she shouts, interrupting herself, as we near the gas station I get my licorice and beer from.

"I found something that's different. Fill Up's sign has been painted!"

I crush her excitement by saying, "No, they just washed it."

She huffs. "Well, it's a *little* different, then."

"Sure," I placate.

"Now I'm craving chips. Can we stop?"

"Sure. I could go for licorice. I just ran out."

"Gross. You're still eating that? Here I'd hoped you'd grow out of it."

"Jess, I'm forty-five years old. I've been eating licorice since I can remember. It's long past when I'd 'grow out of it,' don't you think? Besides, when was the last time you tasted it? Tastebuds change every—"

"Seven years. You tell me this all the time," Jess says. She feigns irritation; I can tell she's missed our banter. I think I have too.

"So?"

"So, what?" she asks, as I park in front of the gas station.

"Have you tried it since?"

"No. I guess I will. I mean, you were going to make me right?"

I nod, despite not caring one way or the other.

There are two other cars in the parking lot. One's a beat-up station wagon filled with beach duds. *It's November.* The other is a sleek, sports car. A cologne cloud surrounds it.

We head in, and Jess rambles about the other food I eat that she thinks tastes bad. Mostly, they are types of fish and vegetables. She complains that it isn't warm when we step inside, but I didn't expect it to be.

"Poor employees; they must freeze their butts off in here." Her tone holds pity, and it makes me uncomfortable.

"Actually, they often don't wear coats," I say over my shoulder as I make a beeline to my candy. "What kind of chips do you want?"

"Cheesy something. Surprise me."

I hear the unmistakable sound of a flashbulb. "Now suck that lollipop," the cameraman whispers.

Jess is picking out gum, while the checkout person rings up a well-dressed couple. I see a silver card come from an expensive looking purse and tune back into the pervert by the beer fridge.

"Yes, that's it. Let some of it show."

"Are you sure this looks okay? I feel like I look a little whore-ish. My agent wouldn't want me to present myself in a slutty light." The model tries to defend herself and sound like an adult. "It's partially the skirt too. I don't like that it's riding up."

"That's what's making the shot. Just trust me, alright? Your agent set this up, didn't he? He must have thought I could add a little something to your portfolio—liven it up a little."

I finally walk in view of the photoshoot. It's the same man I walked in on taking photos of Jess in her pushed up cheerleading uniform when she was seventeen. She'd been told it would make her a cheerleader for some major football team or something. Though I'm not usually a violent person, without a second thought, I punched the guy so hard he blacked out. Jess pretended the whole day didn't happen. She's terrific at denial.

I knew Silynn bred darkness. I'd heard of teachers and students having affairs, drug deals, prostitutes, fetishes involving animals; it's one of the reasons we moved out of the town. Silynn has a sickness. Predators live on every street.

"Excuse me. Are you *the* Rick Polino?"

"In fact, I—" he starts. When he swivels and sees me, it's instant recognition. My hair's a little whiter, and my face isn't as smooth as it used to be, but not much else has changed.

I'm measured as I say, "I'd suggest you leave."

The teen pointed at me with a long, glassy-looking nail. "Lady, I don't know what you think is going on here. But Rick is going to—"

"Make you famous. He did this to my daughter. Only in her

case, she was on a bed, and he was taking pictures from angles that should have gotten him arrested. I looked into him. None of so-called 'contacts' were real. So unless you really want this guy taking photos for his spank bank or putting them up on porn sites, you'll pull that skirt down, wipe your whore lipstick off, and go call your parents."

Jess is behind me. I don't know how long she's been there. "So, that wasn't some weird mushroom trip?" she breathes.

I'm not addressing that. "No."

Rick needs no extra push. He runs out of the shop. It's unlike me to step in, to care. This is the most motherly I've felt in ages, and I want it to stop. Jess brings emotions out of me. It's why only seeing her once a year is optimal.

"You okay?" Jess asks the girl. Her skirt is now three inches longer, and her top covers both her breasts *and* her stomach. The lollipop has vanished. "I've been there."

"Thanks. I guess I wanted to believe I could get out of this place bad enough that I was willing to grit my teeth and deal, you know? Like, if he's my ticket out, then I'll do what I have to." Her face crumples, and it ages her by a decade.

Jess touches her arm, and I turn away. "I got out for college— no thanks to Rick. Now I'm getting married and traveling!"

As the girl begins to respond, I pick out two different kinds of chips and head to the counter. The checkout woman—who I wish was Marly—scans my junk food. I don't even mean to, but I say, "So, you let Rick photograph girls in the store?"

"He'll do it elsewhere if not here." Slumped shoulders and sad eyes say she knows from experience. I choose not to respond.

Jess meets me at the car. "Thanks for waiting. Alice called her dad; he's only a five-minute drive away. I have a feeling Rick is going to have another swollen face by the end of the day. Happy Thanksgiving to him, right?"

Again, I don't to respond. Instead, I try to figure out how Alice snuck away on a family holiday.

"Can we skip more driving and get food? I'm stressed and starving. Nothing's changed enough to warrant us riding around for ages."

"Starving? We just had a full Thanksgiving meal." I keep my eyes on the road as I turn left.

"Stress makes me hungry, Mom."

Rolling her window down, Jess reminds me of my father's dog. It'd been hard to deal with his devastation when it went missing shortly after Laura Hurst. I had been experimenting; several animals bore the brunt of my learning curve. I wonder if all the owners were so despondent when their pets didn't come home for dinner.

Jess fakes teeth clattering noises. "It's so cold!"

"You rolled down the window in November. What did you expect?"

We both shiver.

"Fresh air?" Laughing, Jess rolls it back up. "Lemme have a piece of that licorice." I blast the unready heat and hand her the bag. After loud crinkles and a curse, she breaks into the package. To her credit, the bite she takes is almost half of a stick of black licorice. Three chews in, she spits it out into the bag. "Still, no. Got any water?"

As the car breaks room temperature, Sodas 'n More comes into sight. I point and say, "Nope, but they do."

The lights are on, and cars are in the parking lot. It's packed and loud, and the wait is thirty-five minutes.

"That's okay, right Mom?" Jess asks as the hostess stares us down. "I could really use a shake right about now."

Be a good mother; be a good mother. I mumble, "Sure."

"Great," the leggy blonde says. Her off-the-shoulder sweatshirt is bright pink and has the restaurant's logo on it. "Since we're limited on waiting room space, you can hop in your car, and I'll come get you." She shrugs as if it were a question rather than a polite demand; her straight hair bends with the motion.

Jess says she doesn't care, so I tell the teenager it's fine. I'm tired of the cold, anyhow, and Sodas isn't as warm as the car will be in five minutes. If I weren't so close to a rest stop that stays fairly active, I'd move somewhere warmer. With my pending divorce, I still may have to. I should research rest stops in warm towns. *Is that a suspicious thing to search?*

Nearly forty-five minutes later, Jess and I get antsy enough to go and check on our table.

"Oh! Oh, gosh!" The hostess grabs menus and waves us in. "I'm so sorry! I forgot what name was what and skipped you when you didn't answer. A table is being cleaned; it's yours."

I picture Juliey—a mistyped 'y' or mean parents—in a pool of blood. Her shirt is soaked, perky breasts are covered in gore. It's a satisfying image; one that has me almost smiling as she seats us. She seems relieved, as if my near-smile is gratefulness or excitement over snacks.

Jess responds when I don't. "Thank you." After Juliey leaves, she looks at me. "You okay? You don't smile often, and that was a horribly long wait."

My lips sink, and I'm more myself. "I'm fine. Glad to get some food. But the wait was nice," I say. "I haven't felt this caught up on your life in a while."

Instead of taking the compliment—the fact that I can stand listening to her for over half an hour—Jess takes it the wrong way. "I'm sorry we haven't kept up. I feel like a bad daughter, but life's been so hectic."

Channeling other mothers, I tell her what she wants to hear. "You are a wonderful daughter. Everything's okay. I'm glad you're here now."

"Me too." She reaches for my hand and squeezes. "Me too," she says again.

Our waitress comes and saves me from having to squeeze back. Anne is another version of Juliey, a forgettable woman in an off-the-shoulder sweatshirt. The only difference is that hers is lime green. The '80s have come back to Silynn.

A voice sounds over the hum of conversations around me. I'd know that voice anywhere. "Oh my god!" The words scare away our waitress.

Jess raises an eyebrow. "Mom, I think that woman's freaking out over you. She looks familiar..."

"Why would she be doing that?" I ask as if I don't know.

"Samantha Pruette, as I live and breathe!"

Not turning, I say, "Hailey Corvin, as I sit in this chair." It's been over a year since I've been to Sodas, been longer since I've seen her.

Jess snickers before saying, "Oh, wow! It's been ages!"

"I've been saying that a lot lately," she replies. "Did you know Adelynn Bailey came back?" Hailey asks without turning to me.

"We saw it in the newspaper!" Jess says. "Who knew someone visiting would make the papers?"

I finally turn at Hailey. Her hair still reminds me of the ballerina in jewelry box my mother gave me when I was little. I dropped it out of our attic window the morning after I shot the doe.

"Interesting, right?"

"I guess," I say, guarded. "We haven't had much to talk about in a while, so to some, she *could* seem like news. But with the dead girl found..." I wait.

Hailey pulls a chair up to our small two-person table. "Ada's come back to see her mom, she said." Hailey does this, always tries to sneak back into someone's life; it's sad.

Trying not to sound too interested, I pick up my napkin and put it in my lap. "You've seen her?"

"Yeah! She came in a few days ago, and we got drinks. I called her cabin, but it seems she's gone somewhere else. Of course, Mark played it off like he had authority. When I asked where she went, he told me he's only supposed to give that information to the police." She tsks. "Shame, I wanted to see her again before she left."

Remain calm. "Police? Everything okay? Does she have anything to do with the murder? We didn't read the whole article." I don't ask the question I really want to. *"Do you know how long she'll be staying?"*

"I assume everything's alright since she hasn't left yet. Dave came in for breakfast this morning, said she got some groceries yesterday. As for the murder, I have no idea. It's so unlike Silynn. Still don't know her name, age, nothing. Ada couldn't be involved. That's too silly. If anything it would be the La— So... How are you?"

She was going to say Lake Killer; I'm almost sure. Even dumb Hailey is making connections. That's not great. I don't respond immediately; I'm crafting a response that will both quell her curiosity and make her leave. "Fine, Taylor and I have been fixing up the house as always."

Jess stills.

"Ever a project on the horizon, right?" Hailey jokes.

"Right. Other than that, the usual." I don't go out much, and I see her less than that, so she doesn't know what I mean. I'm fine with that. The last time Hailey and I spent time together we were teenagers. Since, we've stayed cordial.

Hailey launches into a story about a man she met a few days ago and their love tryst—hardly a "tryst" if she's telling a very old friend. I try to get a word in, mostly so we can order, but she's good at pretending she doesn't know things are happening.

Jess nudges my knee under the table. "That sounds great," I say. I hope it's an appropriate time to say that. "Hey, can we order our shakes? Taylor's cleaning up and waiting for us to bring one home."

"Of course!" I get her usual, cheery waitress voice; the glare that comes with it is reserved for me. She's thinking about all those years ago, I can tell. Police and Adelynn go hand and hand in our memories.

I order for both of us, and she leaves. "Thank god," Jess says when Hailey is out of earshot. "I just want to have a milkshake with my mom, is that so hard? What were we talking about before she showed up?"

"I can't remember. Must not have been that important," I parrot my father. "How about you pick a new topic?"

Her next sentence is lost to me.

Across the restaurant, Juliey leads a family to their table. The mother is unremarkable, the father too. But their daughter has my heart thudding in my chest. Long, silky black hair falls onto the satin poof she's wearing—they must have shopped at Polly's.

"Did you hear me?" Jess asks.

"Sorry, can you repeat it? I spaced a little. Seeing Hailey reminded me of a different time, and I fell down memory lane." *I'm so quick.*

"I totally get that. It's like when I saw Quinn a few months ago. Remember her?"

A sound of acknowledgment.

"Well, she didn't even seem to care that I was—"

"Eleanor, sit up straight," the girl's mother chastises. "You'll give yourself a hunched back if you keep slouching."

Small hands with jagged fingernails straighten her dress. *I'll need to avoid those nails.* She sits up, and side-swooped bangs slide into her eyes.

"Mom? Mom?"

"Sorry, I think this place is just filled with too many memories." *Did that sound sincere?* I pull my brow together in faux concern. It's what people do if they're haunted by too many memories on television.

Jess looks around and considers the photos on the walls, the tables, the ice cream counter. She's going down memory lane too. "We can get the shakes to go, see Dad faster." Jess's face wrinkles so fiercely with worry, I can imagine her in twenty years.

"Yeah, let's do that."

"I'll flag Hailey down." Jess reaches for my hand again, but our waitress interrupts by bringing us waters.

I pay attention the rest of the time we are there, but I worry that not listening in on Eleanor's family will keep me from getting my new sweetheart. Then I hear her father tell her to be more careful of her dress—she's going to need it for church on Sunday. There are only four churches in Silynn. So, if they're from here, they'll be at one of them.

Hailey strolls up with the milkshakes and to-go cups. "Here you go. Oh! You said you needed another one?"

"Taylor can have mine. I'm not hungry anymore."

8:49 P.M.

THE CHOCOLATE COOKIE SHAKE I ORDERED makes Taylor moan. Through a smiling mouthful of ice cream, I can make out gratitude. Bits of chocolate speckle coffee-stained teeth.

"You're welcome," Jess beams.

We've seemingly moved past the snide comments Taylor jabbed at us the moment we opened the door: Jess and I took too long to come home; Jess is leaving soon, didn't I remember that? "Plus, I was getting worried."

"I'm making cocoa," I announce. I regret not ordering another shake.

They don't respond, but I get three mugs out anyway. I don't want to have to do this again.

Standing over the stove, stirring chunks of chocolate into warm heavy cream, my mind drifts back to Eleanor.

With Lori having just been found, I *shouldn't* be planning for another sweetheart. If they don't make the connection to the Lake Killer at first, a second girl going missing will tip them off. Inwardly, I wince again at the name I've been given.

The smell of Irish whiskey steams up from my drink, and I'm reminded of Hailey and her parent's liquor cabinet. She knows something I don't, something about Ada. Hailey had looked at me that way when Laura was found too. There was a worry in her eyes that made my palms sweaty. The police knew about the baptism, she told me.

"What if they suspect us? Wouldn't they do that? I can't have my mom finding out about that day! They didn't tell her, so I lied. I can't go back now."

"Calm down. We didn't do anything wrong—then or now."

"Mom? Can we play Masterpiece?" Jess cut through 1988. "Did you make enough cocoa for us? I could use something warm now."

I nod. "Sure we can, and yes, I did."

"Do ours have some of that delicious smelling whiskey I see on the counter?" Taylor asks.

"It can. Let me grab the game first."

Juggling three cups of spiked hot cocoa and a board game, I head into the living room. They are both smiling at me, grateful. *We're your average family on Thanksgiving.*

11:19 P.M.

· · ·

JESS HAD US SWITCH TO SCRABBLE and kept us up until 10:45. By then, snow blanketed the driveway, and Taylor was falling asleep.

"Why don't you stay here?" I suggested.

Taylor asked to grab some blankets and a pillow—"*my* pillow." It should've hurt, and I suppose it almost did. To Jess, it was shattering.

"Dad, this is still your house. Right, Mom?" *That word again.*

"Of course. Taylor, what's mine is yours. It will be long after we get a divorce," I say. I don't mean it, but I say it. "We have a beautiful daughter together, so that's just the way it is." That beautiful daughter beams, and Taylor nods, knowing I'm full of shit.

"Well, I'm off to bed. I have to call Cole to say goodnight. What time is it in Prague, anyhow?"

Taylor and I both shrug. "It shouldn't matter," Taylor says.

"Good point! Night, Mom. Night, Dad. Happy Thanksgiving! Thanks again for a wonderful day. I'll see you in the morning." Her voice is one step away from a delighted squeal. She's so pleased that we're under the same roof, despite her understanding of our decision.

When we hear the guest room door click, Taylor turns to me. "I'm sorry about this. I should have paid attention to the time."

I finally say something I mean. "It's fine."

"Well, thanks."

"No problem. Night." I lean forward and kiss Taylor's cheek —muscle memory. It earns me a raises eyebrow which has become more salt than pepper in the last year. *I'm just as shocked.*

"Night, Sam."

In my bedroom, with the door closed, I find solace with my sweethearts. I know I should wait for Taylor to settle on the couch and Jess to get off the phone, then wait even longer until they're both asleep. But the day has been filled with fakery, and I need to feel something real. Rubbing their hair brings me that.

Knock.

Before I have a chance to put Jessica's lock away, Taylor steps into the room. I slide the box under my pillow in the nick of time.

"What's that?" Taylor's cheeks flush, blue eyes widening at what I'm holding.

The childish part of me, the part that chased other girls down at recess wants to snap, *"Nosey much?"* Instead, I ask, "Can I help you?"

Taylor strides to the bed, sits beside me, and drapes a gentle hand over mine. "Who's is that?"

One of Jessica's only remaining unbloodied blonde locks wrapped in her signature pink ribbon peeks out from in between my cupped hands. "Go to bed, Taylor."

After a long moment of quiet save the whirring of my personal heater, Taylor whispers, "I thought Laura had red hair. So, who's is that?" *Why did you have to remember her hair color?*

There are two universal truths: pain and death. In my life, there is a third: caution. I've piqued Taylor's curiosity now. "Taylor, go to bed."

"Sam." *Warning tone noted.* Taylor's conscious has been a parasite eating soft innards. Knowledge of my teen 'indiscretion' has been gnawing for years. The day Taylor found out, I figured the police would arrive at my door. Instead, I was held and told it would all be okay. It was tender and loving.

"Go to bed." I stand and usher Taylor out.

The sound of teeth gnashing on intestines and breaking through rib bones keeps me awake long enough to find or think of new hiding spots for everything.

Before I drift to sleep, Laura Hurst's green eyes flash in my mind. If it hadn't been for her, life might be so different.

November 24, 2017

Ada

SUN BOUNCING OFF BRIGHT SNOW CLEAVES my head in two. Sometime in the early morning, the storm had calmed. Now, the warming cold is melting the sheet of fluff I worried may keep me trapped in this dull cabin. I checked, and it wasn't turning to ice —thank god. Another full day of nothing but lackluster books and an odd assortment of food may kill me.

I've had three cups of coffee and the last dredges of wine, along with gummy worms and the last two bites of chicken. With the fortitude sugar is giving me, I decide to talk to Polly. I want to talk to my mother again, too—*maybe*. And I have to go to Lynn Pond, that's the main reason I came. Still, in the middle of the night and early into this morning, I questioned if I would be safe. I wondered if I should go home the moment it was clear. I could use that trip I was lying about. *When was the last time I saw the Golden Arches?*

It's broad daylight on a Friday, and I am ready to find out some ugly truths. More importantly, I can't stay in the room with my boxed-up childhood anymore. My fingers have itched to open them twice this morning. Once, they landed on my eyebrows; the second time, my eyelashes. The bare space I have created since planning this trip, not to mention the raw skin under my jeans, devastate me; I had been almost fine for so long. I need to do what I came to do and leave—with or without the police's approval.

Few cars are on the road, and they all drive like it's Sunday— fifteen miles under the speed limit when the lines are double yellow, then five over when broken ones appear. By the time I arrive at Polly's, I'm starving. I don't want to lose my nerve, so I ignore the grumbling in my hungover stomach. I have to park three blocks away because no one in Silynn can parallel park correctly. I am shivering and sweaty when I step into the warmth of Polly's dress shop.

"Be right with you," a pleasant voice shouts from a back room.

"Thanks!" I respond.

I wander and flip through dresses and skirts like tabloid magazine pages. *Nope, nope, nope—wait, nope.* I am half-way through judging the store's wares when a woman pops her head out from a curtained doorframe. I don't recognize her, though she was supposedly my mother's best friend for decades. I didn't really know my mother, so that shouldn't surprise me. Had Polly never come over to the house, or did I blur her face with the other faces of Silynn when I left?

"Are you Polly?" I ask the woman with thin pale skin, an age spotted neck, and smoker's line around her mouth.

"My goodness! Little Adelynn!" I loathe the 'lynn' bit more and more each time I hear it. She draws me into a ferocious hug. "It's been… what? Twenty-five years?"

"A little more than that," I say.

I'm five years away from being over-the-hill.

"Let me look at you." A slight whiff of booze lingers on her breath. Polly spins me around and holds up my hands. She frowns when she sees my palms. I step backwards. "Your mama said you were comin' to town. Guess that's why she told me; musta knew you'd come see me. I guess you didn't recognize me earlier. What brings you to Silynn? And how's your mother? It's been a while since we've talked, is all. Well, 'cept that phone call." *Why the hell would my mother warn Polly?* And I am almost positive I wouldn't have recognized her when I lived here, so it doesn't surprise me that she says I didn't earlier. But when and where would I have seen her?

"I'm here because I had some holiday time, and I wanted to see how everything had changed," I say.

Her right eyebrow shoots up; it's a feat I've never mastered. "Sure, sure, sounds 'bout right. So, what can I do you for? You didn't come for a dress, I'm sure."

I'm pleased with how quickly the conversation has gotten to the point. Despite the store's warmth, I haven't taken off my coat. I use the pockets to hide my palms and dive in. "Honestly, I came to ask if you knew anything about my mother's affair."

Polly's mouth puckers, yet she doesn't seem taken off guard. "Well, that's not really for me to say, is it? Have you talked to her 'bout that? She'd know more than me, is all."

"I have, but she won't tell me much. I think I deserve to know, though. Hailey told me you might know something. She said you might be willing to tell me." Name dropping my old babysitter again—*how sad.*

"She's right. I do know things. We used to be best friends— your mama and me. We were each other's confidants. When all that nasty business with Laura happened, things changed 'tween us." She shakes her head. "Let's not chat on an empty stomach. You hungry?"

Absolutely. "I could eat."

It seems she may have the dirt I need.

Polly waves at Hailey, who is not our waitress. She smiles and gives me a thumbs up as if to say, "You go, girl! Get all that juicy information that destroyed your family!"

"Okay," Polly says after we have both ordered sandwiches, fries, shakes, and a slice of pie; the pie tips the lunch portion out of wack. She's a lady after my own heart. "So here's the deal: your mama loved you." I nod. I hope she doesn't preface every negative statement with a positive one. This lunch will take twice as long. "She was flawed, is all," she continues. "She and your daddy weren't happy. He wanted one thing; she wanted another."

"What do you mean?"

"He wanted a housewife, a mother to his children; she wanted to be a workin' woman. Needless to say, both weren't happy with how things were goin'."

"I'll say."

Polly smirks. "She tried for him. She had Peter. She had you. I'm bein' honest, is all—and hell, why not at this point, you're old enough to hear this. Anyone who thinks things through knows that havin' kids won't help nothin'. Your parents weren't any different. Soon enough, your mama started havin' an affair. For a long time, I had no idea. It was her best-kept secret, and your mama's had many. After four years or so, your daddy found out. He left. Told me it was the hardest thing he'd ever done, not stayin' for you kids—hurt too much, is all. Still, no one knew who the man was. My guess? He was married too."

Our waitress stops by our table with a tray. *The gods are against me.* "Pimento cheese, fries, blueberry pie, and cookie dough milkshake for you." She places plates and the shake in front of me. "And Polly, your usual: steak and cheese, fries, strawberry milkshake with sprinkles, and an apple pie. Need anything else, ladies?"

"I'm good." I glance at Polly, and she shakes her head.

Our waitress—who has a name—swishes her hips as she walks away. I immediately forget everything about her and play the piano on my legs as Polly takes a big swig of her shake. "Delicious!" Polly licks the whipped cream and crunches hardened, dyed sugar. "Want some?"

"No, thank you."

"Suit yourself." Polly pulls a flask from her purse and takes a big swig. "Jus' a quick sip. So, where was I?"

"You were saying my mom told no—"

"Yes! That's right. She didn't tell no one for a long time. Wasn't 'til you found Laura—" My face screws up, and Polly steamrolls on. "—that she told me who it was. I couldn't believe it, really. Felt like a bad joke, or maybe jus' a lie. Sometimes your mama did that, you know: lie. She'd make up a good story for attention, is all."

I squirm in my seat. "Yeah." *Polly just validated my childhood*; I'll unpack that later.

"You know, it really should be her tellin' you this." If I screamed at her, would she tell me faster? "But I'm guessin' she's clammin' up again? Fine by me. I'm a blabbermouth—probably why she waited so long to tell me. Not sure I'd want to tell me secrets either. Anyhow, if your mama wasn't lyin', she was sleepin' with Mike Hurst—Laura's father."

Her words are headlights, and I am a frightened doe.

"You're turnin' white, dear." *Dear. Ha!* "Should I not have told you? I messed up, didn't I? I do this sometimes, is all. Start mouthin' off 'fore I get all the facts. Didn't know you were a *sensitive* type'a woman."

"N—no, I'm not. I'm glad you told me. I wanted to know."

"Good. Hate to have ruined your day, is all." Polly stops to eat, and I follow suit. We chew and drink and chew without any more conversation. It's for the best. When we switch to our shakes, the silence persists.

She looks up as she dips her soggy fries into swirled ketchup and mustard. With a glob of orange condiments on her face, she says, "I heard about Luke." *Oh?* I nod and take a bite of pie. She leans in. "You know about him?"

Crunching on syrupy pie crust, I shrug. Nonverbal is all I can manage now. My mother had an affair with *Laura's father?* The man at the door that day was a grief-stricken man leaving his mistress. It's pathetic. Tragic, even. Is their relationship why I have flashes of memories with Laura at a young age that end abruptly?

"He makes great drinks, but he's a pedophile, he is," Polly declares. She crosses her arms for emphasis. I put a hand to my cheek. My head hasn't exploded; it could still happen. How many blows can one person take in a matter of days, hours, *minutes?* Leaning back, she adds, "At least, sure seems like it after what he said to you, is all."

"How do you know what he said to me?" I muster.

Polly looks at me as though I am the unwashed child at school parents feel sorry for but don't help because it "isn't their business," and pats my hand. "Everyone does, is all."

"But *how?*"

"Dave, dear. He's a talker, that one. Can't believe Luke asked you out because he had a thing for you when you was little." As if she smelled my sour breath, her face contorts. "It's disgusting! We're all *so* sorry. *But* we did think it a bit odd when you showed up at Bar, is all. I didn't know 'bout everything then. Found out in the mornin'. Dave told me everything—showed me the paper too. That Jane Doe! You must be feelin' a lot, is all." The flask makes a second appearance.

How would Dave know anything? "I haven't been to Bar since that happened. What are you talking about?" I reach for a fry to stuff my face with, hoping it will give me a moment to process. I am disappointed; at some point, I had eaten them all. Even the pie crust crumbs are gone. I slurp the water my ice has made. *Where is that ever-bothersome waitress when you need her?*

"Wait, you weren't at Bar on Tuesday?"

"No." The papers must be keeping some things to themselves; that, or they don't know. So more than one person at Bar thought it was me. I should call Officer Frueller. I bet the drunk patrons didn't tell him that.

"Did Luke call you after?"

"No." Why tell her he doesn't have my number? She's a talker. This whole place is filled with gossips.

Her face fell. "But a woman ends up at Lynn Pond the next morning? That what you're sayin'?"

"I'm not saying anything."

Polly grabs her last few fries and jams them into her mouth. "Oh, Adelynn!"

"It's Ada." Mike Hurst, Laura, Luke, Jane Doe, this drunk across from me. *Nothing makes sense.* "I have to go."

"You think Luke did somethin' bad to that woman? I told him I thought that was you talkin' to Kit. You think he thought he was doin' somethin' bad to you? I was too drunk to stay and help. Could I have? Is this my fault?" She retrieves her flask for an encore. Only this time, she takes two large gulps; if she isn't careful, it'll be empty in a swig or two. "His insides are all wrong, is all." I can't tell if she is justifying this to herself or me.

This is a shitty town filled with monsters, *is all.* "Right. Well, thank you for everything. I'll get the bill. Have a great day."

"Oh no! I fear I've said all the wrong things. I was only tellin' you what I know, is all. Bits and pieces in some cases. I'm sorry, Adelynn!"

"It's Ada," I reiterate, then claim the handwritten ticket left by the forgettable, worthless waitress.

Paying the bill takes so long it becomes an awkward joke, like rushing into an elevator only to have to wait for it to close. Polly sidles up beside me. "Adel—Ada, I'm sorry. I shouldn'ta brought up Luke. We should'a jus' stuck to your mama."

"Unless you have something else to say, I think we're done for now." My chest thumps and hums; I'm buzzed on bad news and disappointment.

"Jus' one more thin'," she slurs—sounding like she had downed those swigs after all. I wait. "Wasn' the affair that made Laura get a new babysitter. Thought you might wanna ask yer mama 'bout that, is all—you know, jus' in case you cared."

"What?"

"Thanks for lunch. Gotta get back to the shop. You come by anytime if you need to talk. I think I'm gonna call the police. Feels like they maybe oughta know we thought it was you there the other night at Bar. Luke and CK weren't too happy 'bout that, is all."

CK? Isn't he the owner? *And did he not say the cameras weren't working?*

Sam

JESS SUGGESTS PUZZLES AGAIN.

"I'm puzzled out," I say. "What about—"

"Wait!" Her hand flies to her face; she's thinking. "I saw you had a 3D one, and it's been forever since I've done one of those!"

"Sure, why not." I'd rather be collecting, but Jess couldn't come with me. It would be hard to explain why she had to stay at the house while I ran an errand. "Your father should be out of the bathroom in a minute." *How, after all these years, is it still weird to say, "Dad"?*

Taylor shouts from behind the door. "What am I doing?"

I try not to sigh. "You're grabbing the Big Ben 3D puzzle."

I know deep-set eyes are rolled so far back you can only see the whites. Puzzles are to Taylor what sports are to me: bearable. I have always been the one who's wanted to do them. They keep my brain active, alert, and focused on an activity, rather than collecting. I've needed that often over the years. When Taylor started working from home more, it hampered my ability to drive to and from rest stops freely. What was meant to "bring us closer" created a sixteen-year drought. I shudder thinking about my desperation.

"Sure thing." Taylor sounds as excited as I feel.

From the outside, we're the perfect family. A snapshot of us would make most people jealous: mom, dad, and spoiled-rotten daughter spending the holiday together, playing games and drinking our thirty-eighth cup of cocoa. I know the charade we're putting on. After twenty-five years, Taylor's gotten good at playing pretend. *What are a few more days?*

"I'll grab the paper; I should've done that already."

I flinch. "I can get it."

"I'm literally right by the door. Why would you get up?" Jess laughs. "It's not like I'm a guest, Mom." *Mom.*

"Right." *What if there's more news on my Lori?*

Jess gasps before the wind stops blowing into the house. My heart sinks. I wish she would stop looking at the paper, especially with the damned door open. I can't ask what she sees. Taylor doesn't seem interested and heads to the closet where we keep the games. Luckily, I'd moved my sweetheart's locks from behind the games before Jess came home. "Mom! Did you see this?"

"Well, no, Jess. You're holding the paper."

Jess begins reading an article. "Early this morning, a young Jane Doe was found near the Lynn Pond bridge. She brings back a chilling memory of one Laura Hurst, a young girl found in Lynn Pond almost twenty-nine years ago to the day—"

Taylor steps back into the living room. "Got the puzzle!"

"Dad, are you listening? It's an almost identical article as yesterday! Only today, it's a young girl."

Yesterday's wasn't about Lori? I have a hard time breathing. They hadn't come to the door after claiming they had persons of interest, so I'd felt a small weight lift off of me. *Premature, I see.*

Taylor's face pales. "None of that today. We are trying to have a good old fashioned family holiday. Let's do that without gruesome details of dead girls."

I almost say, *"She is not a dead girl. She's my sweetheart."*

"I'm just trying to stay informed, Dad." Jess stomps into the living room.

"I think your dad has a point."

Jess plops on the couch with the paper still in her hands. "I'm just saying, this person is sick! Only perverts kill little girls. They say there was no sexual assault. But why would they add that in a small town's paper? It seems like something they'd add so people wouldn't ask the question. Besides, usually it happens. That's just statistics. I've taken Abnormal Psych."

My stomach clenches as my daughter accuses me of the unthinkable. Somehow, it pangs my heart. Taylor strides to Jess and snatches the *Silynn Times* from her hands. "Enough. If they say there wasn't any sexual assault, there wasn't. Besides, what did I say? No more of this." Taylor's neck splotches.

"I thought this town was safe. I mean, two dead people in two days? That Adelynn Bailey comes back to town, and now this. Holy crap! Do you think she could have done it?"

"No, Jess," I say.

"No, Jessica," Taylor says at almost the same time.

Before we start a family puzzle made of foam and paper, Taylor puts together one of flesh and bone. Stormy blue eyes widen and skin mottles into a rainbow of fear. I await Taylor's heart failure.

"What a friggin' co-inky-dink, then! She finds a dead girl when she's six. Then she moves away, and no more deaths. Almost three decades later, she comes back, and two girls wind up dead in the same place? It feels fishy." It's a nice bow. It's a good theory, even. The police won't make the connection, because they've found many other sweethearts and hadn't yet.

They wouldn't even listen to the reporter who had connected my sweethearts before. "Don't you think?" she prods.

"Well, Jess, maybe she is the killer. Who knows? That doesn't matter. What matters is this 3D puzzle won't put itself together." Taylor dumps the box on the kitchen table. "Ladies."

I'm obedient for one of the few times in our marriage.

Jess brings up Adelynn Bailey, Laura Hurst, Lori Michelle Prescott, the Jane Doe, and her theories four more times before we complete Big Ben. Taylor shuts her down each time. During most of the build, I've been lost in thought. I want to be focusing on the fact that my daughter thinks I'm a pervert, the puzzle, Taylor's story about the albino deer, or the tingling in my left leg that demands I uncurl it, but all I can think about is Eleanor.

Once I finish three more cups of cocoa, I have a fish tank sloshing in my stomach. "I feel nauseous," I tell Jess more than Taylor.

"Aw, Mom. Too much cocoa's probably the culprit. Maybe you should go lie down," Jess says. "I won't be heading out until around eleven, so we'll still have some time to be together before I leave."

I hear a sharpness I don't think Jess notices, as Taylor adds, "I'll come check on you in a bit."

"I hope rest will have you back to puzzling in an hour or so." Hugging me makes goldfish in my belly splash around. *Jess may make me vomit if she squeezes again.*

I make a noise which seems to be enough for her. The moment she releases me, I escape to the bedroom. It's dim already. Rippling shadows on the wall remind me of Mary's tubby, clutching fingers.

Taylor knocks on the door.

"Yeah?" I answer.

"Everything alright?"

"Yeah."

"You need anything?" *Privacy, space, the car, Eleanor.*

"No, I'm fine."

"Can I come in?" *No.*

Taylor steps in and closes the door.

Ada

I HAVE BEEN SITTING ON THE FRONT PORCH holding my little felt coat for an hour and six minutes, unsure of what comes next. We'd both been inside—me and the coat—until we weren't. I guess I was on emotional-masochism auto-pilot. *Let's go outside, freeze, and try to relive some of the emotions from that day, Adelynn. Adelynn?*

It has since resulted in physical pain. Courtesy of the cold porch underneath me, my back and tailbone are throbbing. An invisible blow torch burns my nose, and my eyes will not stop watering. Puffs of breath in front of me fade into the winter evening the canopy of trees brought on early. Creaking like an old machine, I stand. I take one last look at the bruising sky, then head back inside.

Either the heater broke while I slept or the power went out. Probably the latter, if the flashing numbers on the oven were any indication. *Damn.* I shiver and glare and the tan antique dial with no degree marks. I push the only button there is and tick it as far over as it will go. Burning plastic and car exhaust pump from the vents. *Halfway it is then.*

The stained quilt and two cold comforters are the only blankets I see. A stack of firewood sits by the old stove in the center of the room. The latch in its center is rusted over. After a few jerks, I force it open and brown stains my hand. With crossed fingers, I toss logs in. Some break as I do, and I try to remember if wood can be too old to burn. I use the long-handled lighter and watch as the tiny flame touches the logs. Nothing happens. I blow it a little, still nothing. *What happened to wood just catching fire?*

Frustration almost clouds a memory of my mother spraying a canister of lighter fluid on the chunks of wood, cautioning me not to let it get on anything—least of all the carpet. Not having to start fires in the city has allowed that knowledge to be shelved. I concentrate and vaguely remember her shouts about grabbing it from underneath the sink.

It seems to be a common location to keep it, as the cabin owner has done the same. It's beside a dirty paper towel roll, bug spray, gallon-sized liquid soap, and metal lubricating fluid. A spray of said fire-starting fluid and I'm rewarded. It's a small flame at first, but it picks up. The smoke leaves the house—no clogged chimney here—thank you very much. *I hadn't even thought of that.* By the time the fire is roaring, I can feel my fingers again. I close the door to its innards, peek at my pink watch face, and turn my attention to the childhood boxes still sitting in the middle of the floor.

Beary lays beside it, discarded in my haste to pull the jacket out. Now, with false, flame-fueled bravado, I am willing to voyage into my past. The first thing is a quilt I do not remember. I wonder if it would be a good apology quilt for the cabin owner's wine-stained one. Dragging it out, I see it is lumpy and torn. *Guess not.*

The cardboard releases it, and pieces of a plastic tea set tumble to the floor.

It's as if I am back on the fuzzy rug in my time-capsuled room. I hear Peter yelling about me getting everything I want, which is terribly untrue. He stomps into my room and screams that he hates me, hates my mother, and that the world is unfair. Then he runs to his room and slams the door behind him.

I recall the ripples he created in the overfilled plastic tea cups. I used to tell my dolls it was a stampede of dinosaurs.

A brave Saturday afternoon, I even borrowed one of Peter's plastic stegosauruses to mimic it. Of course, *that* day he wanted *that* toy. So, instead of retreating to his room, he rushed into mine and slammed the door. His eyes were wild as he stepped away from my only escape. He broke the porcelain doll my grandmother gave me and kicked me in the shin. Then he stepped on my tea party plates, snapping them in half for good measure.

Tossing the memory bits back into the box, I decide I am better off not exploring; I'm better off drinking wine by the fire. But the wine is all gone. It's become the worst holiday week ever, which says something. One Easter, I think I was ten, my friend's parents had the bunny make an appearance. He told us there was a special egg by the tree at the edge of their property—away from the party. When we followed him and his big puffy tail, all hopping in a line, he showed us his penis. Megan kicked it, and we ran. Her father punched the Easter bunny a lot that day. His dick was still out, his mask still on. When he stood to leave, blood ran down the front of his bunny costume out of his mascot head as if its throat had been slit.

I re-stuff the box without looking further into its depths. I will take it out to the car—long walk be damned—and not think about it anymore. *I'll leave the jacket out.*

Shoes on, I open the door; the snow has begun its descent to Silynn once again. Looks like the boxes will have to live in the corner—a punishment I suddenly recall having. Peter had smacked me with a doll. I had a cut on my arm, yet I was the one banished to the corner of the kitchen on a small stool. I stared at a small water stain for thirty-four minutes and fifteen seconds—four minutes and fifteen seconds longer than I was told I would have to. I now understood my loathing for those ugly dolls from craft fairs—the ones who have no faces, only bowed heads and sad postures. What kind of person wants to use a mock child being disciplined in a corner as a decoration? I hope I never meet one of those people; I'm not inclined to hold my tongue on my stance.

Staring at the snowfall, I think about the night's vast possibilities. With countless choices, I decide closing the door is a good start.

Sam

AN HOUR AGO, I avoided the desire to burn the house down and joined my family for dinner.

"I want to go outside," Jess says. "I'll miss the snow soon, and I still haven't played in it!"

I try to sound like a *mom*. "Sure, Jess. Let's all go out and play around in the snow a bit before you go. Your dad can turn on the big outside lights so we can even get a picture of you for your new fiancé." I may want the photograph for myself too.

Jess falls to the rug like the dancers from that competition show (of which she made me watch all twelve seasons). They celebrate good news, such as getting fake plane tickets to the next round of scrutiny by throwing themselves onto a hardwood floor. She slips her flimsy fashion boots on and hops back up.

"Dad? Did you hear that? You're on light duty. Also, get your snow gear on! We're playing in the woods." I never said anything about the woods. Secrets are buried in my woods.

"No woods; we stay in the yard." It's firm. Maybe Taylor

discovered one of my secrets once upon a time. It would explain a lot.

I feel Jess's, "But *Daaaad*" coming on. Taylor quells it with a look. She puts on her leather gloves. Silver buttons run along the outside and wrap around the wrist. Like her boots, the gloves were intended for impractical, fashion purposes, not actual use in freezing weather, so they have no liner. The chill of the metal will be fire when the wind blows.

I walk over and peek out of the blinds. *Jess will be miserable.*

10:15 P.M.

HER LAUGH IS THE MUSIC behind a story I've heard Taylor tell a hundred times.

"And your mother—" *Two deep breaths.* "Your mother told him she'd rip you out of her so they could fight if he didn't back off." This story shows more of me than I want to share, and I've told Taylor that.

"Mom! You didn't! You threatened to get rid of me?" Jess's cold pink nose flares as her eyebrows disappear into her atrocious haircut. She half-heartedly throws another snowball at the branch Taylor declared their target. A shiver interrupts her laughter, whether from the cold air or the coldness of dear *Mom*, I'm unsure.

"I was eight months along. I was trying to tell the man that if he was going to try and take the wallet of a pregnant woman, we should be on even footing. I suppose I sounded crazy enough because he ran away. Honestly, I was scared out of my gourd," I say. *I wasn't.* The gun in my face caused a rush, similar to the one I get when I collect.

Jess's eyes are still wide. They remind me of a staring contest we had when she was young. After only a few seconds, she broke her gaze away. I knew she could've lasted longer, so I asked what was wrong; I pretended to care more back then. Her answer: "I don't like what I see." *Fair enough,* I thought.

"Why didn't you just give him your purse?" Jess asks. "Why bother with the grandstand? You were a *woman alone.*"

So many things my daughter doesn't know. Can't know. "I was pregnant," I say. "I cannot be held responsible for my actions."

"She's right. Your mom was a little batshit when you were cooking, Rugrat." *And after.* Taylor's arm is a mechanical toy as it winds up—*tick, tick, tick*—and nails the target. Again. We don't clap this time.

"Can we go in? I can't believe how cold it's gotten," I interject to avoid further conversation. I clatter my teeth and rub my hands together.

"Good!" Jess lets out a sigh of relief. "I didn't want to say it first."

"It's not that bad." Taylor mocks us but is the first one to the door.

Inside, I shake off a snow-crusted coat and step out of my boots. Relishing the warmth, I head straight for the kitchen. Before I can reach for anything, Jess has three mugs, the drinking chocolate, and milk out on the counter. Melting snow and dirt clods trail from the door to where she's standing.

"You didn't take off your boots," Taylor points out.

She shrugs. "I want cocoa. Everyone wants, I assume? Mom, you feel up to it?"

"When you take off your boots." *Eleanor is my next order of business, not mopping up your mess.* Without Taylor to do the cleaning, I have so much more work on my hands.

"Sounds good. It'll be my last bit of sugar until next year." Taylor jokes. "Are you sure you don't want one of us to make it?"

Jess kicks her shoes towards the door. "No. *I* want to make another cocoa for us all before I go." I want to ask if we need any more cocoa.

"Okay, can mine have some whiskey?"

"Of course." Her lip quivers for no real reason. She's seven-years-old and faking a knee scrape for a popsicle. She's eleven-years-old and needs a purple bike; her pink one's too girly. She's sixteen-years-old and desperate for the green mini skirt in the shop window.

"No tears, Jessica," Taylor says like all of those other times when she got what she wanted. "You'll see us in a month or two, right? For Christmas or Second Christmas? *Maybe both*?" The hope in his voice is disgusting.

Second Christmas is a faux holiday that happens anytime after December 25th and before February 1st. Taylor made it up so it would sting less when Jess inevitably skipped out on seeing us throughout the years.

Disappointment still clings like a skin suit as our daughter says, "Yeah, Second Christmas. Cole and I are staying in Prague for a while. We'll be with his parents for First Christmas. I'll miss you so much!" I hear nothing about school in her extended vacation.

"Us too," I say with all the sincerity I have when I sing to my sweethearts.

Muffled from the bedroom, I hear, "We'll miss you too, Rugrat." *When did Taylor leave?*

"Mom, can you grab the whiskey again? I thought it was with the oils and vinegar, but it's not," Jess asks, dividing my attention.

"Sure, yeah. Why would it be there?"

She shifts the pot, and it scrapes along the stove. My ears wince. "Because it's for cooking."

"It's for drinking, Jess. We put it in hot cocoa, so it's in the cupboard above the stove with the rest of the booze."

"I forgot about that. Ooh! Tequila. Let's have a shot before I go."

Taylor emerges in a set of our shared flannels. "No, no shots." Since Jess is leaving in less than an hour, I can't see a reason why Taylor would stay. The snow's been much worse, and we've gone grocery shopping. I table that conversation for forty-five minutes from now.

She sighs. It was a stalling tactic. "Mom, I'm really going to miss you."

"Me too, Jess." I rub circles on Jess's back, one of my mother's nurturing gestures before she took to hanging my dolls from a tree in our backyard. The motion numbs my hand, and I think of Laura and the tissue-filled Saturday night I rubbed globs of menthol on her chest and back.

The whisk clangs against the pan, and Jess smiles. "Thanks, Mom. You always know what to do." *Do I?* "Chocolate and liquor incoming!" She pours the thickened cocoa into mugs picked out for nostalgia's sake. Mine has a green T-Rex with an open mouth. In a thought bubble, it shouts, "ROAR! I love you, Mom!" It's blurry, and the mug's innards have cracks underneath the glaze; still, I've held onto it. It's a nice size and holds a value I can't put my finger on. "Here you go."

She hands Taylor the next cocoa in a blue mug with etched pine trees and a cabin that looks like ours on the front. "Thanks, Rugrat." A small sip. A sigh. "Perfect drinking temperature, as always. And just the right amount of spike."

"Glad you like it! Did you see which mugs I picked?" Her left eyebrow wiggles, and she holds hers ceremoniously. "It's been a while, right?"

"It has," I agree.

During a paint-a-thing party Jess's friends put together "ironically," I painted the mug Jess holds. Three gingerbread people are connected paper doll accordion-style with "Jess" scrolled below it. She and her friends were so caught up, she didn't notice me painting it. Nor did she notice the gingerbread people had eyes the colors of her friends: green, blue, brown, and the hair colors of my last three sweethearts. When asked why they didn't look like us, I shrugged. "Artistic license?"

Jess proposes a toast to the last winter she'll be unmarried. I have questions about that, but like Taylor's pajamas, I let it lie. She said winter, not month. It doesn't have to be today's problem.

As soon as the taxi arrives, we help Jess put her bags into her car. It happens so quickly, I barely register it. Mixed emotions swirl in my stomach like the snow still coming down outside. I'm weightless, floating above the scene of her leaving.

Taylor wishes her a safe flight and kisses the top of her head. I hug her goodbye, and the edges of her bobbed hair smack my mouth. I wish I had cut a piece of it while she was sleeping last night. Even in its wrongness, I want to keep its new, adult smell forever.

I try to clutch this moment, like last night's dream. Then, too, I floated. I wore a peach dress with flowers, and Hailey sat at the edge of *the* backyard pool. A small puddle of blood lay on the chlorine water like oil and soaked my dress between my legs. The warm sun slowed my heart. I didn't scream as Adelynn sunk beside me. As quickly as my dream came and went, so did Jess.

"I love you both! I'll call you when I land," she lies. We all know it. There's a comfort in it though, even for me. If I can't have her ugly hair, at least I can have her lies.

"I'm exhausted," Taylor announces, grabbing a blanket before I can speak. "Mind if I stay on the couch again?"

"I do, actually." I need to spend a few hours with my map. I didn't have a chance to add the heart marker for Lori. I've already picked out the colored pencil I'll use: Mid Green. I also need to plan a new route for my latest hopeful. And, as when anytime anything vaguely emotional happens, I figure I'll have the dream where I'm drowning; I've been trying to see the end it since 1992. I thought I'd go to bed early in case that would help. "Jess is gone now, so you need to go back to wherever you were staying. You made your choice. A divorce is in the works." I try to sound a little affected but am genuinely uninterested in anymore overly emotional exchanges for the evening.

"Alrighty then." Taylor drops Mami's quilt on the ground with watery eyes and trudges towards the key bowl, scooping up a neatly stacked pile of clothes on the way. "I wish we'd talked more." *Was the divorce a bluff? Was I supposed to push back for our marriage?* "I tried." *What?*

Opening the door and ushering Taylor out feels nice. I don't have it in me to navigate the nuances of this situation. "Sure. Goodbye, Taylor."

"Goodbye, Sam." A cluster of nerves in my chest unwinds when I press into the lock and click it to the right. *Safe now.*

11:21 P.M.

HOLY SHIT.

My bedroom has been ravaged. Drawers gape open. Pajamas and jeans lay scattered on the floor. Hangers dangle naked, their clothing in piles on top of open boxes at the bottom of the closet. The basket that holds my book, reading glasses, nail scissors, and a small jar of lotion is upside down. The contents of my bag are strewn out on the bed.

Where is it? As I rifle through my chapstick, wallet, and receipts, I violate myself. The nail file is there, licorice, pack of gum, ibuprofen, check. There are only a few items, yet it seems to take an eternity to find—the mint tin. *The mint tin is gone.*

Panic sucks the moisture from my mouth, and breathing becomes a luxury.

Taylor found Lori's hair.

"I tried."

June 2, 1985

Sam

STRINGS OF BROWN HAIR FLOAT around her head. I wait, not telling Hailey of the silly game the girls are playing. The seconds tick by, and her soft-cheeked face doesn't lift from the chlorine. *What does a person look like after they've drowned? Does their skin change colors? Do they bloat immediately?*

Her legs sink a little.

Laura pushes her shoulders, and she is unmoving.

I don't want to deal with police officers and questions and shrinks and adults asking if we're okay. I remember the colored flashes that broke the fading sun in my room the night my mother was carted away like the rabid dog she'd become. I don't want to have the blinding lights spot my vision for days.

"Hailey, it's been quiet outside for a while. Wanna go check on the girls?" I ask.

She nods. "Good idea." In her world, reading a rag mag, she didn't notice me staring out the window. She slides her feet off of the counter and leaves a scuff the Hurst's will notice. The stool squeaks as she swivels it away from the island.

Three. Two. "Oh my god!" Hailey screams and tears out of the kitchen through the sliding glass doors. "Sam, I need you!" she shouts over her shoulder. "Laura, go call 9-1-1!" *So much for no fuss.*

The next moments happen so quickly I can barely keep up enough form snapshots of them. I'll need to be able to recall them for questions later. Hailey's face is wracked with emotions I don't understand; I try to mirror the expression.

Laura pushes herself out and over the edge of the pool and takes off. Wet footprints dry almost instantly on the cement behind her. When she reaches the deck, I hear her stumble into something. To her credit, she doesn't cry out.

Water splashes as Hailey jumps in, shoeless now. She hitches the small lump of a child under her arm. "Oh my god! Oh my god!" Hailey's words become a chant, a prayer, and a curse as she paddles towards the steps. Nearing the shallow end, Hailey yells, "Samantha, grab her!"

I jog over, hoping my face still matches Hailey's.

"The woman says they're on their way!" Laura shouts from inside the house.

Hailey sighs a little and shoves her arms forward. I match her sigh and reach for the unmoving girl. Sun-kissed skin proves my color theory to be wrong, and there's no bloating in sight. Either she's not dead, or everything I thought I knew about drowning is wrong.

Maybe both.

Before my hands have left peach fuzz covered arms, Hailey's smashing her lips against the still little thing and forcing life into her lungs. Palms with half-moon nail marks from Hailey's checked rage towards her father compress the child's still undeveloped chest. The girl's soaked pale blue sundress tangles in Hailey's shaking fingers.

I count the seconds: *one Mississippi, two Mississippi, three Mississippi*—my father taught me to use Mississippis because that's how *he* learned. From the youngest of ages, I realized he wanted to impart as much wisdom as he had into me. He didn't, however, want to learn more than he already knew. One day, I will be much smarter than my father.

Eleven Mississipis later, Hailey stumbles back onto her heels coughing. I push the little spasming thing away from my friend. It seems I'll have to find out about drowned bodies another day.

As she purges chemical-laced water, Hailey begins to cry. "Adelynn!" *Ah, that's her name.* "You scared us, sweetheart!" *I like that better.* "You'll be okay; just take big, deep breaths," Hailey says, drool dripping into Adelynn's mouth.

I'm pretty sure that's a horrible idea. In case I'm right, I stay silent. Maybe I'll get to see a dead sweetheart after all.

Hailey

ASTRINGENT WATER GAGS ME as Adelynn vomits into my mouth. *This is the most disgusting thing that's ever happened to me.* Less than a second later, relief sets in. "Adelynn! You scared us, sweetheart!" I hover over her, spittle still dripping from my lips. "You'll be okay; just take big, deep breaths." *Is that right?* My voice must hold authority because she tries; it doesn't go well. Shouting, I wave my arms, panicked. "Just breathe normally!"

Samantha looks terrified, and she's not speaking. *Oh god, I broke her.* She comes to visit me on what should have been a routine babysitting day, and what does she stumble into? Trauma.

Laura swoops in beside me. Her sniffles are low but present. Thin hairs from her drying legs tickle my smooth ones. My mother shaved my legs on my seventh birthday because the feel of them made her shiver. That seems like so long ago, not just six years. If Laura were my sister, she'd only have one year left. I think the baby hairs are soft and sweet like her innocence.

Words come out like jagged glass. "I didn't mean to." Laura

catches my arm. Uncut nails dig into the squishy flesh I still blame on Valentine's Day and Easter candy. "I really didn't."

"Don't say anything else!" a man's voice shouted from the side of the yard. "Laura, get away from Hailey and Samantha."

Mike Hurst charges towards the pool with an outstretched fist. Laura's slight body tenses; her legs bob up and down, unsure.

"Calm down, Mr. Hurst!" I say. "There was an accident. I'm still trying to figure out what happened." *How did he get here so quickly? I thought he'd been called in to work.*

"My six-year-old daughter called 9-1-1, and *you* did nothing. That's what I get for letting a thirteen-year-old babysit! I thought it would be okay, but—"

I sputter, and Adelynn starts to speak. Mr. Hurst no longer matters. "What, sweetheart?" I lean in closer.

She coughs in response.

"I beg your pardon, Mr. Hurst, but that's not what happened." Samantha sounds mature and in charge. "We came to check on the girls, and Adelynn was floating in the pool. Hailey told Laura—no—screamed for Laura to call 9-1-1. She needed me to help get Adelynn out. Then, she gave her the Heimlich Maneuver." I glance up; Samantha's eyes have gone dark with indignation. "Adelynn is breathing because Hailey saved her. Do you hear that, Mr. Hurst?" Samantha pauses a moment and lets the ghost of a siren answer. "That's the sound of Hailey's quick thinking."

Not only does he not apologize to me, but he also ignores Samantha.

"Laura, come here." With hesitation, she does. His hand crushes Laura's as he drags her away from us. "We're going to flag down the ambulance."

Adelynn's quiet, raw voice rips through the silence. "Hailey? Did I win?" she asks, just as Laura says, "Daddy, that's too tight."

The sun dims.

I lose track of everything but Adelynn's fingers from that

moment until the ambulance doors shut with me in it. I sit on a barely padded bench; the paramedic works around me with ease. Adelynn grows tinier with every piece of medical equipment he attaches to her.

"Will she be okay?" I ask.

Smoky gray eyes flick my way. The man who hadn't stopped moving stops moving. "We thought you went mute." That makes sense. Adelynn being lifted and put on a stretcher left me speechless. Anything that happened to the children in my care was my fault. *I nearly killed Adelynn.* Maybe I'm *not* responsible enough to watch kids yet.

"Thanks for letting me ride with her."

"You wouldn't let go." His face wrinkles as if he's solving a riddle. "As for Adelynn, she'll be just fine. Thanks to you." He rubs his buzzed hair and swivels his head around the ambulance. "Oh, right," he says and reaches over me.

He rips a comically large needle from its sterile paper and plastic pouch. Adelynn's fallen asleep, so I don't have to sing her the calming song I sing to Laura—whose parent's told me she needs it now, even when I'm not around now. *"It won't hurt, little bug. It won't hurt. Look at me, sweetheart, and you'll see. It's already over, as quick as one, two, three."*

I hum it out of habit, anyhow—adding the middle addendum I did the two times needles were involved: *"Just a poke, little bug. Just a poke."* The paramedic says nothing.

Wendy Bailey is at the hospital when we arrive. Her gasping screams are overdramatic; Adelynn's stable now.

"Shh, she's sleeping!" I almost snap.

Looking at Mrs. Bailey makes me sick. Last month, The Hurst's had a barbecue. I was headed into the kitchen to grab ice and another bag of chips when I saw Mr. Hurst brush against Mrs. Bailey. I didn't need to be an adult to understand what he was doing, what he wanted. I've heard things, *seen* things. Instead of stepping aside, or even moving along quickly out of embarrassment, Mrs. Bailey turned her body towards him and slinked by. My feet melted to the floor, and I was helpless to look away. A tingling I'd recently started experiencing when looking at a boy named Billy settled in my stomach.

I kept a close eye on Mrs. Bailey that day, but she didn't end up alone with Mr. Hurst again. The looks exchanged in the crowded backyard spoke of future moments like the one I saw my parents have on New Year's Eve. I picture Mr. Hurst's hand under Mrs. Bailey's skirt, and her pushing down, moaning and begging for more. *More what?*

After the barbecue, I started babysitting Adelynn too. Today's only my fourth time.

As Mrs. Bailey stands in the waiting room lobby of the Emergency Room, I imagine Mr. Hurst on top of her, grunting as I saw in a movie once. I bet they've kissed even though they are married to other people. That's against married people rules; I don't need to be an adult to understand that either.

"Oh, Hailey! What happened?" Mrs. Bailey rushes to my side. Frizzy, root-like hair tickles my nose as she leans into me. "Mik—Mr. Hurst was telling me that Laura called him and 9-1-1 but didn't know my number. You were so quick, Hailey! Samantha just got picked up by her dad; she didn't need to be here for this. I told her I'd call her the moment Adelynn was in the clear."

Anger makes me rashy. "She's breathing." I'm suddenly aware my glasses have gone missing. They must have fallen off in the pool. It makes me question my need for them.

"I know, honey. She just needs to get checked out."

I saved her life. "Right."

"So, what happened?" Mrs. Bailey ignored the edge in my voice. "Laura keeps saying it was just a game. What were they doing in the backyard? And why weren't you with them? I don't mean to accuse you of anything, but—"

"Mrs. Bailey," I say before she makes me cry. "I have no idea what game they were playing. I'll see if Laura will tell me. As for why they were in the backyard without me and Samantha, well, they were playing with chalk on the cement. I told them to stay out of the front yard because Adelynn tried to follow a piece that rolled into the street last week. So I had them play away from the pool. I guess, while I was grabbing a drink or something, they got bored. Them roaming the backyard has never been a problem before." My mouth is dry.

"Adelynn *did* get bored, Miss Hailey," Laura pipes up. I wonder why Mr. Hurst brought her here. The Emergency Room is scary—no place for a child.

"Did she?" I ask and bend down to her level.

Her vocabulary at six is incredible. "Yeah, she didn't want to draw anymore. So I said, 'We should jump rope.' She started to cry—said her legs are too short. That's a lie, Miss Hailey! I had legs like that too." Laura's voice begins to quiver.

"I know, sweetheart."

"She said we could swim, but she didn't bring her suit, Miss Hailey! Before I could ask you, she got in the water. I told her, 'Adelynn, we shoulda asked!' " Laura says, her face contorting.

I open my arms; she rushes into them.

Snotting into my hair, she continues. "Adelynn said we should play like in church. Like this." Laura plugs her nose and squints her eyes closed. Crossing her arms, she tilts her head back a little and nearly stumbles. "We tried. Our dresses made us fall down. And Miss Hailey, Adelynn can't swim as good as me." Laura drops her voice to a whisper, "And Daddy's only taken me to one lesson."

I've picked up an extra day a week for the last few weeks. I wonder if Mr. Hurst is supposed to be dropping her at a swimming class instead of at my house. *Where is he when she's with me?*

An announcement of a color code in a room drowns Laura's next few soft words out. I almost forget where we are, swept up in the visuals she's painting in small sentences. When the loud-speaker quiets, I mutter a sound of encouragement. "Okay, what happened next?"

"That was it. She crossed her arms and put her face in the water. I counted, one," she took a deep breath, "two." Another breath. "Three, four, five, six, seven, eight, nine, ten, eleven, twelve, thirteen, fourteen. Then the bubbles were gone."

With each counted second, my breath hitches. In less than a fifteen seconds, Adelynn went from playing to drowning.

"Samantha saw us, thank goodness." *What?* White flashes in my vision. "Can you hug her for me?" she asks.

We did not have the same thought on what to do with Samantha. If Laura was right, she could have kept this from happening. "You got it. Thank you for telling me, Laura." I hug her tightly. "Now, let me talk to your daddy and Adelynn's mommy." I took a deep breath but didn't count; I'm not sure I'll ever count again. I release Laura's hand and wave them over, only taking one step forward. "Would it be okay if I explain stuff to Mrs. Bailey first? Then maybe she can sit with Laura while I talk to you, Mr. Hurst."

They exchange a look I *am* too young to understand, and Mrs. Bailey says, "Let's get a snack. You talk, and I'll listen."

I decide not to pull any punches. "I think Adelynn was trying to baptize herself."

Mrs. Bailey's face turns a shade of pale I'd only read about in fantasy books—cave dwellers were supposedly this color. "Excuse me?"

A doctor stops in his tracks. "Yes, ma'am?"

"Sorry, she was talking to me." I wave the doctor away. "We're going through something."

I'm more of an adult than ever, and I hate it. I want to be a kid, maybe even younger than thirteen. I wish Samantha and I had stayed outside with Adelynn and Laura, drawn hearts and stars with the smooth chalk. My hand would be pink and dry right, now not clammy and chilled. I want to go back to two hours ago when I invited Samantha over to the Hursts' in the first place. Riding to Laura's house, I passed her. *Company would be nice*, I thought. *On a hot day like today, I bet I'll get bored with the kids*. I wish my legs had kept pumping the pedals, keeping up the momentum from the hill. They wouldn't be sore now, and Adelynn wouldn't be in the hospital.

I'm not sure I want to babysit anymore.

"I'm sorry for your loss," the short, rotund doctor says. Sweaty and harried, he takes off running the moment he finishes the sentence.

"Loss? What loss?"

Welcome back, Mrs. Bailey.

With false confidence, I regurgitate Laura's story—including Samantha's part. I have a lot of questions for her. She should've told me that they were in the pool. I know Laura will mention it if I don't.

"So, this was Adelynn's idea? Oh, Mike's going to kill me!" Face going red, she coughs, "I mean, Mr. Hurst may blame me. Adults do silly things."

I bat my eyelashes and bring my voice up an octave a little to feign innocence. "Why would he blame you? You weren't even there."

It's cold, I notice. It's almost like a breeze is brushing my bare legs. My cousin told me if you felt cold "real quick like," you're near a ghost.

Mrs. Bailey's response quells the urge to swivel my head. "Well, he doesn't like the church we go to. And he's right, you know. We've only been a few times, and already they've tried to baptize us. Look what it's done to Adelynn!"

A wheeze comes from a room we pass—room 5A. I shiver from the sound, the temperature forgotten.

My hand reaches my mouth too late; I can't stop myself from blurting, "Why is what church you go to any of his business?"

"Out of the mouths of babes," Mrs. Bailey sighs. *Babes? Which kind of babe does she think I am?* "He wants the best for us. He's been friends with Adelynn's dad for years."

We've walked in a circle. Just as I'm about to ask if he's her friend too, I see him hop up from a worn charcoal chair and rush towards us. Laura sits obediently on the chair beside his now empty one, eyes downcast. Too-big sandals kick the air violently. I want to scoop her in my arms.

"Wendy! What did Hailey say?" I'm the ghost I felt earlier, only before I knew I'd become one. "Tell me everything," Mr. Hurst continues.

Mrs. Bailey rolls her eyes. "She's right here, you know. You could ask her."

That's the way my mother talked to my father last week when he stormed into the kitchen demanding dinner after I pointed out eating at 7:45 p.m. instead of 7:00 p.m. wouldn't kill him. She said, "You know what, you're right, Hailey!" *I mean, I know.*

"Alright, alright." Mr. Hurst raises his arms. "Hailey, what did Laura tell you? She won't talk to me at all."

I snicker; his glare puts an end to my amusement. "In summary, Laura said Adelynn wanted to swim. Then she suggested a game that's basically like floating or being baptized, so sh—"

"I told you that church was no good, Wendy! What did I say? I told you to go anywhere but there." *What a jump.*

"Or *your* church," Mrs. Bailey mutters.

Mr. Hurst soldiers on, "Did you listen? No! And now you've scarred Laura, and Adelynn nearly drowned." His emotions were more heightened than I've ever seen my dad's—even when talking about a child that wasn't his.

"So—" I begin raising my voice above his. "That bit doesn't matter. What matters is that Samantha saw them in the pool and said we should go check on them. I'd only looked away for a second. She must have thought what they were doing looked weird."

"So I've Samantha to thank for Adelynn's life, not you?" Mr. Hurst asks. Again, he sounds like he's talking about Laura, not Mrs. Bailey's little girl. "I don't think you should babysit Laura anymore."

Whether Mrs. Bailey or I say, "What?" first is unclear. But we both bombard Mr. Hurst with thoughts and questions with the same theme: how dumb he is. I never say the word; he's an adult. Again, he lifts his hands, a sure admittance of being weak-willed —according to my dad.

"We'll talk again later—after Samantha and I talk," he says.

Salty liquid leaks from my tear ducts. Mr. Hurst offers no comfort; Mrs. Bailey's arm wraps around me. "No tears, darling. Adelynn will need us when she wakes up; her dad won't be here for another two hours. Who knows, we may be home by then."

"Wait. I can still sit for Adelynn?"

"Of course! You saved her life. As for Laura... I'll work on Mr. Hurst."

"Thank you, Mrs. Bailey." I sniff.

"Hailey, call me Wendy."

November 25, 2017

Ada

TRY AS I MIGHT, I have yet to convince the sun to rise early to please me. As if it were my mother, it always disappoints me. I will have to wait for it to wake and offer its light. It's 5:14 a.m. now. Sunrise is two hours away.

A fluffy, thin layer of snow blankets everything. I'll be scraping the car before I leave. Sadly, that will not take hours. Time would fly by if there were a television here. Silynn isn't a place where you go to unwind and unplug. Despite the lack of cell service, it's never your intent. *Who thought skipping on a TV and DVD player was a good idea?* Even if they only had boring movies, I would be able to fill the silence.

I start a fire if only to occupy my time. I wish I had to cut down a tree to get the wood. Me using an axe is a recurring dream I have. I stand in a darkened forest, much like the one I'm in now. Instead of trees, copies of me at every age fill the spaces. Some are elongated; others have shrunken heads. A bulbous-eyed version of me in my late twenties whacks at a grotesquely pudgy three-year-old me with an already bloodied hatchet. The gashed-open child-me retaliates, picking up a dagger made of roots and gutting a paper-doll cut-out of me on my wedding day. I watch on as thirty or so different versions of myself hack each other to bits. When each of them is bloody and sobbing, I fling the original axe back onto myself. Only then can I wake up. The first time I had the dream, I was thirty-three. I woke to soaked pajama bottoms and a urine-soaked mattress. Since, I have had a plastic sheet on the *new* bed and carried a plastic picnic blanket with me whenever I overnight somewhere.

Just thinking about the dream keeps me from going back to sleep.

As an avid reader, I chastise myself for not trying another book. I am in chaos, so my attention is divided. I pick up a new thriller and attempt a page. The first line is—*I am going to visit Lynn Pond.* I pick up a romance—okay fine, it's erotica—and read a page. Laura Hurst's face appears as a pattern in words. I sigh. These books aren't poorly written, but they aren't attention-grabbing enough. *It isn't the books, Ada.*

I have done this since I was in middle school.

For my tenth birthday, my uncle bought me a beautiful bike. When I couldn't ride it, I blamed Peter for scaring me the first time I tried to switch from a tricycle to a bicycle with training wheels. I put my hand on my hip and proclaimed, "You don't understand! Peter gave me PDST. Do you even know what that is? It's Pose Dramatic Stress Troubles." I knew *everything* when I was ten. In high school, I blamed the C I got on my geometry test on a friend. "She passed me notes during the test. I was distracted!" I wasn't telling that to my uncle or aunt—not really. They were not upset about my C. I was.

So am I surprised that I am blaming literature for my inability to shake fear and worry? *Not in the slightest.*

I will have an early breakfast. In the dark, still nauseous from a sweat-drenched sleep, I will make eggs and drink flat soda.

I know I have made the right decision because my stomach curls in when the refrigerator light fills the room. The chill is a welcome reprieve from the heat.

Stove coils warm to orange under the oversized sauté pan— the only cooking vessel I could find. Rachael yaps on my shoulder like an angel. *"Don't you put your hand on that, Ada. Do you hear me? I can see you're thinking about it. Don't you do it."*

I crack the eggs directly into the pan. I smash them harder than I had planned to; the yolks burst and bits of shell float in the clear 'white'. I don't fish them out. The roof of my mouth anticipates the tiny cuts I will get; my throat, the quick gag and momentary soreness. Watching them get lost in the cooking egg as the 'white' finally earns its name, a memory hits me. If it were a physical object, I'd be doubled over begging it to stop—like in college when an asshole named Kelin punched me in the gut. When I fell, he kicked me in the chest. As his leather boot swung for the third time, a hottie named Derek showed up and clocked him in the face.

Bubbling, cooked eggs bring me back to the pan in my hand, then toss me backwards in time much further than college.

I ate eggs with chunks of eggshells and Lucky Charms marshmallows the day I found Laura. Peter overfilled my bowl of rainbow freeze-dried cow bone, sugar, and chemicals with milk. The pink color it turned matched my jumper; the melting horseshoes matched my tights. Hungrier than when I woke up, I left the house without winter wear—a dare to my overworked mother. After trudging through a long day of first grade, coloring letters and numbers as if we were still in Kindergarten, Hailey sent me off to walk home alone for the very first time. I took the less populated route back over the small bridge. Wind bit through the thin corduroy fabric and whipped at my skin. My cheeks stung from the snow fall's violent swirls.

The thick green jacket currently stuffed in my childhood box still hung by the front door. Bitterly, I blamed my mother for being too distracted and rushed, packing graded tests and pop quizzes in her tote, to notice I had left without it. The next ten minutes or so is a blank wall of static—unimportant. Birthdays and names of co-workers have taken its place.

I smell smoke. Lost in a shaping moment of fear, I forget to flip my egg. Though the edges burn, the center is only a little too fried. I've eaten worse at diners. The eggs are crispy and slimy and need little chewing. But I hate wasting food. The fragility of my nervous stomach gives way, and I rush to the bathroom. Heaving yields the egg bits in their whole form but more needs to come out. Acid settles in the back of my throat.

Without looking, I know my face will have red freckles—burst capillaries—which I usually find to be a satisfying visual of a job well done. It's like seeing a badge of honor. When I go through hell—or at least a few levels of it—the least I can get is some proof. Like bruises after a fall.

I curl up on the bathroom floor. It's not very clean; the grout is stained, and there are a few dark curly hairs under the sink pedestal. Tilting over the toilet, I stare at the filth—still nothing. The roots of my eyelashes itch and burn. *I thought I cleaned this place well enough.*

I give up after another five minutes of dry-gagging and address my trichotillomania. Trying to remove only the most painful of lashes, I use my nails to gently pull at each one until I find the culprits. When my eye begins to water, I've found them. There are four. My eye feels relief once they're gone, but I do not need a mirror to know that my eye is near-bald once again.

Luke

SHE PACES THE CABIN, talking to herself. My Adelynn surrounded herself with friends; this woman—*Ada*—is foreign in her isolation.

I'm glad I didn't kill her. After the first swing, I regretted it. Shame, disappointment, and grief hit me like the crashing wave when I was five and my parents left me alone, not knowing how to swim. But relief set in when I saw the face of some woman with faint acne scars on her chin; it wasn't the adult version of my Adelynn. It was too late by then. The spotted face with full lips and doll eyes mocked Adelynn's. After I snuffed out the last of the impersonator, I took her to *our* place in tribute.

I almost left Adelynn the missing charm from a bracelet she wore to school once, but I didn't want to cause her pain. She'd gotten in trouble for losing the hammered silver unicorn her grandmother had given her for her sixth birthday. Wendy Bailey took the bracelet away, and Adelynn was sent to bed early for a week. I had no idea unclipping a charm would cause such a ripple effect. I became strictly an observer after that.

Lost in memories of days when Adelynn brought peaches with her lunch and I ducked out of class to watch her eat them, I nearly missed Ada getting in the car. She's clutching her hands over and over, self-talking under her breath. I want to bottle the steam the words make.

I wonder if she puts her seatbelt on before she puts the car in reverse. I picture her gloved hand reaching to adjust a mirror only she uses. Is her console set to play music, talk radio, a podcast that makes her feel like an intellectual?

There's no time for me to watch how she settles in her car, though. I take off running. She can't hear the sounds of branches cracking under my boots with her windows rolled up, so I worry less about being careful and more about making it to my car in time.

It doesn't take long to figure out where she's headed.

I can't remember how long the drive straight there is; the back way takes about half an hour. I pass the lake's little official green and white metal sign and three paved parking lots. The second and third turn-offs will allow me to go through the woods to watch her. I can stick to the tree line again. *Will she see me this time?*

The moment I whip into the third parking lot, I practically leap from the car. Each stride I make is longer than the last. I need to see her reaction to where I left Knockoff Adelynn.

I slow when I see her jacket through a break in the forest. Hunching, I slink towards the edge of the trees. She's tense as she stares at caution tape.

It's too far over to be for Knockoff Adelynn; I'm sure of that. Ada turns left and shakes her head. I swear it's as if she's laughing.

As she nears our spot, I challenge myself. *Run to her.* I want to tell her everything. Slowly, she sits on a snow-covered rock and stiffens. *Go, be bold. Would she believe me?*

Ada

MY NUMB FINGERS FUMBLE with the handle. I have opened a car door before; now, I cannot remember how. Clouds of breath puff from my mouth; the urge to stop breathing overwhelms me. I pinch an eyelash from my stinging right lash line; a small patch of ten to twelve remain. I'll have to switch to my eyebrows again soon.

Because I'm sitting in the car, I must have figured out how to finagle the door while contemplating how poorly I cope with stress. The rest is so automatic, it barely warrants brain space: start car, turn on heat, crank stereo, put on seatbelt. I put the car in reverse and crack my ankle into the gas pedal. *Not how I want to start moving.*

Shards of light, striations of dark, a rising sun, and finally I'm at the small parking lot meant for the part of Lynn Pond I need to visit. A thin layer of snow coats the four-car-space blacktop. My tires mar the pristine surface.

The accidental slamming of the car door breaks the stifling silence only a heavy snowfall brings. Birds awaken.

Snap, zip. Puffy layers of fabric add an inch to my body. It may be a short walk, but I have no idea how long I will need to be where I found Laura, where I nearly drowned in the freezing lake. Dread rears its ugly head. I become a calf, my limbs fresh and wobbly.

Two steps away from the steaming car, and I am six-years-old. My gloves and layers upon layers of clothing do not protect me from the imagery.

Bits of frosted grass and snow mounds crunch under my too-small Mary Janes. I rub my gloveless fists into leaking eyes, smearing snot onto the inside of my sleeve. Shivering, I grumble at my backpack for shifting my skirt up as wind nips through my leggings and panties.

Stepping towards the frozen-over Lynn Pond, I am myself again as something yellow flowing in the breeze under the bridge catches my attention. Never mind that it's the brick structure that has haunted me for decades, morbid curiosity draws me closer; it is few pieces of drooping barricade tape. I thought Jane Doe was found *near* it. They could have told me that to see my reaction, try and trip me up.

But as I get closer, I see a slightly more weathered piece of caution tape sticking up from the snow further to the left; she may have been found *near* the bridge after all, just as the under-qualified officers said she was. Then, wait. A thought pops into my head—ludicrous though is it. *It could be another crime.* Two crimes in Silynn in the same location? If I weren't standing in front of the crime scene, or scenes, I would laugh. *And why, oh why, do bad things happen when I'm here?* This damned place hates me.

There are too many thoughts in my head. I will have to go into town, sit in the car, and call Rachael the moment I leave. I can't just journal this one through.

"I'm worried the cops will think I was revisiting my crime when I was just really trying to get over seeing a little dead girl when I was six. I didn't do it—I should write that down here in case anyone finds this. Right? I didn't murder that woman."

How's *that* for a journal entry?

Whistling wind fills me as the Haystack Rock-shaped stone comes into view. Half-buried under snow, it marked Laura's spot. My muscles tense as if I were in middle school awaiting the head mean girl's chubby hand to slap me when she thought I kissed a boy she liked. I hope Lucy grew up ugly and alone.

I brush white fluff away and sit on the rock. The spot draws my attention once again. I digress to memories, jeans soaking through with every moment I'm lost. Laura Hurst's presence is beside me. I remember very little of the time we spent together: a pool, fairy wands, crowns drawn from yellow chalk, screams—of laughter or fear, I'm not sure.

Is my mother to blame for thirty years of emotional damages? The desire to say yes is irrationally strong. If Hailey had never stopped babysitting Laura, we might have walked home together the afternoon she was murdered.

Pine and snow fill my lungs as I breathe in. Something moves beneath the surface of the water, and fragments come to me. My book bag was filled with a folder, some papers, a lunchbox, and a pencil. I threw it down before I ran to the edge of the lake. Someone screamed my name then, or as I was on the ice, or as I was falling in. I think it was a male voice, but I must have shrugged it off. I don't remember turning. When asked by police and reporters, I told them I climbed out. It made me heroic and brave; it also made me a liar.

For the longest time, I was convinced I *had* crawled out—memories are very pliable. Only a few years ago, I was honest with myself. I stopped and thought about that day; I rationalized and figured it had been Peter. He'd probably followed me home like a good big brother and pulled me out of Lynn Pond when he saw the ice give way under me. It explained why when I came to, there had been a Lucky Charms marshmallow near my book bag. He had taken some to school, I guessed. He couldn't have told anyone he had saved me after the claims I made without making one of us a public liar.

Staring at the fish swimming under the water, I wonder if it could have been the Lake Killer. *Could Laura's murderer have been my savior?* Goosebumps erupt on my skin. I whip my head all around, looking for something, *someone*. My imagination runs wild: her murderer is in Silynn on the same day I am, and they have decided to revisit the site where they dumped her body at the same time as I did. *What of the latest murder?* I wonder if that was the Lake Killer's handiwork too. I laugh at myself. The sound brings an unease as I hear a wheeze from the trees.

A shiver that has nothing to do with weather shocks my spine, and I decide to sift through the rest of my thoughts later. I will tear the memory to shreds and choose which pieces to keep on my shelf once I am settled in front of a roaring fire with two new bottles of wine. For now, I will listen to the instincts I wish I'd had decades ago and leave.

I shake as I stand. The rental car is a million miles away, uphill in the snow. The same walk that held a solemn quiet now feels eerie and dangerous. Every small crack of an icicle or hoot of an owl in the distance is threatening.

Behind me, snow crunches off-beat with my steps. A wheeze punctuates every few feet. Sweat prickles my palms, and I pick up my pace. The steps keep up.

I dare a glance.

A shadow enters my vision and confirms I'm not hearing ghosts. It's a man, I think. I take off, feet pounding. The solid ground sends shockwaves up to my knees. *They are going to catch me.*

Their breathing gets louder, feels closer.

Running in the cold makes my lungs ache, eyes dry up and water. I slow out of necessity, and they get closer. Grunts of exertion match rhythmic thuds. Two coughs they don't try to hide sound inches away. I feel them breathing down my neck—*the Lake Killer?*

When I see the limp plastic tape, dagger-like fear spikes—I will add to the body count. *What's the end game?*

As if the crime scene is an electric fence, the steps stutter behind me. Though I want to face whoever it is, see them after all these years, I don't dare turn around. Pushing the skin-encased beaten muscles previously known as my legs past their limit, I keep running until I see my car.

My sigh of relief is lost to the returned silence ringing in my ears.

Sam

MY CALLS ARE GOING UNANSWERED. Taylor ignored them late last night too. The talk we need to have should happen sooner rather than later. Until then, I await the police's arrival with bated breath. If it's all about to end, I'll collect one more sweetheart. Hopefully, she'll be more satisfying than Lori.

11:30 A.M.

PERRIN IS A SMALL TOWN an hour east of Silynn. Taylor and I have had dinner here a few times in the past few years. Taylor came once a month or so to visit our favorite chocolate shop; I joined every fourth time or so. The shop is quaint, no larger than the attic where my mother used to hang nooses from the ceiling like mobiles.

Without Taylor around, I have to replenish everything for myself. So, Chocopop is where I've decided to start my probably disappointing day.

The parking lot only has a smattering of vehicles, so I find a close space. Perrin's most-uppity shopping center is covered in orange stucco and cursive writing. Faux grapes and vines dangle from lattice overhangs. In flannel and ill-fitting jeans, the few customers milling about gawk at me.

Walking into the posh, overpriced store is a reprieve. I don't like being seen, and the store is empty. I make a beeline for the wall of drinking chocolates. A creature of habit, I get the 85% dark and head to the checkout counter.

"Find everything?" the short blonde asks without looking up.

"Yep." I slide the brown glass bottle over to her. "This and three chocolate cheesecake bonbons." *We all have weaknesses.*

She pulls the cabinet below her open obediently. Tossing the candies in a bag like they are greasy french fries, she asks, "Have you seen our November lollipop, Squash Casserole? As with all monthly lollies, it isn't included in our three for $13 deal." Chocopop carries a line of "designer" lollipops with bizarre flavors like pimento cheese sandwich and lavender blueberry. The monthly offerings are no exception. There are no typical flavors like bubblegum or grape.

I grunt.

That gets her attention. Finally, she makes eye contact. "Whoa!" She leans forward. "How old are you?"

"Excuse me?"

The employee hedges. "It's just that, well, we look so much alike! I was gonna say you could be my sister. Or mother. It's hard to say because I can't tell how old you are."

Mother. I have a mind to spit. *Am I above slapping strangers?* I've been known to make an exception before. I stare at her through dim yellow lighting meant to create a calming mood.

White blonde hair, green eyes, straight teeth, short—shorter than me—and pale skin. I did look like that once, I guess.

"Suppose you're right," I say. Still, I don't say my age. Good thing I hadn't planned on collecting in Perrin. This teen would be able to give the police information about the stranger who is an older version of her.

"I'm Carrie." She thrusts her hand across the counter.

"Hello," I say. My hand never leaves my side.

As soon as she realizes I don't intend on participating in her social norms, Carrie pretends to stretch both arms out to cover my rudeness—or her forward friendliness. "Uh, okay. Well, let me ring these up for you."

"Great."

Before she tells me the cost, I swipe my card. "I don't need a receipt," I say.

"Of course. Have a great day! I hope to see you in again soon!" Carrie's smile is too much.

I'm exposed as I leave the chocolate shop, seen in an unusual way. Few recognize me as more than a human being taking up space and oxygen. I prefer it that way. But Carrie saw herself in me; I doubt she would if she knew me.

Walking back to the car, anyone who's gaze flits my way unnerves me. *Would they remember that Carrie's doppelgänger stopped in Perrin on her way to hunt another sweetheart?* I thought I'd wised up when I paused my Eleanor obsession—too close to home. *This could be a wrench.* At the moment, I care more about destroying this younger me than I do about Taylor and Jess combined.

Miles away from Perrin's downtown, and I'm still considering going back to Chocopop around 6:25 p.m. after it closes. It should be dark in the storefront but not the employee area; Carrie may be counting the money. *No one will expect me.* I'll probably get messy; she's able to fight back.

September of 1989 brutally took over that image. Jessica's

face and blue-gray eyes were frozen in a way Laura's hadn't been. Slick, thick, warm life poured out of her. It coated her long, blonde hair. Maybe Carrie could have a pink ribbon like Jessica —the first to be duplicated. Either way, my insides crave the destruction of this younger version of myself. If on my way home it seems feasible, Carrie will become my first sweetheart who can drive.

With that decision made, I continue east for another hour and a half.

2:58 P.M.

I DROVE AROUND Tropview for nearly half an hour before landing on Hollow's End Park. It's part of my favorite neighborhood in Hollowview; I should have started here.

When Taylor and I were looking for a home a few years ago, we visited a few places in Tropview. Taylor loved the suburban feel of the cookie cutter neighborhoods and upscale chain shopping areas. I saw cul-de-sacs of sweethearts and grocery stores filled with soccer moms. So I said I'd rather stay in Silynn.

In some way, I think Taylor knew that the scent of moon glitter and bouncy curls were what kept me from saying yes to Tropview. Mind you, our biggest gripe would have been about house paint colors—Taylor would want pastel robin's egg blue, but I'd want muted sea foam.

I've been sitting here for almost an hour and a half. School should be getting out at any moment. Chewing on the last twists of licorice helps me count down the minutes—each tiny bite a second, each strand thirty seconds. I wait. At 3:16, a lone girl runs to the jungle gym. She looks around a hundred times or so, as if she's desperate to find the friend who swore they'd be there by now. I imagine the sound her snow pants make as she hops up on the merry-go-round. The metal bows as it spins, and she steadies herself.

I observe her and open my bonbon bag. I savor the first one, enjoying the way my teeth crack the white chocolate drizzle over the dark chocolate shell. As I reach the smooth, tangy cream cheese filling, I close my eyes for a moment. Something about a bonbon; each one is a special squirreled away moment no matter what's going on around me. The chunk of cheesecake dissolves on my tongue.

Jess thinks the Lake Killer is a pervert—thinks that I am. Moment ruined.

When the cheesecake is nearly gone, I grab the paper bag. The second one is between my teeth before my mouth tastes like itself again.

I only want to *collect* sweethearts. Jess has it all wrong.

My mother was a collector too. She left the basement door unlocked one week before my seventh birthday—mere months before they took her away. It finally gave me the chance to see what she kept down there, something I'd desired for years. A foul smell wafted through the door now and again. When my father would mention it casually over a breakfast of globby, plain oats or eggs with shredded cheese bits, she'd nod dismissively. The smell would get fainter over the coming days—if not gone altogether. I still don't know if he knew the horrors our house contained. He was a decent, if not passive, man. I assume he never saw her remodel of the basement, or things would have gone differently. I want to think he didn't know she needed help for as long as I suspected she did.

I pop in my last bonbon and begin to chew. *Damn it all.* I planned on letting that one melt from start to finish. I may not believe in signs much, but this felt like one. *I should go back to Chocopop.*

A high-pitched yell shatters my train of thought.

"What are you doing over here?" the girl I'd stopped paying

attention to demands, as she runs across the road without look-ing. With my window up, she shouldn't be so loud. I hate that I have to roll it down. It's bitter outside, and now, she'll know my face.

I motion for her to give me a second.

She approaches the car with more hesitation than she had moments before, her bravado fading. "What are you doing over here? Are you *watching me?*"

At first, I shake my head. I roll my window down, and say, "Well, actually, kind of. I'm new here; just moved right outside of town on Sycamore." Though I've rehearsed it, my words sound natural. "I want to be part of the community, and I have free time since my two boys are off being successful men. So I thought I'd join the neighborhood watch."

Her hand flies to her pre-cocked hip. This girl is older than I thought, so I'm ready to head home. I'll be early; Carrie will be granted a reprieve for today.

"*You* have two sons that are old enough to be called 'men'? *Really?*"

"I do."

"You look younger than that," she says, coming closer to the car. Her hair is stringy, greasy, and unwashed. I know it's my imagination, but I can smell her from here. I try not to wrinkle my nose at the phantom stink.

"Thank you."

She smiles. "I'm Vanessa. I live just two blocks up on Theodore Rd. It's nice to see people trying to keep the streets safe. It's even nicer to see *women* doing it." *Great, a feminist in the making.*

"Nice to meet you, Vanessa. I'm Carrie." Her name slips out of my mouth before I say, "Rosemary," as planned.

"Nice to meet you too. Well, I'm going to go back now. My friends should be here soon. Thanks for helping keep the pervy guys away. Sorry I freaked out on you—never can be too safe.

That's what my mom says, 'V, you can never be *too* safe. Vigilance is your friend.' She's always said that, even before I could pronounce 'vigilance'."

I put my car in gear. "Smart woman. Nice vocabulary too." Before she can say anything else, I drive away disappointed.

Ada

I HAVE DRIVEN AROUND for hours; my gas tank is near empty, and I still haven't picked up my wine.

The clock mocks me. I look at my watch—perfectly synced with the car. It's 3:01 p.m. on the day I found Laura Hurst. At 3:01 p.m. twenty-nine years ago, I was listening to Sarah-Jane's lies.

She was the funniest girl I knew. At six, that said very little. I remember snorting milk once when she told a story about turning into a mouse. I tried not to eat or drink around her for a while after that. Peter said she told tall tales. "That's a fancy way of saying she's a liar," he said. She was okay in my book. Now, when I look back, I see how cold her parents were. It explains why she never hugged me back and couldn't tell more than a partial truth to save her life. The sky couldn't have been described as anything but *cotton candy* blue. To simply say blue was either pedestrian or too real for Sarah-Jane.

At 3:03 p.m., she was telling a story about a stranger offering her free ice cream. Her mom had said no because she had to "work the circuits." Karen and I laughed because turning ice cream down is ridiculous. We should've consoled her for having a pageant mom and been worried that a stranger offered her sweets.

Hailey snuck up behind me at 3:05 p.m. and tapped me on the shoulder. She did it every day—sneak up on me at 3:05 p.m. I never stopped jumping out of my skin.

Visiting Lynn Pond has wiped some smudges from my memory, it seems. The hypnotherapy that hadn't worked—or so I thought—may be contributing to the vivid movie-like recollections.

Hailey's words come back as clear as freshly-cleaned glass. *"You can walk home by yourself like a big girl. Right, Adelynn?"*

Embarrassed, I emulated a teenager by cocking my hip and sassily putting a hand on it. I probably looked like a spoutless little teapot as I said something about not being in Kindergarten.

Hailey told me to go straight home, said she would see me the next day. As always, she called me sweetheart and kissed my cheek. I skipped away like Dorothy towards the only path on the scenic route. Following the snow road shouldn't have been hard.

The first time I heard noises, I was sure it was a rabbit coming out of the forest. I almost turned around to see it hopping, dusted in snow, pink nose twitching with the chilly air. But I was cold and wanted to warm up, so I told myself I could see our class bunny in the morning—snowless, but still cute.

When the sounds came again, they were more like footsteps. I instantly started thinking about how stupid Peter was. He had always said he didn't want me around, didn't like me, even said he *hated* me sometimes. Then, he would be there in the shadows watching. I started looking for things to slow the walk down but never turned around to see if it was him.

Footprints. *No.* Tennis shoe prints. *No.* Bootprints. I couldn't see them clearly; I only knew they were larger than mine and led to the edge of Lynn Pond. I leapt from one to the next, making sure to land in them. That's when the shadow grabbed my attention. I shed my backpack and ran. A voice followed. At the time, I pictured Peter; then, I imagined no one. To this day, I'm still unsure if it was even male. I've spent years flicking through good and bad men and women I've met throughout my life, trying to find a voice match, and have always come up empty.

Without replying, I dropped into the snow. My bare hands burned. I shuffled onto the pond—one scooch, then two. Instead of counting one, two, three, I counted each movement like seconds. *One Mississippi. Two Mississippi. Three Mississippi. Who taught me that?* I found the interesting spot after the fourth Mississippi. The face trapped and frozen in a scream was familiar.

I have dreamt of that moment: my seeing Laura, my scurrying back, the blood I couldn't stop from pouring, so many times I don't know which is a memory and which is a dream. The version that feels the most visceral and real starts with my silence.

Peter didn't come to save me and Laura, so I was on my own. Fear-sweaty palms stuck to the ice and tore skin as I wrenched my hands towards me. Deep red warmth oozed down my wrists from the gory, muscle-exposed space. I stumbled back onto my butt to discover my jumper had ridden up. Only stockings and cheap underwear protected me from the ice.

Crackles filled the air with more immediacy than an electrical storm. The violence with which the ice shattered stunned me. Frigid water snatched my breath. I flailed, and outstretched fingers tangled in my hair. As I squeezed watery eyes closed, my eyelashes fused and became little rows of brittle icicles. I tried to see *her*, but a blistering pain wouldn't allow for more than a peek. Bubbles formed around my face.

I clawed above me in vain; a nail I had bitten ragged ripped backwards in protest. Flailing had shifted me away from the hole through which I'd fallen. Tendrils of Laura's floating red hair found their way into my mouth as I cried out. I choked on the water that froze in my chest.

The memory—something I have never dreamt about—picks up with me lying next to a popsicle child.

I heard sirens before I thought to move. My head was frozen to the left, leaving me to stare at my unzipped backpack and a Lucky Charms heart marshmallow. A bare right cheek stung until a numbness took over. I told myself to become invisible and freeze like Laura. No one would miss me. I just ate a lot and took up a bedroom my mother said could be better used in other ways.

When the voices and hands and faces appeared, I let myself go away. I woke up five hours later with a tall tale bigger than Sarah-Jane's ever told and the hope that Peter would tell on me so I could thank him. Part of our breakfast had fallen out of his pocket, for god's sake.

Instead, I hid my truth, as I thought he had.

3:34 P.M.

I WILL GET three bottles of wine this time. *No. Four.* I will drink until I forget about Laura and Lynn Pond, being chased and my old name. The grocery store is in sight, and I'm relieved. *Merlot, here I come.*

November 25, 1988

Luke

SHE'S LAUGHING.

I tingle when she throws her head back. So far, no girl in my grade has made me feel like she does. Greg acts out the sensation in a gross way, grabbing himself when he says he wants to boink Kelly or Theresa. Maybe it's because I'm a year younger than him, but I don't want to do those things to Adelynn. I only want to be around her. She's my everything.

Greg follows Kelly behind the bleachers, so he doesn't notice or care when I slip behind the bus to watch my secret favorite show: Adelynn's Life.

"Guess who?"

"Hailey," Adelynn giggles. "We play this game every day."

"Then why do you jump?" I want to punch Hailey for making her.

Shrugging, she says, "You can't prove I do."

Billy sneaks up behind Hailey and wraps his arms around her. He whispers something in her ear, and she smiles.

"Whispering's not nice," Adelynn's friend, Karen admonishes. "If you can't share it with everyone, then don't say it when other people are around. Mama says that all the time."

"I'm sure she does. Probably tells you to eat your peas to grow big and strong too, huh?" Billy snarks.

That earns him a smack from Hailey. "Hush up, you. Girls, he's a big silly, is what he is. Peas are great for you. I eat 'em all the time; that's why I'm taller than Billy, here."

"Better eat my peas then," Sarah-Jane says. There's something wrong with her; I just don't care enough to figure out what. "I have two I got from a traveling salesman—"

"Not now, Sarah-Jane," Hailey interrupts.

Though Sarah-Jane stomps her foot, I've watched people hush her enough times to know she's got to be used to it by now.

"I need to talk to Adelynn for a second." Hailey motions her head like she's got a secret for her. "You can walk home by yourself like a big girl. Right, Adelynn?" *Don't patronize her, Hailey. She's six, not three.*

Hailey is too tall with a boyish figure, and her boyfriend sleeps around. I've watched them some also. She moans quietly when Billy slides his finger down into her underwear. It seems as earnest as my love for algebra or interest in the girls who've told me that we were going to the dance together.

Adelynn's hand flies to her hips. "Of course, Hailey! I'm not a Kindergartener." *Don't I know it.*

"Okay, great! You go straight home then. I'll see you tomorrow, sweetheart."

Adelynn smiles and lifts to her tiptoes. Hailey laughs and meets her cheek with a kiss. My breath gets shallow and shaky as it always does when lips touch Adelynn.

"Bye, Karen. Bye, Sarah-Jane. I'll see you two tomorrow!" Adelynn's arms go around them one by one. My jeans constrict.

"Bright and early," Karen says.

Sarah-Jane says, "See you."

Underdressed for the weather, Adelynn skips towards the back way home. With a thick forest to one side of the pathway, it'll be easier for me to enjoy watching her. She slows to a steady walk before she's out of Hailey's eyesight.

"See, Billy?" Hailey purrs. Though she wraps herself around him, her eyes are dull and bored. "We'll have tonight all to ourselves."

My window is short. Sticking to the tree line is simple. Adelynn kicks up snow and hums, unaware of the need to check for watchers. When her happy fades and she looks uncomfortable for a moment, I consider finally saying hello. *Oh, me? I go this way all the time. My name? My name is Kevin.* I hope one day she can know my real name. But today, if she were to tell her parents, they might not understand that I'm looking out for her— following her because I care. Looking myself up and down, I decide I'm not presentable enough; I should look like I did when I first saw her.

She shivers and rubs her thin arms. Wendy Bailey should be ashamed, letting my Adelynn out in the snow only dressed in one of my favorite pink dresses and some ripped tights. And why isn't she wearing boots?

We walk side by side divided by trees for some time: her on the path and me to her right, hidden in the small forest. It becomes the kind of peaceful Greg's mom and dad have together in bed while she knits and he reads. I've watched them through their bedroom window a few times, jealous of the calm they have. And now, with Adelynn, I have that. *Does she feel it too?*

Lost in imaginings of a future version of us—Adelynn baking a cake while I chop vegetables for stew—I nearly miss her sudden stop. It almost makes our footsteps fall out of sync.

I watch her jump in shoe prints—an endearing sight. After five two-footed hops, she shrugs her book bag off and runs towards Lynn Pond's frozen surface. I swallow my heartbeat.

"ADELYNN!" I've made myself known; I wonder if my days

of observation are over. But she doesn't turn; she drops and crawls onto the ice.

Stilling a few feet away from the edge, her naked hands shove snow away from a spot with the vigor she opened her birthday presents with. A shrill scream slices through the stuffy air; a crack follows. I blink—*blink*—and Adelynn is underwater.

Snow sinks as I race past her backpack to the frozen water that won't hold me as well as it had her. I slink on the ice towards the hole. I can't see her; I can't see anything. I'm reminded of ice fishing with my grandfather. He had too much time on his aggressive, wandering hands. That thought and fear for my Adelynn make punching the solid water easier. I pound the ice again and again, as far away from my body as possible, ignoring the cracks my knuckles experience. Each bit of blood left on the ice is another hit I'll have to give some poor schmuck on the way home to explain this all away. Let's hope someone does something to deserve it.

The weakened ice finally breaks and creates a chasm, connecting her shattered space to mine. Time is limited. Adelynn is there. Hair and fingers sink faster than the snow melted under my boots. I yank at them. She's dead freezing weight. I tug harder and horizontally climb towards the snowy bank. Ice tears with her body. I can't look back anymore; I just go.

It's not until I'm on land, gasping for cold, dry air, that I realize Adelynn isn't the only girl I've pulled from Lynn Pond. Laura Hurst is tangled with Adelynn. I pull her hair from Adelynn's mouth and swallow my heart. She's not breathing; neither of them are. Laura's skin is wrong, so I know it's too late for her. But not my girl.

I get to do the unimaginable. I lick my dry lips and press them to Adelynn's. *I love you.*

November 26, 2017

Ada

I HAVEN'T SLEPT YET. With the oncoming blizzard whirling against the window, the power started to flicker around eleven. *Good thing I hadn't bothered fixing the oven's clock yet.* I've had to stoke the fire every so often since to keep myself from freezing.

I worry I may get stuck here, with no phone, no electricity, no way to leave. I shudder. Fear of every sound I hear outside isn't helping. The almost-certainly-not-Peter's voice is out there—I know it. When the window fogs, it is their breath that's steamed it. Instead of imagining a shadowy form peeking through my window, I try to focus on what Rachael would tell me if she were here. After yesterday's ordeal, I was so far gone, calling her while I still had decent service didn't even dawn on me. I go on previous conversations and hope they apply here too. *"Let the thoughts come."* She might add to ground myself because I'm in a foreign location.

A branch thuds against a window—the voice trying to get in. As the tree's fingers scrape down the glass, my ears clinch.

The man that broke into my home when I was young has come back; he's been the one all along. I feel his hand over my mouth. "Shh, shh. I'm Justice, and I'm here to see your Mommy. I need you to stay quiet, so no one gets hurt. Can you do that?" No, it couldn't be him. My mother shot him. It's Luke. He's the voice. Watching me wasn't enough, so he made contact. He stands in the woods as snow morphs into schools of fish around him. No, Hailey did it. She realized her mistake of sending me home alone and came after me. Maybe her's was an innocent reason. The voice and my pursuer did not have to be the same person. Dave, the grocer, seemed to have a problem with me. Did he follow me to keep me from talking to his wife? People have done worse for less. Polly knew a lot for someone who hadn't seen my mother in years. Old Enough may have felt scorned by me at Bar. It could have been his hands that bludgeoned the woman who resembled me. Surely there were other people from my past, now grown, with lives I may wreck if I remember something. And what if it *was* Peter? Should I call and demand answers once the storm allows?

I feel dizzy with names and faces. The endless possibilities, the missed opportunities—if only I had turned around twenty-nine years ago; if only I had turned around yesterday.

Using my foot, I scooch my pen and paper close to me. I write my fears to Rachael. I pretend we're conversing. I am just at the part where she asks me if I was sure I heard footsteps behind me at Lynn Pond when another loud noise breaks my concentration.

I guess I'll ground myself now, I scrawl in chicken scratch. I tap the paper with the pen over and over as I think but do not write. I am sitting in a rocking chair that squeaks if I go too far back. From here, I can see most of the cabin. No one can come in behind me. The stained quilt I've draped over myself is doing little to nothing to keep away the chill invading my bones.

I squeeze the fireplace poker I deem a worthy weapon.

I wish I'd had the sense to bring the butcher's knife from the kitchen drawer with me. I'm as safe as I can be in a cabin with no real weapons, electricity, or access to a phone or car.

The wind picks up outside.

11:45 A.M.

MY MOTHER AND I had a breakfast "markered in" for today. I *can't believe* she would not try to get ahold of me by now. We've only gotten to see each other for a few hours this visit. It's all so terribly unlike her! *And... scene.*

I am so exhausted. I spent hours watching shapes form on the wall, in the knots of the wooden floor. I'm not sure I have the defenses to be in the same room as my mother even if we had somehow gotten in contact.

After tracing the stitching on the quilt twelve to fifteen times, I snuck towards the kitchen to have some 4:03 a.m. wine. Then I enjoyed 5:15 a.m. wine. Some more at 7:38 and 9:34, and now it's 11:45 a.m., and I'm polishing off my second bottle.

It became official about half an hour ago: I cannot leave Silynn. After a night spent with one eye open, waiting for monsters to sneak in through the window, the snow hasn't let up. My flight has probably been delayed. I can't call to confirm, and I can't drive to find out. I am stuck in a real daymare—*which is excellent.*

Breakfast will be coffee. I am craving Lucky Charms marshmallows. Running my tongue in the grooves of my teeth, I can practically taste the lodged sticky sweetness. I could go for some pink milk too. Though I put in extra grounds, my cold-steeped coffee is weak to the point of tastelessness.

I get a chunk of cheese from the fridge. A cold slime has formed around it, so it sticks to the roof of my mouth. I let it melt as I add two logs to the stove; I am running low and have to conserve more than I have been.

As I stoke the fire, my back tightens. *Someone is on the other side of the window.* I don't see them, but I feel their gaze. There is a rustle by the unnecessary back door. The wind is all but non-existent now, gone in the wee hours of the morning. I watch the handle, sure it will jiggle or turn. It doesn't. Nothing more than a low crackling flame fills the cabin. I'm a Victorian horror novel character.

Chewing the glob of processed milk fat, I relax my fight-ready muscles. Another bath may be in order. I do still smell, and after all, *where am I going?* To eat one more bite of unsatisfying cheese.

From my peripheral, I see a red smear flash by the window. The fire poker is on the floor in front of me. I grab it, and pain throbs from the bruised indentation my unease created last night. "Who are you?" I'm a moron—a terrified moron. "What are you doing here?" I shout from safety.

No answer; not that I expected one.

Unlocking the door and rushing out is a terrible idea. I have watched enough horror films to know that the first person who does it dies. So I do it. "Who are you?" Snowflakes fly into my face. "What do you want?"

The same rustling from before is closer now and much louder. I hear a soft voice. "I'm so sorry."

A woman emerges from behind a cluster of trees in an arterial red plaid shirt, jeans, charcoal work boots, and no jacket. "I'm so sorry," she says again. "I didn't mean to scare you! I came to check on the place and was very surprised to see you in it. I had no idea Taylor had rented it. That's why I was sneaking away; I didn't want to scare you. I see by that iron poker in your hand, it didn't work." She attempts a laugh.

My jaw drops, the poker does not. "Why were you checking on the place? It was a man who rented it to me," I say. The broken words and bad signal technically *could have* been a woman with a deep voice—one this woman did not have. "Who are you?"

"That man's wife. Well, soon to be ex-wife. I hope to get this in the divorce," she says. Her warm smile does not reach her eyes; they are colder than the air I'm letting into the cabin. The ice in them is familiar. White blonde hair surrounding apple-cheeks and a heart-shaped face tickle a memory too.

Shivering, I say, "Ah. Well, I'm okay—so is the place. Thank you, though. I appreciate you checking."

She takes a step forward. "No problem. Do you think I could get a hot drink of some sort? Hell, whiskey or beer would do. The walk was long."

Social norms compel me to continue the conversation. "And without a coat!"

As it is her place, I have a niggling sense of obligation to let her in. I don't, though. *Is my hesitancy due to Silynn-bred paranoia or a real sixth sense?* Should she have not known to wear extra layers? The walk is long; she would know that if this was her place.

"Thanks for understanding," she replies and half-pushes past me.

Gulping, my heartbeat increases. "Of course." This woman makes me uncomfortable in the same way Luke's eyes did when I tried to close the door on him.

With her back turned, she says, "I'm Carrie." Then, she sinks into the rocking chair. *Liar.* I don't know why, but her name feels wrong. Two can play at that game.

"Jill," I reply, using my mother's middle name.

One cup of substandard coffee, then I will usher her out with a jacket she won't need to return.

Sam

IT HAS BEEN A DAY AND A HALF, and Taylor hasn't called. So I will do the only thing I can think of to protect myself: I'll hide my sweethearts' mementos. I can't bear to leave them somewhere unfamiliar, so I'll utilize the "investment" cabin that has yet to pay for itself. If police come for me, it will only buy me a little time.

I hate parking in the front because the walk is long. So I drive at a snail's pace to the back—fully snowed in. I park at the edge of the woods, which is closer to the cabin, but not enough. *Well, so much for being here without anyone seeing my car.*

I leave my coat on the seat, as I don't want to have to throw more clothes away when I get home. Within steps, I see the porch. Smoke is coming from the chimney, and the curtains are open. I freeze. *What?* I take a second to walk back and put the tote bag full of cherished memories in the car. Better safe than sorry.

Now, to find out who the hell is in my cabin.

It takes some finagling to look into the windows without being seen. When I do, my hand flies to my mouth. Seeing her face is like being slapped. *Adelynn Bailey.* Taylor rented our cabin to Adelynn Bailey—*without knowing, right?* No one would be that stupid.

In a split decision, I choose to go home. I see the benefits of snatching her life, though it would be more messy than beneficial. She's already swept up in another investigation. Killing her could draw attention to me. Unless necessary, Adelynn is a loose end I'll have to leave frayed.

Backing away, I avoid branches and leaves. But I can't fade into the trees; my red shirt in the snow is a joke, and I'm so close to the window. I duck down, about to military crawl to my car, when I hear a voice. "Who are you? What are you doing here?"

Shit. No. This could ruin everything. At least I don't have my sweethearts' things with me. Spotted, it's either run or stay. Running may involve the police. I make another snap decision and make myself known. *I'll tell her a half-truth.*

The deadbolt clicks, and Adelynn Bailey rushes outside. *Idiot.* I wish I'd come with a ribbon. "Who are you?" she calls again. "What do you want?"

As if I'm talking to a sweetheart, I soften my tone. "I'm so sorry." I step forward. "I didn't mean to scare you! I came to check on the place and was very surprised to see you in it. I had no idea Taylor had rented it. That's why I was sneaking away; I didn't want to scare you. I see by that iron poker in your hand, it didn't work." Faking a laugh, I imagine Adelynn Bailey swinging her weapon at my face and the metal hook catching my cheek. *Would I then have the right to slaughter her?*

"Why were you checking on the place? It was a man who rented it to me." She waivers as she says it. "Who are you?"

"That man's wife. Well, soon to be ex-wife," I say with a smile. "I hope to get this in the divorce." I *need* to get this in the divorce.

Adelynn stares at me with a hint of recognition. I've seen that spark before. "Ah. Well, I'm okay—so is the place. Thank you, though. I appreciate you checking."

"No problem." *What's the most normal thing to do here?* "Do you think I could get a hot drink of some sort? Hell, whiskey or beer would do. The walk was long."

She is a reluctant Southern belle. "And without a coat!"

"Thanks for understanding." I step past her and hear her heart in her throat. Maybe today will go differently than planned after all. I think she says some platitude, but I'm picturing her broken body filling the tub with blood. "I'm Carrie."

"Jill," Adelynn replies.

What game is she playing? "Nice to meet you, Jill."

"I don't have anything warm, but I have some lukewarm, weak coffee. That okay?" She's already pouring the dredges of the pot and refilling it.

If I said no, I wonder how she'd respond. So I say, "Of course. If it's not freezing, it's better than nothing."

Her face is away from me, and her body is rigid. Adelynn is scared. *I guess I'll treat her like Jess*—half-sweetheart, half-adult. I pop my right ankle, and both knees ache—reminders that I've aged.

"Here you go," she says. "Hope it's alright." At best, it's not cold.

I smile and nod.

"So..." The word floats in front of me like a gnat. Though it's bothersome, I'm uninterested in addressing it. After three sips of the cool coffee water with grounds in it, she finishes her question. "You walked from your car without a coat?"

"Yep." *And no plan.*

Wendy Bailey's words come out of Adelynn's mouth, "It's cold out; you could have gotten sick."

"I planned on turning the heat on quickly."

"As you can see, the power's out. The fire's still roaring, though," Adelynn says with a nervous laugh.

"So glad Taylor chopped down those two trees this past summer." *There, I contributed.*

Glancing at the cabinet drawers, I'm curious. Did Adelynn move the knife? Is it in the sink or dishwasher? I think she notices my shifting gaze because she wanders back towards the kitchen area and refills an untouched coffee.

"Me too. Don't know what I'd have done without the wood. I'll reimburse you for it, of course."

"Don't you worry about that," I coo. If Adelynn were my sweetheart, I'd brush her hair away from her face. "It's part of renting a cabin." This, I believe, is the time in a visit when I either leave or come up with a topic of interest.

"I collect sweethearts. What do you do?" That's not great. *"Do they have any leads on the person who killed that woman someone buried so closely to my Lori?"* I'm bad at small talk. I don't care enough to do it, usually. I need to bide time. I want that knife. Once it's in my hand, I can make another big decision of the day —one I thought I'd already made. But an opportunity has presented itself.

Ada

CARRIE IS STILL HERE. She's had two cups of not-quite-coffee; I have reluctantly nursed half of one. We've lied to each other about our occupations, and she has given me some bullshit excuse about why she didn't have a coat. "I took it off in the car and didn't even notice until I was a ways away. Can you believe it?"

No.

"I have an extra coat you can borrow."

Carrie shakes her head. "No, not necessary. A little while longer here, and I'll be okay to hoof it back."

"Sure." My smile falters.

"I'm starving," she says. Her eyes move to the empty grocery store bag on the floor.

I sigh. "How could I have forgotten my manners? I only have a few things like cheese and chocolate left, but if you'd like—"

Dead eyes twinkle for the first time as she interrupts my lie. "Oh! I love chocolate."

"Well, that's easy." I fetch the chocolate bar from my purse and hand it to Carrie. "It's nothing fancy, really," I start.

By the time I sit back on the edge of the bed, she's already devoured most of it. *I guess she was actually hungry.* I resist the urge to make her eggs.

She stands. Calf muscles tense up, my fight instinct in full gear again. "Just putting some wood in the fire," she says and puts her hands up. "Sorry about that." Carrie crouches and stabs at the wood. I watch on. Tiny bits of ash float in the metal belly exposing a new, angry orange. "It's the silence, isn't it?" she asks.

I jump, having been mesmerized by the flames. "What?"

"The silence is why you're on edge, right?"

I nod. "Yeah, the silence."

An eyebrow flicks up in amusement. Carrie knows something I don't; I am raw and exposed. *Who is this woman?* "I play the radio when it's too quiet," she says.

"Didn't know there was a radio." Even if I did, I'm not sure I would want to block out my only real defense.

Carrie grunts as she stands. The sound ages her in a way her smooth face and unblemished hands conceal. "It's right under here. No one ever thinks to look under here—unless they are nosey or looking for a first aid kit."

"How did I not think to look under the sink?" I sound more upset than I am. After all, I *had* been under the sink. Only I'd been looking for something else.

Her mouth crooks. "Could be you just aren't curious in nature." She knows I've been under the sink, though. How else would the lighter fluid be by the fire?

"Usually, I am." I shrug then thank her for the radio. "You sure you don't want a jacket?" This time, she takes the hint.

"You know, I will take it. Thank you." I bring her a gray and white coat that is two sizes too big; my mother bought it for me when I was a whopping five pounds heavier than I am now. I carry it most places, though I've never known why. "Maybe we'll see each other again," Carrie says as she slides it on. It's loose on her too, but not as much.

I usher her to the back door—five whole steps away—and open it ceremoniously. "It was lovely to meet you, Carrie."

"You too, A—Jill." Blood rushes out of my face, and I'm struck still. She meant 'as well' but realized she already said 'too.' *Right?*

"Good luck out there! Sor—sorry I can't drive you," I stutter out.

Carrie shakes her head and pats me on the shoulder. "No problem. Take care of yourself, and be careful of that curiosity you have." She winks. "I hear it kills cats." Every nerve in me demands I run away. It's not what she said, it's *how* she said it.

She steps outside, where the wind has picked up. I expect her to turn around, ask for another cup of coffee or to wait until the wind's died down. She doesn't. For a reason only Rachael could dissect, I don't close the door until she's out of sight. Before I do, I glance down.

Carrie's boot prints remind me of Lynn Pond and Laura Hurst. *Silynn's making me crazy.* I know that Hailey, Justice, Carrie, Dave, Peter, or the waitress at Sodas 'n More did not kill Laura. Yet I cannot shake the feeling that an amalgamation of them did. A chill has spread to my bones, and until the faces of Silynn's residents leave my mind, I'm not sure I will be able to shake it. I curl up in a ball on the floor in front of the fireplace. Journaling can't help me now.

Luke

I THOUGHT ADELYNN WOULD RUSH into my arms when I came to pick her up for the date I never imagined I'd get. Small scissors and a plastic baggy were in my back pocket for that moment. A snip of her top, a clip of her hair. They could have gone next to the ones from age six and seven and eight. The perfect photo of us was going to hang beside the framed front page of *Silynn Times* that boasted her heroism. Her small, shivering body captured in time after she'd "crawled from the icy Lynn Pond" with Laura in tow. I imagined having the Daily Specials menu from our first date next to articles from the few national papers the story made it into (many of which had small photos of Laura Hurst's face; fewer had my Adelynn's).

I pull out her pink scarf and wrap it around my neck. The bubblegum she'd chewed at her first sleepover is preserved in a glass jar. I open it from time to time, give it a chew. It's the closest I've gotten to tasting her since the lake. I still savor the moment after I compressed her chest. She hadn't started breathing yet. I slid my tongue inside her bottom lip before I shared my life with her again. Though the wintergreen gum is now flavorless, I pretend it tastes like sour milk, sugar, and stale tater tots.

I stare in my closet at the top of the dresser that takes up most of it and the wall behind it. It's not a large enough collection.

If Adelynn is gone, if only Ada remains, maybe she'll do. I'll try and learn to love Ada as much as I love Adelynn, and she can learn to love me back. After what happened at Bar, I can't imagine a life without her. Tonight, we'll start our life together—if we can get past her differences. First, I need to work up my nerve.

9:37 P.M.

WORRY CREASES HER FACE. The youth I once craved is gone. But my feelings for her go beyond the skin.

I won't hide this time. I'll explain everything. I'll come clean, about watching her, my collection, Lynn Pond, even the unicorn charm. She'll love me then; she'll have no choice. It will all fall into place once she hears how much and how long I've wanted her. Maybe she can be my Adelynn again.

She's talking to herself, and it doesn't seem to be a pleasant conversation. *Should I knock? Should I wait?* There's no time like the present, I've been told.

As Ada paces the cabin, I wonder if my unannounced visit would only make things worse. My patience has done me a disservice. She leaves tomorrow—if her travel plans haven't changed. And yet again, it's not the right time. Before, our age difference would have been scorned. Now, she's too broken, too different, and I pushed.

Tossing her hair up in a ponytail, her sweater sleeves slide up.

Quickly, she pulls them down. Adelynn was never so self-conscious; she lived with reckless abandon and torn stockings. Even alone, *Ada* tries to hide her scarred palms. I want to kiss them and apologize for not making it to her sooner. I imagine her blushing, standing on tiptoes to steal a kiss.

She's only here one more day. I'll have to try and find an opening then, a moment when she's smiling or laughing at a passage in a book. She'll be more receptive to me then. Or maybe we're doomed to be star-crossed lovers—Adelynn and I. *We'll find out in the morning, my love.*

November 20, 1988

Sam

LAURA JOGS UP TO MY SIDE. "Hey, Samantha!" Her breath imprints my name on the air.

"Good day, I take it?" I tilt my head enough to wink at her. "How was your math test? Did it go well like I said it would?"

"I got a B. It would have been an A, but I couldn't remember things fast enough. The Hairbrush Game helped a lot, though." She flips the few pieces of hair that can be seen under her hat for emphasis.

I'm proud of the 'game' I invented. With each stroke, we'd go over the quiz questions. Stroke one: "What is six times five?" Stroke two: "What is 4.89 rounded to the nearest decimal point?" Stroke three: "How many dimes and nickels are in a quarter? For this one, there are multiple right answers." Stroke four: "What is one times any number?" Stroke five: "What grade will you get on your math quiz?"

Last week, during a question she needed a pen and paper for, I snipped a lock of her hair. It was so small she still hasn't noticed.

Using a peach ribbon she left at my house, I tied it up and put it in my jewelry box beside the wrinkled sandwich baggy keeping Georgia's curl safe.

Laura jumps up and down twice. "Let's walk the long way home today."

"You got it."

I slide her backpack from her skinny arms and carry it like a handbag. My back is already breaking from the homework I have to pretend to do. Mrs. Thompson drones a lot in Biology, so I finish my pre-Algebra and English homework there. Biology gets done during lunch. All of my other classes require very little of my attention, so I work on the papers and projects throughout the week. If I didn't, I wouldn't have enough time to babysit and run around town with the few people from school I haven't imagined snuffing out.

For a while, Laura and I enjoy the light snowfall. The grass resembles a perfect pastry dusted with confectioners sugar. My dad buys me sweets whenever he goes to Hartfield or Perrin.

"Skip with me," Laura says.

Suddenly, I'm nervous. She's never asked to do this before. We step out of the more wooded area, and Lynn Pond is just ahead. The usually still water ripples with the heavier snowflakes.

"Of course." A pre-loaded response I use, second only to nodding. Our gloves are too puffy, and I can't close my hand around hers. "No gloves?" I suggest.

Out of the corner of my eye, I watch her pull the puffy material off. Her mittens crinkle as she balls them up and tucks them in her zippered pockets. "Better!" she says, laughing.

When her small hand touched mine, her warmth fills me with a sensation I haven't felt before. *Maybe longing. Maybe just an honest connection with another living being.* It occurs to me that I've never laced my fingers with anyone. I'm unsure of how I've gone sixteen years without it. Then again, I have a monstrous mother and a father who understands me as much as my gym teacher understands the word ovaries. I also have no real interest in dating.

So, I go out on a limb and try to slide my fingers between hers, but her hand is too small. Laura tugs a little, probably with discomfort. I tilt my hand just a little and try again. This time it works, and our fingers dangle, hooked together. Hummingbird wings beat in my chest, and the puffs of air in front of me become a steady stream of steam.

We slow, and Laura asks, "You okay?" Her face screws up with worry.

I fake a laugh unconvincingly. "Just cold."

"Put your gloves back on, silly!" She tries to drop my hand. I squeeze a little. *I can't let go yet.* Her voice changes as she adds, "I don't mind."

I can't read her, but it doesn't matter. My thumb touches the back of her hand as I'd always wished my mother had touched mine. Admitting this to myself makes me ill.

After a few steps, I begin rubbing circles on her satin skin how I imagine I would have wanted comfort. I find myself humming as my cheeks warm. Venturing, I trace the outline of her small fingers.

Laura makes a choking sound and rips her hand from mine. "What are you doing?"

"I just—" Scrambling, I say, "I thought I felt you slip."

"No, you didn't." Her eyes narrow. "You were rubbing my hand like Mom does to Dad. You shouldn't be doing that to me! I didn't like it." Things begin to slip, and she starts to stomp away. Laura's next words are a barrage of fists. She calls me a pervert. She shouts that I must like little girls and that she is going to tell her mom—and Adelynn's too. *How did we go from skipping to this?*

I don't like little girls—*not like that, anyway.* I have never felt much of anything, and compared to my friends and their height-ened emotions, I still don't. Girls are innocent and soft and make me want to take care of them. I've always wanted hair that shines like theirs.

Snow starts to pour down like rain, and Laura takes off. But I have her book bag; she has homework to do tonight. *And what will her parents say?*

"Leave me alone!" Her voice bounces around me as trees reverberate the final straw.

A primal urge attacks my senses, and I'm the hunter my father told me not to be. I give Laura a second or two before I chase her. Copper hair peeks out from under her knit hat. I see it all unfold; she trips and falls to the ground. It's almost a shock to me when I realize this isn't a fantasy. Everything I've ever imagined is happening—more even.

I slide her backpack down my arm just enough to hold it. One swing and it connects with the back of her skull. She stumbles forward. I don't like the sounds she's making; they make me queasy, as if I'm doing something wrong. I drop her bag and hit her with my heavier one.

She's quiet then.

When I flip her to face me, she's still breathing. "Laura? Laura?" I'm frantic. *"It won't hurt, little bug. It won't hurt. Look at me, sweetheart, and you'll see. It's already over, as quick as one, two, three,"* I sing, as I steal her breath with my two hands. Her struggle brings more discomfort, but I'm too far in; I accept the feeling.

Time passes. I know this because my fingers cramp, and my bones are cold. Laura's eyes go glassy and snow piles around us, outlining my crime. A dark sky looms; we should be at my house finishing her homework before we watch a movie.

I look around the field for some way to hide Laura. All I hear are animals and the soft sounds of Lynn Pond. I brush fresh snow into the hollow space Laura's little frame created and walk to Lynn Pond with her body in my arms.

In case I forget where imaginings became a reality, I choose a spot near a rock that's embedded in snow. Here's hoping it's deep in the earth. When I slide her into the still water, something feels incomplete.

I rifle through my backpack. Books, papers, pencils, a magazine I borrowed from Hailey, a notebook filled with scribbles from friends, a bag of pretzels. *Nothing*. Until—at the bottom, in a squished box—I see the candies Hailey gave me earlier this week. Valentine's Day conversation hearts with sayings like, "Kiss Me" and "Be Mine". She told me they are basically chalk, so they taste the same as the day she got them eight months ago.

The cardboard box shreds as I tear it open with frozen fingers. I shake a few hearts out and land on a pink one that says, "Be Good". Close to the lake, but not *too* close, I place the candy in the snow.

"Thank you for letting me take care of you, Laura," I say.

Taking both of our book bags is a final goodbye.

I'm at my house when I realize I didn't cover my boot prints. Before I can turn, the front door opens. Mr. And Mrs. Hurst rush out.

"Oh, Samantha!" Mrs. Hurst cries. Her heavy eyeliner is smeared under her lashes, and her shoulder-padded dress is wrinkled. "We were so worried about you two. Wait... where's Laura?"

Mr. Hurst stands stone-faced behind her. His suit looks as pressed as the day it was picked up. They aren't touching or comforting each other—*Hailey's right.* I wonder if Mrs. Hurst knows. *Does Mr. Bailey?*

The lie is an oil spill. "I don't know." I sniffle—hopefully at the right time. Leading us back towards the house, I say, "We met after school, but she said she needed to go grab something from the gym. We were already part of the way home, so she said she'd just run back. I waited, of course. But when she didn't show up—"

I pretend to falter as we enter my home. My dear father stands in the living room. His face flickers like a skipping film. He's disappointed and angry, worried about Laura, about me. My father saw too much of me the day I shot the doe; now, he may be able to put the pieces together.

"I'm so sorry! I know I should've gone with her. I was so tired; it was a rough day. A football player said something nasty to me, and—that's no excuse. I wasn't thinking. She's only nine! *What's wrong with me?*" I wish I could pat myself on the back. I didn't plan on using my friend's story. I only wish it all sounded a little more believable.

Mr. Hurst speaks first. "No! No, Samantha. We've let her walk home alone before, too. It's not like we live far from the school. You can't blame yourself for this! We have an idea of where to start. You stay home, in case she comes here. Carla—Mrs. Hurst—will go back home and wait there." He turns to my dad. "Vernon, you and I will head to the school."

"Samantha, we love you. Stay safe," Mrs. Hurst says.

The house reeks of fear. I could tell them not to waste their time looking, but I'd rather not deal with the emotions or potential of them finding anything. Her backpack is in a muddy part of a ditch off of an out-of-the-way back road.

Is that good enough?

I nod. "I will."

Mrs. Hurst drops a quick kiss on Mr. Hurst's cheek, and I turn away from his ambivalence. "Now, honey," she says to her cheating husband. "Go find our sweetheart."

She's my sweetheart now.

November 27, 2017

Ada

HE IS THE SCENT OF A DARK STAIRWELL. Rust clings to his breath, piss to his jeans, fear to his clothes. Decaying teeth and roadkill hide underneath it all. My vomit sits on the edge of everything.

We have been like this for hours, maybe days—Luke and I—as if he were my green coat. I cannot remember when I sat beside him or when I slid my murderous, cramped hand under his—my heartbeat pounding into his lifeless fingertips. He's stiffened since, pliable fingers tensing with time, and the blood pooling under him has thickened like wet paint.

My eyes snap open, and I look around. Luke is nowhere to be seen. The visceral memory of him breaking in, telling me secrets, of me beating him with the fire poker, all dim until my brain puts together that it was only a dream. Despite the scent of death burning my nose and my hand still feeling warm and slightly sticky, I never sat in Luke's blood.

Movement outside last night set my jaw on edge, and I fell asleep in a cocoon of the fear. I woke to my stench, not Luke's.

A flash of warning hits me: *he could be waiting in the woods, watching from behind a snowy tree.*

Two eyebrow hairs sting. One is on the far left; the other is underneath the arch. If I plucked either I would end up looking angry and confused. *Great.*

8:29 A.M.

THE FIRE POKER IS ODDLY HEAVY. Its weight has everything to do with me having to kill Luke after he broke in and beat me with it—nightmare, though it was.

If I wasn't shivering, I would let the flames die out. Mere hours ago, in the longest dream I've ever had, I saw the dying fire spit out a small spark, and Carrie's cabin went up in smoke. Cartoon flames flickered in my eyes. Books caught fire first, pages of words turned to ash in seconds. Fibers of hand-stitched quilts shrunk and blistered as flames nipped at their sides. The cabin walls suffocated as the roaring fire consumed Luke's corpse and my crime wholly. *I need to get out of here.*

The sun is bright, and the ever-falling snow is white glitter. Fresh air could do me some good.

Even with a coat, it's frigid. Chunks of wet hair turn to icicles, and my nose starts to run before my boots get snowy. Firmly focused on the tingling in my fingers, I am not worried about disturbing nightmares.

I can't feel four toes. That's a sign I'm done with the outside. No frolicking, it seems. At least I am no longer focused on Luke and death and fire and—*Carrie?* Her tan coat doesn't stand out in the woods and flurries; the blue flannel peeking out from underneath it does.

She waves, and I know it's not a mirage. "Hey, Jill!" she calls. *Right, my name is Jill.* As she comes closer, I see a disingenuous smile and a tote bag on her shoulder. This time, she's fully prepared for the weather, wearing gloves, snow boots, and a two-toned tan trapper hat. I give her a half-hearted hand movement some *may* call a wave and don't go in yet. Carrie comes up beside me quicker than seems possible in the deep snow. "I thought I'd come give you some newspapers to read."

"Really?" I accidentally say out loud. "I'm sorry. I mean, that was thoughtful. Such a long walk just to give me some papers."

"Well, I had to drop something off at the cabin too." She walks in first.

And you had to do it today? You couldn't wait until I left tonight or tomorrow? "Of course. Can I get you some water?"

Carrie shakes her head and sets her bag on the kitchen counter. I'm embarrassed at the crumbs and wrappers, the empty wine bottles and unwashed mugs. She gets out a clean kitchen towel from a drawer, then empties the contents on it: a child's shoebox and a stack of *Silynn Times* newspapers.

The reverence in which she touches the box makes me think it's her child's memories. Nana had a hat box like that. Her age-spotted hands pulled it from the top of the closet, holding it as if it were a Fabergé egg. Neatly stacked inside were photos, three baby teeth, my mother's first bow and rattle, and a drawing of the whole family. I try to picture what Carrie's holds but come up short.

"So, here are the newspapers. You won't believe what's happening in Silynn right now." Though her words sound shocked, her voice holds little inflection.

I glance at them; they are from early in the week. One is the issue Dave had given me—the one I'm in. Goosebumps threaten my covered arms and legs. The next two have headlines that could have been copied and pasted with only two to four lines changed in the first paragraph of the article: Jane Doe's were found on back-to-back days. The issue dated the oldest mentions no age but talked about me. I think that's the one Luke's good for. The second says it was a young girl. "Adelynn Bailey Questioned" is the final headline. I sense a theme. One that makes me want to take another walk.

"That is crazy," I say to gauge a reaction.

Carrie goes to the bathroom with her shoebox. "I'm surprised at all this talk about Adelynn Bailey."

She knows. "Oh?"

"Have you heard of her, Jill?" she asks over the sound of porcelain scraping. "She found a girl named Laura Hurst about twenty-some-odd years ago in Lynn Pond. Both of the newest Jane Does were found there too. I've been hearing locals worrying that she's the killer. We don't have a lot of dead folk around here." She steps out of the telephone booth sized bathroom without the box.

I gulp, hoping that says I know nothing about this Adelynn person.

"I've wanted to thank her for years. I was babysitting Laura the afternoon she went missing. What if Adelynn had never found my sweetheart?" *Sweetheart?*

I recall little of this woman if she is who I think she is. Hailey used to talk about her a lot. They had a falling out—something to do with me and Laura. But I remember almost white hair and a song about things not hurting. It was Hailey's song, yet another voice rings clear in my head. I believe her name starts with an "S".

"Good thing she did."

"Yes, good thing." Her eyes narrow. The liar is waiting. "I'll have a glass of water, after all. Want one?"

I am a caged animal. "No thanks."

"Suit yourself." Downing two full glasses of water, she says, "So, *Jill*, tell me more about yourself."

"Not much to know. Married with two kids and a dog, no picket fence. You?"

"Getting a divorce, one kid." Carrie slurps her third glass of water.

I stand. A momentary flashback to my dream hits: me leaving to get the police, I turn back to Luke's corpse and tell him I'll be back soon. Ignoring the instinct to check for blood splatter, I say, "Well, I was going to go for a walk, so I'm going to head out. Sorry to be rude, just got all pumped about it."

"Ada—that's what you go by now, right? You shouldn't go anywhere just yet." All pretense falls away, and I'm left with Laura's babysitter—and a woman who knows too much about me.

"And you are?" I ask.

She sets her water down. "Tying up loose ends."

Seeing her lunge, having one second of a head start, makes no difference.

Luke

A WOMAN WITH A SOFT LOOKING FACE I vaguely recognize is standing in *Ada*'s cabin. She looks straight at me, but I'm hidden in the trees—always unseen.

Watching this woman as I wait calms me. She's lost in thought. If I were in the room, I bet I'd hear humming. When she cracks her neck, I feel stiff, overly aware of myself. I mimic her action, and my relief breaks the silence.

Sam

CRUMPLED ON THE FLOOR like a used tissue, Ada is nothing like she used to be.

After the attempted baptism incident, I didn't see her for over a month. Laura's best friend was turning seven—I think—and all the neighborhood kids had been invited to bring her presents. It had the bonus of giving the parents another reason to openly drink during the day. Adelynn had just turned four not long before. It was the only reason Hailey talked to me again; she wanted to gush about the party. Laura had been there with her dad, and Adelynn's mom had spilled a drink on him. Then, they'd gone to the bathroom for "a really long time just to clean up some juice."

At the birthday party, Adelynn was confetti. Her white poof of a skirt had multicolored sparkles on it. When I asked where she'd gotten it, she beamed with pride and told me she'd glittered it herself. Knowing the little I do about her mother, I don't know how she managed that.

Her outfit and smile lit up the backyard, stealing attention from the tiara, tutu, and wings the birthday girl wore. Laura spent more time with her four-year-old friend than she did the ham she called a best friend.

Now I see Ada, and she's drab. Gray sweater with gray leggings, black boots, and a dark burgundy coat. I wonder where the glitter went. *When did she stop being Hailey's sweetheart?*

The tote bag on the counter has a few items left in it. One of them is a rainbow ribbon. I hadn't thought about collecting before Laura. If I had, Adelynn would have made the list. In a way, she still will.

I wrap the ribbon around my right hand. My breathing calms. Just in case, I grab the wine bottle I incapacitated her with. To what extent the ribbon's strength goes, I don't know.

A click to my left is a wave crashing into me. Suddenly, I'm swept into the undertow as Ada runs out the back door, and it's Heather Carter all over again. Seems I can't gauge my strength. Heather's head had caved in like a chocolate bunny giving way under excitable teeth. If only that was the problem I was having now. But no. This is all my fault, of course. I didn't think to tie her up. It's not as if I carry rope around with me everywhere.

Stuffing Ada's ribbon in my pocket, I give chase. She's only got a few seconds on me, and I know these woods. Taylor may have chosen the cabin, but I'm the one who spent hours outside learning the landscape. I was planning for the day I'd have to escape and run from the townsfolk like Frankenstein's monster or from a small-town police force that had finally caught up.

Yards into the trees, I stand still and listen. The scurry of a small animal is to my left, a larger mammal straight ahead. Boots crunching days-old snow under the fluff from this morning are up ahead to the right. I move with a purpose, trying to find boot prints I can hide in.

I hear a hiss of pain. With any luck, she's twisted an ankle. My hat's doing little to keep snow from my eyes; I can still see the indentation she's left. At least one thing's going right today. Inwardly, I hunch down and pull out a rifle. Following the gouges Ada's leaving in her wake brings back memories of my father's wide eyes and his hand reaching out. *"We don't kill young things."*

The rush I only get from sweethearts pounds in me. Ada's no sweetheart, though. She's not young or innocent; she's something new.

I wonder if she remembers me yet.

Ada

A TREE LIMB SNAGS ON MY WATCH. Its leather band cuts into my wrist; I hiss in pain. Laura Hurst's babysitter is seconds behind. She probably hears me. *Does she see me?* I undo the buckle with reddening fingers. The watch falls into the fresh snow. With it, time slips away as if the ticking hands were the only thing that cemented me to the here and now.

Her face nags at me, as it did the first moment I saw her. I test out names as I struggle through the white forest. Sally. *No.* Sarah. *No.* Sandra. *No.* Samantha. *Yes.* With her name comes a memory of getting my hair brushed and cold fingers on my neck.

Cavities in the snow lead her to me like breadcrumbs.

Despite having lived in Silynn for the better part of my early childhood, each part of the woods is a foreign language. The snowy ground covered in branches and leaves is Spanish; I can move freely if I go slow. Trees with monster limbs are Italian— too far removed from familiarity. Falling snow is French. I recognize it, but wading through is harder than it seems, even though a cute exchange student in high school taught me how to say, "I love you." And the canopy is beyond a spoken language—it's Braille. The very *idea* of learning it intimidated me into defeat, leaving me feeling small and lost.

In the bright day, only miles away from a home I spent years in, I may as well be in the Bermuda Triangle. Even worse still, I cannot call for help in case my voice carries.

The morning light is almost humorous. Monsters are supposed to chase you in the middle of the night.

I am oddly aware of the wispy hairs on the top of my feet caught in between fibers of my socks. They are my older brother's fingers pinching the back of my young, soft arms. *I hate Peter.* The fear-fueled realization urges me to live a life beyond this place. I pretend I am running in water. The mud-drenched sensation weighing my legs down is a force I can push past. A friend's mother—a kind woman with hugs to spare—taught me to swim. She told me that the water was mine to command. *Snow was water once.*

My throbbing head fills with pressure. As if I jumped from the deep end and the solid surface shattered, sounds around me muffle. The lack of clarity unsettles me. I only hear my heart and lungs. Every breath I take is louder than the one before until I'm an overheated dog. The air-puffs in front of me warm my cheeks as I race through them.

Tired thighs burn with each high step I take, and I know my pace slows. Samantha, the babysitter, breathes down my neck—like at Lynn Pond. I'm forever being chased. *This* is why I hide. If I'm seen—if I stand still too long—I may be caught.

A branch behind me groans, and the sound becomes more than important than my physical pain. *She's close.* If I get away, I'm never coming back to Silynn.

Luke

SHE'S CHASING HER.

I watch it all unfold, as I did the day Adelynn and I found Laura Hurst. This time, I choose not to act.

The woman looks so at home in the woods, pacing herself despite *Ada*'s head start. Even if I wanted to, I couldn't keep up. My legs ache from the fifteen steps I paced for hours last night, staring at the newspaper clippings when I feared I had run out of chances. *I should have stayed after I pulled her from the lake.* When it comes to my Adelynn, there are a lot of things I should've done.

Now, hearing the crunch of boots and imagining her heartbeat thumping in her throat, I know for sure it's too late. The woman will catch up. She'll catch *Ada*—a woman I'm still unsure I could grow to accept. Still, thinking about saying goodbye fills the very marrow she'd infected twenty-nine years ago during the first prayer on Easter with white-hot fire.

As *Ada* tries to outrun her chaser, I see Adelynn's mother

telling her to open a Bible. She tugs on my shirt and suggests we leave. The tulle of her yellow dress catches between our fingers as we run through the church doors.

"No one will miss us," she says. Adelynn drags me towards the park. Laughter echoes in the streets as we swing around poles and splash in a wishing well. Our hands are still interlaced when a large plastic slide comes into view; we are sweaty and stink of chlorine and old pennies.

She heads straight for the merry-go-round. It squeaks as she hops on it. She pulls me down, and we lay flat side-by-side. Invisible hands on the metal bars push us, and my stomach twists. Adelynn giggles, and the ends of her hair wave. We spin so fast the trees are blurs, and everything else disappears.

Adelynn is only a dream now. Our possible life, a ghost story. I'll have to find a replacement. I can't imagine anyone as good, but if she's gone, I have no choice.

Sam

FEAR BOUNCES BETWEEN TREES and dies in the snowfall. Ada's discarded watch warms my pocket. I already envision it next to the lock of Laura's copper hair; I'll tie the rainbow ribbon around it.

Her pace has quickened, and so must mine. Following Ada's snow trail, I veer right towards the road. She's either lucky or has gotten her bearings. Either way, the time to catch my last reason for being in Silynn is dwindling.

Conversation hearts clink in their lipgloss tin, and an imaginary peach scent wafts up to my nose. I've chosen Ada's; it's blue and reads, "Be Mine". I can't treat her like my other sweethearts, though. For her, I'll eat a candy. Hailey said, "They are sugar and cocaine. I doubt they ever expire." Twenty-nine years after she gifted them to me, I hope they still taste like a teenager's Valentine's Day—too sweet, cheap, and disappointing.

Soft steps are close. The loose end is nearly tied. My eager fingers twist the ribbon around my knuckles. Only a few yards away, I see burgundy. She's getting too close to the road.

Once I've collected Ada, I'll run. My box waits for me under the floor in the cabin's bathroom. With my map—sadly folded to fit in a shoebox—I'll never forget the exact place I collected Laura, Jessica, Mary, Karla, Nancy, Tracey, Francis, Heather, Kendra, or Lori. Revisiting them in my mind will never be the same, but I can have a fresh start. It's only a matter of finding another town with an equally oblivious police force.

I can leave Jess behind; her new husband will console her for the few days she grieves me. Taylor is an anvil hanging over my head. My dear father left us early. He only wanted wrapping paper. But when he found the box of my sweethearts' locks of hair under my bed, the darkness he'd seen in me when I was young crashed around him. It was an act of kindness. A soft pillow, him asleep when it started, the dark obscuring his daughter's face. No piece of him is in my box.

There's a shadow in the snow. The watch in my pocket ticks loudly, counting my slow, measured steps like seconds. *One Mississippi. Two Mississippi. Three Mississippi.* I'm six again, stepping towards the scent of my curiosity. *Four Mississippi.* A card table sits in the middle of the room. *Five.* My mother's borrowed my tea set. *Six Mississippi. Seven.* Thick red liquid fills plastic cups, and chunks of flesh sit on plates. Three bloated people are tied to foldable chairs. *Eight Mississippi.*

A horn honks.

Nine. A silhouette in the snow takes shape. *Ten Mississippi.* I take off my gloves, setting them in the snow. *Eleven Mississippi.* I pull the ribbon taut between my fists. Two bruises mar my wrist; small fingerprint reminders Lori left behind. The purple marks have already begun to mottle. They resemble my mother's guests: the woman in the pink dress holding the teacup, the man with a bowtie and plate in his lap, the child in frills clutching a stuffed pig. *Twelve. Thirteen. Fourteen Mississippi.* I lunge.

She's strong, bucking under me.

Terror stills her after a moment. The ribbon is too short, so I lay behind her, put my knee to her spine, and tug. Threads shred under the pressure. I let the strings of colored fabric go and wrap my hands around her throat. When her eyes bulge, I do not turn away. *"It won't hurt, little bug. It won't hurt."*

I have no idea how long I'll have to hold her like this, bristly fur itching my fingers. This time though, no one will have to kill the doe for me. Adelynn is gone, and Silynn will be my past in mere hours. After I collect my box, I'll leave and not look back. *"Look at me, sweetheart,"* I sing. *"It's already over."*

Under my hands, her muscular body softens.

Ada

FOOTSTEPS CRUNCH BEHIND ME only steps away. The scent of aggression is ripe in the forest, somehow overwhelming the ever-falling snow and pungent game. Still, I do not turn. I hike my knees higher and push harder. I see the end of the trees. Beyond it, the highway is my yellow brick road.

She is ready to drag me into the arms of danger. And here I thought revisiting Lynn Pond would be the hardest thing I would have to do while I was in Silynn.

Just get to the open road, turn right, and run. It's only yards away. I count the steps like seconds. *One Mississippi. Two Mississippi. Three.* Samantha taught me that, I realize. *How involved was she in my life?*

My first step out of the forest is a sharp inhale; the second, a sigh. Headlights shine through the morning snowfall. I don't rush out into the arms of danger. I go against my better judgment and slink back into the trees.

A honk shatters the quiet that has hidden me. The pick-up

truck slows to a stop. Its oversized wheels remind me of a field trip I took to a historical museum in Lorla Falls. When the window rolls down and a hand motions for me, I almost stay put. But Samantha knows I've made it to the road by now. Shredded muscles propel me to the car.

A hand opens the door. I slip in, and the wind slams it shut. I turn to see my savior. "You looked mighty cold out there," the blonde says.

I nod in agreement to the asinine comment and press my nose against the glass. Looking into the tree line, all I see is white. *Where is she?*

The blonde turns up the heat, and I hold my hands to the vents. The warm air is molten lava in my veins.

"Helluva storm! I can't believe it. *And* I'm still going to work." She looks down at her Sodas 'n More sweatshirt. "Obviously. It was supposed to be clearing up today. What happened?" I have been wondering that myself. My leg hairs catch fire, and all I want to do is rip them out one by one. "I guess Mother Nature had a few things to say about our assumptions. The weatherman will have a hard time backtracking from his prediction of sunny skies. I hope we're still open. How can I feed my kids without a paycheck? And the shitty tippers around here—let me tell you." Unnamed Waitress tsks and turns up the radio. Twang and sadness pour through her speakers. "Oh, I love this song. Really gets you, you know?"

"Mhmm," I mutter.

"And I don't mean you—'bout the tipping. You've been great. Everyone else—especially people passing through, though... This may be a small town, but it's not the '50s. Why am I getting one or two dollar tips on a $30 meal? Should I wear a sign that says, 'I have a deadbeat husband, and I'm supporting his two miserable brats and fat dog while he's on a cruise with a dental hygienist'? Or maybe I should start stripping; I hear that's good money. But after two kids—"

The town proper is minutes away; how many is hard to keep track of without my watch. Samantha is behind us now. I almost breathe a sigh of relief.

Unnamed Waitress has not stopped talking. "—get a bite to eat? On me. Or did you want me to take you back to wherever you're staying?"

"Can you take me to the police station?" I ask in one breath.

"Sure thing, doll."

The heartstring-tugging song ends, and a commercial for a local hardware store blares. There's a One-Day-Only Sale on leaf-blowers—fifty percent off. Unnamed Waitress nods as if this could help her and her "miserable brats." She flicks her ponytail to her left shoulder, and asks, "Whatcha going there for?"

"I need to talk to Officer Frueller."

Shrugging, she clicks her radio to preset number three. "Have you heard this one?" she asks as a girl's auto-tuned voice sings, "Be good to me."

Her surprising lack of curiosity is refreshing, if not a little disappointing. Regaling her with my harrowing escape sounds as exhausting as it does satisfying. I could turn the music down, shut off the heat, and let the pounding in my chest say it all. In reality, I wouldn't know where to start.

When I was a child, I had a babysitter named Hailey.

A Note & Acknowledgments

I wanted to share with you a short story about trichotillomania. Well, it's not a story so much as a factoid about me. I've battled with hating my body in some way, shape, or form for almost two decades. It has come out in the form of self-mutilation and trich —which my character, Ada, has. Every person experiences these things differently, of course. I know some people who've never felt the burning I have, nor the itch, but it still plagues them. (So be mindful of everyone's experiences, and be kind.) In my case though, I wrote it just as I felt it. I still feel it now and again, too. Why am I telling you this? Maybe so you know it's real, so you know everyone's isn't the same, or maybe just so one person out there can know they aren't alone.

Novels are not completed by oneself. As a writer, I have the fun —if not solitary—job of putting words on a page. I edit and edit until my eyes are blurry and then hand my work off to Tessa Garrett. Without her, you'd see "and and,," a few times throughout the book, I'm sure. So I'll thank her for her unending patience in dealing with continuity problems, confusing sentences, the same grammar errors pages after page, and staying up late night after night so I can meet a deadline I set for myself without consulting her.

The therapist in this book is loosely based on mine. She is warm and spends most of our sessions laughing and smiling, and I'm an emotionally healthier person thanks to her. So thank you, Alexis, for teaching me to love myself again and helping me work through my own emotional demons, which thankfully lack dead girls.

To say that I could stay motivated without my writing buddies would be a lie. I don't get writer's block, but I do get writer's lack-of-motivation. There are days and weeks at a time where I feel like a fraud. My husband told me once it's called Imposter Syndrome. If it weren't for my support system, I'd never see past it. Luckily, I can sit down at a good coffee shop—Townshend's is my favorite—and laugh with friends about the trials and tribulations of creating people and worlds, and suddenly, I'm an author again.

Thank you, Beth Cook and Angelique O'Rourke for checking in online, because leaving the house isn't always an option for me. Margaret Pinard, Tuesdays at my house were so special, and I am grateful for them. Jessie Kwak and Lexi Bafford, thank you for including me in your Thursday writing dates; I've learned more about the industry and gotten more work done since you have. You five ladies have shaped my work in quality and speed, as well as enriched my life. I appreciate you all.

My sister is amazing. Her smile is perfect, her laugh is adorable, and she *almost* always knows the right thing to say to keep me sane. You talk me down from the craziest of worries at all hours of the day—even though we're in different time zones. For that reason, and so many more, Jennifer, thank you. I would be less whole without you.

I'll always thank my parents. In this case, Padre helped me

with the title of the novel and watched as I flipped through font after font for a cover I didn't use. Mum listened to me talk about the same plot points so many times; I'm not sure even I would have done that for anyone. But above the novel-related things, they've supported me and loved me.

Gramy deserves a thank you for her unwavering love and support. She's lifted me up in ways I didn't know existed and spoiled me just because. I'm proud to be her granddaughter. Thank you for being my heart.

To my Bubee, my husband, love of my life, and father to my Littles, Wesley, I thank you for being you. You and I have been through more in seven years than most couples have in twenty. *Can you believe it's only been seven?* By now, you know me better than I know myself—and you still love me. I can't imagine a better life partner, best friend, or human to have by my side. I appreciate you sharing your love and life with me; it's an invaluable gift that I hold precious. Thank you for your silliness, your sexiness, and your love. I'll never repay you, but I'll spend the rest of my days trying. I love you.

And, as always, if I missed you, I'm sorry.

If you and I have ever come in contact with one another, if I have ever seen a photo you've taken or street art you painted, if you have ever walked past me or held the door for me, you are probably owed a thank you.

So, thank you, strangers, acquaintances, friends, exes. I'd have fewer stories without you.

About the Author

ELLE MITCHELL WRITES about the lives of imperfect fictional people. She spends her downtime researching and eating more than her share of homemade baked goods. Being a woman with several invisible illnesses, she enjoys living a semi-horizontal life with her husband and spoiled furbutts in the PNW.

sweethearts

ELLE MITCHELL

Made in the USA
Middletown, DE
30 September 2021